The crowd pressed close. Jenkins drove his four-wheeler between them and the tractor and showed his shotgun. From the road came the sound of sirens and the hectic flashing of blue and red lights. Squad cars bounced up the hillside, raising clouds of dust. Policemen jumped out and jogged in the direction of the tractor, ordering the trespassers to disperse. The man lying in the tractor's path hadn't budged. Two cops pulled him up off the ground and stood him up, but his legs went limp. They hoisted him up again, held him by the arm pits above the ground then stood him down again. His legs collapsed like a marionette's.

"We are not trespassing here," someone cried. "The earth belongs to all. Earth is bleeding, save the Earth."

Someone climbed up to the cab of the tractor. It was Father Ned.

"Look back, Everett!" he cried. "While there's time."

"Get the fuck off my tractor," Pillars yelled. Policemen pulled Ned off and threw him to the ground. Pillars seethed. But he didn't look back. He forged ahead.

A tall, gaunt woman with raven-black hair wearing a shiny black cape and a black beret stepped out of the shadows, waving a kind of scepter at the tractor. She bobbed up and down like a heron, moving her head with strange feints, her face contorted with deranged ecstasy.

"Prairie chicken, qu'est-ce que c'est," she sang. "Spider smile, business feaster, history eater, die on poisoned seed."

She chanted in an eerie, cracking voice. ``Paw-paw-paw-paw-paw. Paw-paw-paw-paw-paw. You better run, run, run, run away." Pillars stared at the apparition as she uttered strings of incomprehensible words, punctuated with odd "Yips." For an instant he was rattled. The woman's eyes were outlined in thick circles of black make-up. She kept shaking her scepter at him, witch-like, laughing and yipping. For a second he imagined she was Gwen. One of the policemen grabbed her by the elbow and led her away. She kept up her crazy chanting, and looked back at Pillars, sticking out her tongue.

"All that you love will wither and die," she cried. "Wither and die."

To Susan

The Griefmaker

Also by George Gurley

Fugues in the Plumbing, BkMk Press

Home Movies, Raindust Press

Press Box and *City Room,* BkMk Press

Cures and *Indian Givers,* Plays produced by Park College and directed by Pulitzer Prize winner Charles Gordone

The Griefmaker

GEORGE GURLEY

Anamcara Press LLC

Published in 2022 by Anamcara Press LLC
Author © 2022 by George Gurley
Cover art and photograph by Louis Copt, https://www.louiscopt.com/
Adobe Caslon Pro, Pulpo Rust, Berlin Sans FB

Printed in the United States of America.

Book Description:
Henry Tenbrook and Everett Pillars, friends and rivals, find themselves on opposite sides of a barbed wire fence. At stake is the fate of the Griefmaker, a thousand- acre virgin native grass prairie. Tenbrook wants to preserve the prairie, Pillars wants to develop it. When Pillars plows up the Griefmaker, the stage is set for a conflict that turns violent and also provides a chance for self-discovery and redemption.

ANAMCARA PRESS LLC
P.O. Box 442072, Lawrence, KS 66044
https://anamcara-press.com/

Ordering Information:
Quantity sales. Special discounts are available on quantity purchases by corporations, associations, and others. For details, contact the publisher at the address above.
Orders by U.S. trade bookstores and wholesalers. Please contact Ingram Distribution.

ISBN-13: 978-1-941237-90-8 eBook
ISBN-13: 978-1-941237-89-2 hardback
ISBN-13: 978-1-941237-88-5 paperback

FIC066000   FICTION / Small Town & Rural
FIC043000   FICTION / Coming of Age
FIC008000   FICTION / Sagas
FIC045000   FICTION / Family Life / General
FIC019000   FICTION / Literary

Library of Congress Control Number: 2021951920

CONTENTS

Enter the dust devils, the dervish grasses,
prairie schooners creeping in their ruts.
Enter sod busters and ploughshares,
settlers in dugouts raving in the wind,
John Brown in a God-rage,
Bible in one hand, rifle in another,
bleak whitewashed farmhouses
blinding in August light.
Awl, adze, hoe, axe, and maul,
reaper, thresher, harrow,
stone boat, corn crib, farrow pen,
slop barrel, pitchfork, hay rack, ice hook.
Egg bulge in a black snake's neck.

Sky filled with wisps of Judgment Day trumpets,
cicadas prophesying drought,
hedge balls, sand burrs, thistle down,
cedars shivering in greatcoats dusted with snow,
buffalo wallow, arrowhead.
Shoat, boar, anvil, tong,
bullheads hanging from a trot line,
coyote pelt stretched on a fence,
bob-white whistle, cuckoo chuckle,
dickcissle's chew-chew-chew.
Mocking bird and copperhead,
lambsquarter, morning glory, curly dock,
dead fall and sheep-eating dogs.

Enter the thousand acre Griefmaker,
Chief Blue Jacket, enter the dog star,
black Nicodemus and Haldeman-Julius,
Beecher Bible and Rifle Church.
Kansas, Acansis, Konzas, Ukasa.
Santa Fe and Union Pacific
braying in the bottoms,
townships, metes and bounds,
rain-worn gravemarkers
and organ pipe columns
of grain elevators washed in moonlight
beyond the deserted towns.

—*George Gurley,*
"Entering Kansas," 2021 Tri-Quarterly

My Dear Ora:

The boys have gone hunting again and I have been running the sawmill. It is a wonder. Indeed, the quickest or easiest description for the plant is that a tree starts in one side and comes out the other as a house with a family living in it.

We have had three days magnificent sport shooting quail. The old fields between the mountains or hills are filled with them and as they scatter and alight with a whir on the hillsides our dogs "mark them down." Soon the old gray fellow has them located, goes staunch on point. The other three back him. Liking those dogs grows into absolute love for them as they all four freeze on a covey, heads up, tails extended, one foot raised, motionless except for a visible twitching of their fine muscles. Their pointing is the only sign that there are birds hidden in the grass. Then, with a rush of wings, the birds explode, our guns crack and if we're lucky, each dog comes back laughing with a quail in his mouth. Oft times, on the way, he finds another cowering bird and with the dead one in his mouth he makes a stand that causes your blood to surge with the supreme thrill: The other dogs see him pointing. They "back him up" and there they are, about a foot apart always in a line, standing as a sort of a compliment to the first pointer's intelligence.

The last farmer we took dinner with was an old timer. He had the usual quota of lean, lank, howling, cadaverous, speckled red and yellow hounds. Our dogs and his bunched and circled, facing out, greeting one another with angry snaps plainly to show their disapproval of native familiarity. 'Twas funny to see the yelping pack circle around in almost battle array until Sam dispersed them with the kindly aid of stove wood.

His house was really aristocratic. It actually had little windows, doors with latches, a mill-sawed floor, the customary, honorary fireplace with an old cannon laid across the top to help support the rock. The women were always busy, the old one at the spinning wheel, the younger carding the wool. She had two things that looked like curry combs with which she combed the stuff into little strings. The old lady would then take one, fasten it to the end of the wire spindle, give the wheel a whirl, hustle back a few steps as she drew the string back, then shuffle forward as the yarn wound itself into a ball. All the time, she gave a mournful sort of a chant, keeping time to the rasping voice of the curry comber. They work about 3 days for a 1.50 worth of yarn.

Every house has the regular old Missouri chair— hickory back, untanned deer skin bottom. The seeds for spring planting are suspended from the ceiling in dirty fly-specked sacks. They are the only ornament excepting the family group, once seen never to be forgotten. The distinction between animals and human beings in these parts is difficult to discern. The trite old saying "If I owned this part of Missouri and Purgatory, I'd trade Mo and keep Hades" is not a particle wrong. Snuggled among the hills are the log huts, some with the holes daubed full of mud, others without, chimneys built on the outside out of nothing but mud and sticks. Usually 'tis a long building, the families huddled in one or two rooms on one end, the horse or mule in the other, while the open space in between serves as a sort of shelter for chickens, geese and razorback hogs whose incessant snuffling and grunting is not far off from the conversation of the family.

But a man who loves nature forgets all this and is almost lost in admiration, in the grandeur, the magnificence of God's handiwork. The scenery is beautiful —clear creeks, deep-running pure rivers, majestic pines waving gently, seeming to bow their heads in reverence to Him who made all things, grand old hills whose sides show formations of rock which in the distance look exactly like a flock of sheep lying down. One certainly realizes among these hills how infinitely insignificant is man, what pygmies we are and how when life goes out 'tis no wonder we are not missed. Still it is a pity and we almost allow a reproachful thought that the Supreme Architect of the universe would place such a miserable lot of cannibals in such a natural palace fit for kings and gods.

Tomorrow we reach the Missouri–Kansas border and Middleton which I hope we will come to call home. Middleton is scarcely a place at all yet, though it promises to soon be the land of milk and honey, or so I pray. It gives us a second chance to do things right.

Having had a splendid time but am longing for Tuesday evening when I will see you again. We start Monday night at 8. Well dear, the one mail a day is ready to go out and I will quit. Am anxiously awaiting the delivery of today's mail pouch and am expecting you by letter together with my kisses or kisses for me.

With my love, Ten.

—Letter from Henry Tenbrook to his betrothed, 1879

PART ONE

THE PLOUGHMAN

"The cut worm forgives the plow."
—*William Blake*

"From now on, prayers and penance shall be my plow..."
—*Piers the Ploughman*

Chapter 1

Henry Tenbrook the First was known as "The Patriarch" in Middleton, Kansas, where he reigned for a short time. He brought a mixture of naïvete and cunning to a county that wasn't rich in anything but the absence of rules. Most of his pioneer ilk failed to leave anything behind but ruined, moss-covered foundation walls of homesteads, with forlorn lilies still blooming at the threshold. The Patriarch was one of the few who made a mark, though it too proved transitory. His dynasty terminated in the blades of a plow, in Henry Tenbrook IV's pile of debt and in the person of his daughter, Channy, who married a Polish house painter from the Missouri side, burying the Tenbrook name in a welter of slavic k's and z's.

Some people disparage a man like the Patriarch for being greedy. But if it was just a matter of taking more than your share, more of us would be rich. What distinguished him was voracious energy, a crude kind of creativity, an aptitude for seizing opportunities and the willingness to risk everything over and over again. He was also lucky. His true genius was the recognition of the openness of Middleton, Kansas, where an enterprising individual could do almost anything without having to ask permission. He entered the landscape as an itinerant lumberman and Chautauqua speechifier and, almost overnight, transformed himself into an entrepreneur and civic leader, all this before Middleton was worthy of even the name of "town." Within ten years of his arrival, he'd built an empire which included five lumberyards, a bank, a newspaper, an automobile dealership, a flour mill powered by the Middleton River—and lots of land.

The Patriarch claimed he'd founded half a dozen towns, all extinct now, before he settled in Middleton. Early in his career he claimed he was captured and taken on a "buffalo hunt" by some of his creditors, whom he managed to disarm by laughing at them.

"Everything's got a handle," he liked to say. All you had to do was take hold and not let go. When the biblical mood came over him, he'd quote Proverbs: "Whatever your hand finds to do, do it with your might." His son, "Junior," never found or even looked for a handle, spent his adult years in a fog of gin and gambled away his father's properties piece by piece. Tenbrook the Third entered the Episcopal ministry and later committed suicide. Henry IV lurched from one project to another in search of a metaphysical handle that probably doesn't exist. Of the Tenbrook Land and Cattle Company only the thousand-acre Griefmaker remained intact at the beginning of this story, the last piece of virgin prairie in Middleton County, and it belonged to Everett Pillars.

Those who fear that this great nation is going to become a plutocracy might consider the Tenbrooks, whose fortune was made and dissipated in four generations. You don't need a confiscatory inheritance tax to thwart the rise of a capitalistic kingdom. Folly, incompetence and quixotic dreams can be counted on to break up empires and redistribute wealth.

Chapter 2

Henry Tenbrook, great-grandson of the Patriarch, crouched in his blind and watched an enormous tom turkey strut forth from woods, filling the air with a thrilling gobble. It was one of those born-again mornings—Kansas has two or three of them a year—when heaven comes down to earth like a preview of everlasting spring. Patches of mist lay in the hollows. Spider webs hung like silver nets in the dewy grass. An early shower had wetted the road dust down and washed the air, which smelled clean, renewed, pure. The sky floated just above the treetops, with a few scarves of cirrus clouds against the pale blue boundless fabric, hung out to dry. Sycamores and oaks were still leafless, but the redbuds already showed their flowers like puffs of purple smoke in the black woods along Kill Creek.

Technically, he was Henry Tenbrook IV, but he never signed his name that way. He thought it sounded pretentious, as if he was some sort of Shakespearean king. But he had been a king of sorts in his high school days, a star athlete, a local legend, quarterback of the state championship football team, the baseball team's pitcher, known for a wicked fastball that burned his catcher's hand, point guard on the basketball team, averaging 20 points a game. He once picked up a tennis racket for the first time and beat the country club champion in straight sets. The expression on his face never changed when he was competing. It was a mask. He never pumped his fist or let out a primal scream. When he ran for a touchdown, he didn't do an endzone dance. He'd just hand the ball to the ref as if he was delivering the morning paper.

***

He and Everett Pillars were best friends—and rivals. They couldn't have been more different. Tenbrook was modest, graceful, laid back. Pillars was aggressive, ruthless, ambitious, hungry for success. But some strange attraction bonded them. They did everything together, hunting, chasing girls, getting drunk, raising hell. The Griefmaker was their hallowed ground.

Tenbrook had peaked in high school, so he thought. Everything had come easily to him in those days. A bout of rheumatic fever had kept Pillars out of sports until his senior year when he entered the last game of the season and went on a tear, racking up a dozen tackles. The moment he put high school behind him, Pillars seemed to know exactly where he was going. It was as if he, rather than Tenbrook, had inherited the Patriarch's knack for business.

Such thoughts were on Tenbrook's mind as he watched the turkey make a beeline for his decoy, its head bobbing up and down like a toy on a rubber stick. He held his breath, heart drumming, and eased his finger to the trigger. Then something happened. He stood up without shooting. The turkey started, bewildered at this apparition. Then it wheeled, ran off and disappeared into the woods. An unexpected thought had come to Tenbrook: He was done with hunting. He'll killed enough turkeys, quail, pheasants. It no longer excited him. He had other business at hand—confrontation with Pillars. "Collision," he thought. Tenbrook dismantled his decoy and walked to his truck watching a gathering of buzzards circling above some carrion on the road.

He had tried to get out of Kansas. He had tried to hate the state. He'd joked about the "Ski Kansas" poster that depicts a desolate, flat landscape, featureless except for a broken windmill and a scrap of tumbleweed. Kansas had nothing. No mountains, no sea, no metropolis. Busloads of senior citizens didn't come to Kansas to witness the turning of the leaves. There weren't any trees. The wind could blow for days with a punishing will that drove settlers to madness and suicide. Drought, dust storms, blizzards. The Great American Desert. Empty spaces without dimensions or shadows. Visitors from other states experience panic when they enter Kansas—agoraphobia. The first sighting of the blue mountains shimmering in the Colorado distance excites cheers and spasms of relief.

But beneath his longing to escape was a powerful attraction. Kansas was like a blank canvas. It stimulated imagination. Emptiness meant infinite prospects. Open spaces meant freedom. A painter said that it was in Kansas that she saw the horizon for the first time. Tenbrook was a romantic man infected with wanderlust who was stuck in empty, desolate Kansas, fixed like a blade of the giant blue stem grass that sends its roots down more than ten feet into the chalky soil in search of moisture. There was a thousand-pound anchor in his heart. He was grounded. Kansas was the stage on which he had to rediscover, prove himself, fulfill himself.

At the heart of the matter was the Griefmaker, one of few remnants of the tallgrass prairie that once spread from Canada to the Gulf of Mexico, 600 miles wide in parts. The Griefmaker, never broken by a plow until the night Everett

Pillars violated it, raped it according to some. Pillars owned the Griefmaker, but the Griefmaker possessed Tenbrook. He couldn't walk away from it. He somehow thought it held the key to a redemption he dreamed of.

He had no power or influence in Middleton. The Tenbrook name no longer carried any clout. But everyone liked him. He didn't say much, but when he did it was usually something unexpected that somehow hit the mark. He could make "It depends" sound like an insight. Tenbrook was tall, gaunt. He had a weathered face, sandy hair thinning on top, one slightly crooked tooth that some mistook for mocking. He had some of the unsettled, oppositional nature of Kansas in his genes, some of the weather that makes twisters, contrary politics, perhaps some of the John Brown legacy, Bible in one hand, rifle in the other. At any rate, his spirit was daubed with blue-grey moods. Hard to imagine him resting in peace.

Chapter 3

Tenbrook drove his rust-pocked Jeep down Cockle-bur Road. Signs of spring were everywhere. Frogs delivered their mating croaks from the thawing muck of sloughs. Amorous pairs of geese paddled on glassy ponds. Shorebirds darted like arrows overhead on their way to northern nesting grounds. Turtles, awakened from their winter slumber, lumbered across the roads in search of love. All nature seemed aroused to the business of procreation, the ceremony of renewal from the dark graves of winter.

Tenbrook's Jeep rattled over the bridge at Means Crossing. Half-hidden among bulrushes was the ferryman's stone hut, still standing beside the ruins of the well where Santa Fe Trail-bound pioneers once filled their pails. Gold-seekers forded the stream at that spot on their way to California. Border ruffians from Missouri ran their ponies across the stream on the day of the Middleton Massacre, a few years before the outbreak of the Civil War. On a nearby barbed wire fence someone had stretched a coyote skin as an example to its cousins.

An immaculate white-washed fence that ran for more than a mile marked the beginning of Pillars' estate. His brome pasture had the manicured look of a golf course. Henbit covered the crop land like iridescent pools of gasoline. Black Angus cattle grazed among walnut trees that

Tenbrook's great-grandfather had planted a hundred years before. Each animal had a red identification tag like a price tag in its ear.

At the top of the hill stood the house which Henry Tenbrook, the Patriarch, had built—slate roof, stone chimneys, leaded glass windows, even a turret, all the trappings of a castle except for a moat and a portcullis. Pillars' grandfather had acquired it after the Tenbrook bankruptcy and expanded it with two wings and a guest house. Three blue A.O. Smith silos loomed above its roof tops. A great stone barn stood nearby. A short distance from the barn was the church, built on the land that Everett Pillars now owned and built for the most part with his money.

Beyond the estate to the west was the thousand-acre Griefmaker, just beginning to green up after the spring burn like the baize of a billiard table. At the crest of its dominant hill was the iconic cedar tree, bent by the prevailing southwest wind, which preservationists had appropriated in their crusade to save the virgin prairie. When the wind wasn't blowing, you could hear the whisper of commuter traffic a mile away. The Middleton Loop would cut the Griefmaker in half.

The circular drive had been freshly coated with shining black asphalt. A sculpture ensemble occupied the island within the driveway, half a dozen bronze children holding hands, playing ring-around-the-rosy. The figures, intended to convey the freedom and innocence of youth, looked somehow alien and aged. The artist had captured them in a centrifugal whirl, skirts and pigtails flying, freezing them as their feet were just beginning to lift off the ground at the moment the leader would cry, "All fall down."

Tenbrook approached the house as if entering his own past, a past that had been ruptured when his family lost the Griefmaker. He'd spent much of his youth there, as the Pillars' guest. They owned the Griefmaker, but the Griefmaker owned Tenbrook. Faintly, from somewhere, he heard the liquid call of the upland plover, a call heard only on pristine prairie. Mary, in her gray maid's costume, was waiting at the open door.

"Henry Tenbrook, where have you been?" she said. "You look thin. Are you sick? That pretty wife not feeding you? Not giving you enough love?" Mary gave her deep, generous laugh. Before Tenbrook could answer, she wrapped him in a hug. Then came Gwen's "You-Who" greeting, her high heels clicking on the flagstone entry floor. "Henry Tenbrook, Henry Tenbrook," she sang, her voice rising on the "brook." She had a way of accenting ordinary words so as to make them seem more meaningful than they really were.

"Let go, Mary," she said, "He's mine." Gwen pulled Tenbrook free, wrapped her arms around his neck and kissed him on the mouth. She seemed nearly weightless and Tenbrook felt a nervous current passing through her arms. She held him at arm's length and looked him over with glistening eyes. Tenbrook could see vestiges of the wrinkles some plastic surgeon had almost ironed away. She still has the original ass, he thought. Her striped skirt was cinched tight to show off her wasp-thin waist. A large silver cross hung from her neck, accentuating her ample breasts. She wore a ring with a huge amber diamond.

"I've been ordered to keep you entertained," she said. "Master is busy closing big deals, bossing people around, firing minions. Mary, tell Charles to bring the roses to the upper house. And tell Jenkins to please park his disgraceful truck in back. I don't know how many times I've told him." Gwen took Tenbrook's hands in hers and gave him a fond, pleading look.

"You know, I hate having servants," she said after Mary had left. "I just hate it. But Everett makes me order them around. I'm supposed to look pretty and terrify the cook and the gardener. Chop, chop. Is that what I was put on this planet for? Ten! Tell Kate I've found the most wonderful new hairdresser. An absolute artist."

"To tell you the truth, I don't think Kate goes to the hairdresser," he said.

"You don't think?" she said. "Don't you know? Do you two ever talk? I like Kate. But I can't get across to her. She's enigmatic, deep. Has she been saved?"

"You'll have to ask her. She and Father Ned have become pretty tight."

"You're not jealous, are you?"

"They flirt. They tease each other. He prances for her."

"Ned prances for all the girls."

"He comes over and has his glass of sherry," said Tenbrook. "They're supposed to be 'talking shop.' When I come in the room, they clam up. He and I pretend to have a conversation, but he addresses all his comments to her. He looks at me every twenty seconds to check me out or make me feel I'm included. I walked into the kitchen the other day and they were giving each other high fives."

"Take it from one who knows. You have nothing to worry about."

"How do you know?"

"People think Ned and I are having an affair. I don't care what they think. Maybe we are. He's changed my life. That's all I know, all I care about. Kate's not enamored of him. It's their little soup kitchen she's in love with. I understand she has a talent for business. I envy her. I wish I had something like that."

"Everett would go crazy if you got into a business."

"You're right. That would threaten him. But he actually likes to leave me alone with you. It gives him a chance to show he's above that kind of jealousy." Gwen laughed and gave him a taut, radiant smile. Her phone rang.

"Julie!" she cried. "I can't talk, darling. I'm just going out the door. No, I can't. I'm tied up. I've got the Cornbelt Dinner Friday and the Sunflower Auction Saturday. I won't be able to do anything for months. Give me a rain check, Sweet Pea." She rolled her eyes for Tenbrook's benefit. Tenbrook's mind drifted. He could feel the Griefmaker's presence, pressing in on the room from the outside. He wished he was out there, walking in the open.

"Julie Blevins," Gwen exclaimed. "I can't imagine anything more dreadful than an evening with her and Ralph. We're giving a dinner where half the guests will get Beef Wellington and half will get a bowl of brown rice. Won't that be a hoot? That ought to raise a little consciousness. See how the other half lives. Come on. I want to show you my Johns." She led him down a corridor past glass cabinets filled with cups and plates, paperweight and ceramic bird collections, past antique tables and chairs meant to be looked at rather than used. There was a rich aroma in the hallway, a subtle incense of preserved flowers and wood polished with tung oil that Tenbrook associated with money. They entered a room that had been made into a gallery. Paintings ablaze with violent slashes and splatters of color covered the walls. One object made out of scrap metal appeared to be a fish with headlights for eyes. A bright orange fiberglass extrusion flowed like a waterfall from one wall and formed a puddle on the floor. In the middle of the room was a playpen filled with heads and limbs of dolls and broken musical instruments. At one end was a kind of totem pole formed by toilet bowls stacked one on top of the other.

"Ta-da!" said Gwen. "That's my 'Johns.' Get it? People expect a Jasper Johns and I present them with a stack of crappers. What do you think?"

"I'll never be able to use a toilet again," Tenbrook said. "You amaze me, Gwen. Who would believe? Twenty years ago you were a Minneapolis, Kansas farm girl and cheerleader. And look at you now. You're a rich woman, a collector, a connoisseur."

"You're making fun of me, but Larry Moe says my stuff is cutting edge. I hate it when people say, 'We're not in Kansas anymore.' This ought to show them that we're not living in the Dark Ages. I can tell you: I paid boo-coo bucks for this art."

"I paid boo-coo bucks for it," said Pillars, who'd just entered the room.

"Everything has a price, according to Everett," said Gwen.

"Somebody's got to mind the cash register," said Pillars. "When stuff like this shows up in Kansas it's not cutting edge anymore." He frowned and shook his head. He was a burly man with massive shoulders, bushy eyebrows and eager restless eyes. He was wearing a coat and tie even though it was Saturday morning. He walked up to one of the paintings.

"A kindergartner could have done that," he said.

"That's one of my favorites," said Gwen. "It's called 'Prometheus Approaches Maximum Entropy.' Larry says it's already worth twice what I—you—paid for it. Think of it as an investment, dear."

"It's ugly."

"Larry says we don't speak of beautiful and ugly anymore," said Gwen. "We speak of presence."

"Larry has a gift for spending other people's money." He put his hand on Tenbrook's shoulder, gave him a little massage and turned him around like a dance partner. "Come on," he said. "I've got to talk to you." Gwen gave Tenbrook a plaintive look, then recovered with a bright smile.

"I'm on my way to prayer group, dear," she said. "I'll put in a good word for both of you." Pillars guided Tenbrook to his office, a walnut-paneled den that smelled of tobacco smoke.

"Did you notice her new boobs?" Pillars said, lighting a cigar. "I paid boo-coo bucks for those too. They're the best money can buy. Of course, I shopped around." He winked and gestured to a pair of leather chairs positioned before his desk and offered the cigar box to Tenbrook.

"Gwen said you were firing someone," said Tenbrook, waving off the cigars. "That must be hard."

"Actually, it's easy," said Pillars. "I always feel better after firing somebody. It keeps staff on their toes." He glanced at Tenbrook to see if he was impressed. Tenbrook tried to give him a blank look and turned to inspect two pairs of intertwined antlers mounted on a trophy board, vestiges of a fatal encounter between rutting bucks.

"You're a hard man, Everett Pillars," Tenbrook said and left it to him to judge whether he was impressed or making fun. Animal heads hung on the walls—elk, moose, grizzly bear, a mountain goat and the Big Five from Pillars' African safari—lion, leopard, buffalo, rhino—excluding the elephant which was represented by a pair of tusks.

"When I bagged that lion, the villagers had a big celebration," he said. "I was a hero, because they hated lions. Lions killed them. One thing I learned from that trip is that people who live with wild animals don't sentimentalize them. You don't find any National Geographic King of Beasts bullshit over there." Tenbrook had heard the story before. There was a companion tale about a little girl who'd wandered too close to the river the same day Pillars had killed the lion and got taken by a crocodile. The villagers had mourned the death of the child with wailing and rending of garments but accepted it as a natural thing. That night they held a joint feast for the death of the lion and the death of the child. Tenbrook had heard it all before.

"Have you taken up polo?" he asked to bait Pillars. He knew that the crossed polo mallets and the polo helmet which also hung on the wall were expressions of Pillars' ego and social aspirations, along with the prints of men in red riding coats on horseback following hounds, anglers dressed in tweeds fishing in salmon streams. Pillars didn't bite.

"That's what I call art," he said, watching Tenbrook look around the room. "That stuff never goes out of style."

"Larry Moe says Gwen's collection is worth more than yours," said Tenbrook. Pillars snorted.

"We've got dueling collections," he said.

Above the fireplace was a portrait of Pillars' grandfather, looking out across an expanse of prairie with visionary eyes. It occupied the space where a portrait of Tenbrook's great-grandfather once hung. The credenza behind Pillars' desk was cluttered with blueprints and files. A gold-painted ground-breaking shovel rested against the wall. There were photos of Pillars shaking hands with commercial and civic dignitaries and the framed Pillars family crest, three Doric columns—grandfather, father and son—supporting a bulldozer. "The Trinity," Pillars called it. In the middle of the office was an architect's model of a town—clusters of diminutive houses and apartments, matchbox office buildings, a shopping mall. Shards of mirror glass for ponds, scraps of sphagnum for bushes and trees. It was the Griefmaker, subdivided, leveled, squared, channeled and plumbed.

"How is Kate, how is Channy?" said Pillars.

"They're fine," said Tenbrook.

"Be glad you have girls."

"Is Tod okay?"

"Tod worries me. He wrecked the Mercedes the other night. He was driving without the lights on, plowing up some sod we'd just put down on one of my construction sites. His way of reaching out to me, I guess. He ran into a parked dozer. Totaled the Mercedes. He told me not to worry about the car—it was just a material thing."

"Sounds like a philosopher."

"He belongs to a band called 'Fecal Matter.' They have all the fanciest equipment, but they don't know how to play do-re-me. You've never heard such a racket. Ten thousand decibels. At the end of their signature song they stick their fingers down their throat and gag. They're 'artists,' you see. Tod dresses like the kind of kid who takes guns to school in a duffel bag. He's after me to get him a rifle and it worries me. He's never shown any interest in guns before."

"I wouldn't worry too much," said Tenbrook. "You and I used to be outlaws, misfits. Remember throwing Molotov cocktails against the incinerator in your back yard? Remember when we butchered the dummy on the road and ten cop cars showed up?"

"Back when we knew each other," said Pillars. He made his crows-foot squint that was intended as a smile.

"Gwen seems lively."

"Gwen is fine. Gwen is expensive. That crap on the walls in there cost me a fortune. I guess it's a small price to pay."

"For what?"

"She doesn't try to keep me on a short leash."

"A lot of men would like to be short-leashed to Gwen."

"The thing about Gwen is she's mercurial. One day, she's a limousine liberal, carping about the rightwing fundamentalists who give Kansas a bad name. The next day she's saved and on a first-name basis with Jesus. You'd better pray that

Kate doesn't get saved."

"Kate isn't religious, but she's tight with Father Ned. They're planning some kind of soup kitchen together. I don't know about these holy men. I don't trust them."

"I don't trust anyone," said Pillars. "You know, Ten, I can have just about any kind of girl I want. I've got a tall, freckled redhead with legs that start just below her arm pits and small buttercup breasts, a chubby blond type with boobs the size of cantaloupes. It's nice, after all the frustrations when you and I were just sniffing around, having no idea what women want. It makes me happy now—for about fifteen minutes. The more I have the more I want and the less it excites me. Didn't Jesus or some other wise man tell us it would be like that?" He got up and walked over to the model town, glancing at his watch, puffing out little clouds of smoke. "And I don't believe in anything—except this." He passed his hand over the model like a priest giving a blessing. "Footings, joists, bulldozers. I don't believe in climate change, I don't believe in peak oil. God, these woolgatherers. I like to see earth leveled, shaped. Come take a look." Tenbrook got up and walked over to the model.

"Recognize anything?" said Pillars.

"Of course," said Tenbrook. "That's the Griefmaker. That's Hangnail Hill. There's the Mare's Tit. That's the booming grounds of the last flock of prairie chickens in Middleton County."

"It's all a goldmine if you know where to dig," said Pillars. "We're talking wampum, Henry boy. Big time." He clapped his hands together like a little boy who'd just opened a Christmas present. "The Mare's Tit is going to be about 400 garden apartments. I believe that's what you appraisers call the 'highest and best use.' Speaking of which, I understand you're appraising the Griefmaker for the tree huggers."

"I need the money."

"You need money? Why didn't you say so?"

"Everyone needs money. Even Bill Gates wishes he had just a little bit more."

"Appraise my house if you need money. I'll pay you twice what the tree huggers will pay."

"That would be a conflict of interest."

"Since we're friends?"

"Since we're friends."

There was a loud knock on the door and Lloyd Jenkins barged into the room, breathing hard. His boots were caked with mud. His overalls were almost white from hundreds of washings. His frayed red flannel shirt was unbuttoned halfway to his waist. A welder's cap perched childishly on the top of his enormous head. Snowy white hair tumbled over his ears and collar. His long beard was tied with a string beneath his chin. In his hands, which were as big as catcher's mitts, he gently cradled a dead squirrel.

"Colonel Tenbrook," he said, nodding at Tenbrook, his mouth curved in a wide smile. "How ye be?"

"What the hell do you have there?" said Pillars.

"Fresh squirrel," said Jenkins. "I wondered if you and the missus might want me to fry him up for your dinner. Dusted in flour, fried in lard."

"Will you get that goddam thing out of here, Jenkins," said Pillars. "Fry it up and eat it yourself."

"I will, if you don't want it," said Jenkins. "Just wanted to give you first dibs." He laid the squirrel on Pillars' desk. "Lookee here, I brought you these." Jenkins pulled a couple of hedge apples out of the pockets of his overalls.

"What the hell am I supposed to do with those?" said Pillars

"Put them in the basement. They'll get rid of the spiders."

"Get those damn things out of here too," said Pillars.

Jenkins set the yellow globes on the desk beside the squirrel, as if he hadn't heard. He pulled an oil-stained rag out of his hip pocket and blew his nose into it with a sharp blast. He examined the discharge for a moment, then returned the rag to his pocket.

"When we go'in huntin', Colonel?" he said. "When we gonna go noodlin' for grand-daddy catfish?"

"Just say the word," said Tenbrook.

"You two spend a lot of time hunting fantasy creatures," said Pillars.

"I'm hearin' quail," said Jenkins. "Real ones. They's fixin' to have three hatches this spring and summer."

"Do you ever do any work for me?" said Pillars.

"Nossir, not if I can help it." They were both laughing. Pillars seemed to be enjoying the disruption and his affectation of annoyance. Jenkins reported a cow hit by lightning and a plugged culvert.

"What do you think about your boss's plans for the Griefmaker?" asked Tenbrook. Jenkins looked over at the model development.

"You can't stop progress," he said.

"That's progress?" said Tenbrook.

"Ask the boss," said Jenkins.

"Get back to work, Jenkins," said Pillars. "You're a trouble-maker."

"Yassir," said Jenkins with a bow. He shook Tenbrook's hand, gathered up the dead squirrel and the hedge balls, saluted Pillars and left.

"Every time he comes in here he brings me some of those damned Osage oranges," said Pillars. "He thinks they ward off evil spirits."

"He left some sort of deposit on your carpet."

"Don't worry, it's just a material thing," said Pillars. "We had some fun with him when we were kids."

"He taught us everything we know."

"He taught us how to shoot, that's for sure." Pillars got up and went to the door and called. "Mary, will you please come here and clean up this shit from Jenkins' boots?" He sat down, leaned back in his chair with his hands behind his head. "God Almightly, Ten. Remember Poo-the-Screamer and the girl who got nettles on her ass?"

"Remember the Well of Piss?"

"And the blackboard sign in the barn that cracked us up?"

"Gymnosperm and angiosperm."

"We nearly busted our guts," said Pillars. "Oh, we get to keep our memories, Ten. I'm not selling those. Listen, if we're such great friends, you ought to be on my side."

"You know how I feel about the Griefmaker," said Tenbrook. "It's sacred." Pillars snorted. Tenbrook went on. "I'm against you on this one. But don't worry, Ev. It's your property. You can do whatever you want with it."

"You can't be so sure of that anymore," said Pillars. "There are some assholes in Middleton who'd like to abolish private property. They think the Griefmaker belongs to the community. Some of them say the Griefmaker is sacred because it's an Indian burial ground. They're even talking about preserving scenic views. 'View Sheds,' they call them. They want to prevent development of prime agricultural land—because we're going to need it when the world runs out of oil. Hell, they'd like to outlaw the gasoline engine. Those pecksniffs want to tell you what to eat."

Tenbrook smiled.

"They're just looking out for you," he said. "Don't you think they know what's best?" Pillars gave another snort and brooded for a moment.

"There's going to be an interchange a quarter of a mile from this room," he said. "You're an appraiser. What do you think the Griefmaker is worth?"

"Based on the sale of Leathers' farm, probably $40,000 an acre."

"More than that after the interchange is in. I've got a study that shows the Griefmaker at the center of Middleton's growth in 20 years."

"It's never been plowed."

"There was a time when you could have said that about every square foot in Kansas," scoffed Pillars. "The tree huggers have offered me $3,500 an acre. Is that some kind of joke? If they want to pay market price, it's theirs."

"You know they can't come up with that kind of money."

"What are you saying—that I should just let $40 million slip through my fingers?"

"What exactly did you call me for?"

"Out of respect for you."

"You're not asking me for permission, though."

"I called you because I want to be straight with you."

"You and I grew up on the Griefmaker, Ev. That means something."

"You still think it sort of belongs to you."

"I love this place," said Tenbrook. Pillars stamped out his cigar. Then he shrugged and his eyes brightened.

"Look at this," he said, his hands cupped over a corner of the model. "That's going to be the World of Oz theme park. You're looking at a quarter of a billion-dollar project. I'm talking to the Injuns about putting in a casino there."

Tenbrook walked to the window and looked out.

"I can see The Cowardly Lion roller coaster, the Tin Man Tilt-A-Whirl," he said. "I can see Taco John's, Taco Tico, Taco Bell, Senor Taco. The whole taco cosmos. The golden arches. Hordes of shoppers piling out of SUVs. A hundred acres of parking lots."

"It's King Solomon's mine," said Pillars.

"You think good times are going to last forever?"

"They're not making any more land."

"The last time I heard that was just before the real estate bubble burst."

"This time's different."

"They always say that too."

"You're a perpetual pessimist, Ten. We're in a global economy. The world is awash in money."

"When money's cheap, people overbuild."

"You think too much," Pillars said. "People like you expect life to give you something it's not supposed to give. And you end up empty-handed. And whether times are good or bad, people like you think of all sorts of reasons to sit on their hands and do nothing. You'll never get rich, Henry. You don't get rich without taking risks."

"I wish I had your confidence," said Tenbrook. "But I don't understand it. Look at all the people we know who've gone under. You don't know what might be lying in wait for you."

But Pillars wasn't listening. He wore a distant smile.

"Just think," he said. "Once upon a time people were living in sod huts in Middleton County. There may have been slaves on this farm once upon a time. Imagine what it must have been like during the Border Wars. You'd be driving along in your horse and buggy and a bunch of ruffians comes up and asks you if you're a slave owner or an abolitionist. You can't tell by looking at them what they want to hear and if you give the wrong answer, they shoot you." Pillars looked at his watch again. "Jesus, I've got to go," he said. "Meetings, closings. There aren't enough hours in the day. Are you for me or against me?"

"I'm against you," said Tenbrook. "But I don't have any ammunition. Don't waste your time worrying about me."

"I'm your friend. I can help you. But you don't want to make an adversary out of me." They were silent for a moment, looking out three arched windows that formed a triptych. Suddenly horses ran past. They were running for the pure joy of it, their tails waving gaily in the wind. They stopped and for a moment they seemed like the work of an artist, an image frozen in time. Then they galloped off and disappeared from view.

"My horses," mused Pillars as if he were talking to himself. "Beauties, aren't they?" Mary opened the door and leaned into the room with a mop and dust rag in her hand.

"Your people are here," she said. "I never thought I'd see such a vehicle in front of this house."

Pillars and Tenbrook walked to the front door. A white stretch limousine was parked nose to nose with Tenbrook's Jeep as if poised to devour it.

"Don't forget," said Pillars, as Tenbrook walked to his car. "Your ancestors stole the Griefmaker from the redskins."

Chapter 4

When Tenbrook left Pillars' house, he drove eastward back to town, past his old neighborhood and the little Victorian house he and Kate had called home for a dozen years. He parked in front of his one-room midtown office, wedged between a laundromat and a liquor store. The appraisal of the Griefmaker for the Friends of the Prairie was due the following Monday and he'd only just begun sifting through figures that would magically reveal the property's value. He'd inherited the office from Sylvester Niestrom, who'd lost a fortune in the Depression and earned it back by bleeding rent from Bottomtown car washes, second-hand stores and slums he referred to as "garden apartments." Tenbrook had shared the space with him and managed some of his disreputable lodgings. The office, with its chipped linoleum floor, ancient metal filing cabinets and cramped back room toilet, was a memento of Depression-learned frugality. Due to his own financial straits, Tenbrook hadn't changed a thing.

The ceiling-hung heater came on with a roar, drowning out the clatter of dryers and the drowsy sloshing of the washing machines next door. Tenbrook opened his file of rural comparables. There were sales of five-acre lots in the county for $5,000 an acre, sales of marginal crop land for $2,000 an acre. One acre abutting a west Middleton shopping center had sold for $100,000. Sales had been few due to the economic downturn and Middleton's anti-growth mentality. The only sale relevant to the Grief-maker had been Dewey Leathers' 40 acres, a quarter mile west: $40,000 an acre. That was all there was to go on. From that slender thread, Tenbrook would have to hang a 100-page document filled with incomprehensible graphs and boilerplate proclamations gussied up as a blue chip, bankable verification of value.

Tenbrook had lost faith in his profession. For all the pretense of empiricism, the three great pillars of the appraisal process—the Cost Approach, the Income Approach and the Market Approach—offered at best mere guesses of what a specific property would sell for or, more important, what it was "worth." Appraisals were really a kind of black-market currency traded between the appraiser and his client and "value" was based on the appraiser's intuition of what his client wanted—a high value in the case of condemnation, a low value for estate tax purposes. The Friends of the Prairie wanted the lowest possible figure to justify their meager offer. Tenbrook had told them that the Leathers sale blew their numbers out of the water. But he hadn't been able to convince them of the futility of their position—partly because, in spite of what he'd told Pillars, he was doing the appraisal pro bono. It was an exercise in futility that would cost them nothing. And a sense of futility perfectly suited Tenbrook's mood—doing something that didn't make sense, for free.

He remembered the smirk on Pillars face when the Leathers sale came up. Pillars had invited him to buy a half interest in the same property five years before for $10,000 an acre. If Tenbrook had gone in, he would have made enough to pay off the mortgage on his home. The value had been certain to go up. But Tenbrook would have had to borrow the down payment. The prospect of maybe 10 to 20 years of debt service had put him off. So he'd thrown away the life jacket Pillars had tossed him, justifying the lecture: "You're afraid of taking chances. You'll never get rich."

Appraising the Griefmaker seemed particularly senseless to Tenbrook. How do you price something that's priceless? But he was getting some satisfaction from knowing that Pillars really was nervous about the tree-huggers' threats to his plans. Given Middleton's powerful environmental lobby, the FOP might be able to get a temporary injunction to prevent him from developing the Griefmaker. The idea that he could lose a fortune on account of a couple of endangered forbs drove Pillars crazy.

Tenbrook opened his field guide to Kansas weeds and wildflowers. Milkweed flowers, he read, were "bisexual, usually borne in umbel-like clusters...Above the petals and elevated on a column, a whorl of five erect petaloid parts called hoods or nectar receptacles, somewhat like small sugar scoops...Five horny winglike projections each with a vertical slit that allows access to the inner chamber... Outside of the gynostegium, a translucent mass of golden pollen."

Some wanton botanist must have written that, thought Tenbrook. The supposedly endangered Mead's Milkweed, found locally only on the Griefmaker, was named for its discoverer, Samuel Barnum Mead, 1799-1880: "Slender, erect, herbaceous perennials...leaves opposite, sessile, very narrowly lanceolate to ovate, pale green glabrous...Corolla lobes reflexed, lance-oblong to elliptic...Hoods short-stipitate, erect, somewhat ovoid with two marginal teeth, nectar horns shorter than the hoods...Rare." The middle lobe of the Prairie Fringed Orchid, the other endangered weed, was "shortly clawed and broadly cuneate."

Tenbrook had no idea what those words meant, but he looked forward to quoting the X-rated descriptions in his appraisal, a little soft porn to hold the interest of the judge. What was the Mead's Milkweed worth? He didn't know. How do you put a value on a plant that would stand up in court?

He would like to digress, to call the court's attention to other considerations of value. To tell them of the hours he'd spent wandering in his own vest pocket prairie, observing how it changed from year to year. White asters covering the hills like a dusting of summer snow one year, disappearing the next, followed by a profusion of sunflowers or the strange webs of field dodder. A single acre might contain two hundred different species fighting for living space, from delicate purple clovers to thorny thistles. He'd tell them that the sage was wrong who said that the lilies of the field don't toil. On the contrary, they were engaged in an eternal, brutal battle for survival with all the other flowers. He'd describe the leaves of the giant resin weed, designed like fluted cups to gather rain water…the seasonal successions of insects, leaves and blossoms, advancing and receding, balance overthrown and mysteriously restored…and the autumn storms of seeds in which were written nature's secret codes, speeches, sermons, prophecies and poems. He would like to find words to express that pageant, words beyond common sense and pragmatism that would excite awe, a rapturous fellow-feeling with that alien world, the liberating revelation of individual insignificance that sometimes comes from looking up at the stars. But he knew an outburst like that would only excite embarrassment in the courtroom and confirm the suspicions of his peers that he was losing his professional grip.

On his desk was a bundle of yellowed papers bound with a scarlet ribbon. It was a copy of the abstract of title to the Griefmaker, saved from the bankruptcy sale. Tenbrook glanced at the metes and bounds descriptions, beginning with 160 acres in bounty land granted to Nestor Griefmaker, private captain, McGuire's Company, Pennsylvania Militia, by the hand of Abraham Lincoln, President of the United States, "made patent and the seal of the General Land Office hereunto fixed in the year of Our Lord, one thousand eight hundred and sixty two and of the independence of the United States the Eighty Sixth." There was the quit claim deed from Chief Tawakonic for a large chunk of Middleton County at seventy-five cents an acre and the will by which Nestor Griefmaker freed his slave Sam Hawkins when he entered Free State Kansas. "To my colored man Sam I give his freedom, his mule, a $20 gold piece and the yellow kitchen wench known as Sally to have as his own."

From seventy-five cents to $40,000 an acre, Tenbrook mused. Life would have been different if the Griefmaker were still in Tenbrook hands. But would it have made him happy? Buffalo-hunting Indians prohibited tribe members from accumulating too many possessions, because possessions hindered mobility. They feared that signs of individual wealth would stimulate envy and undermine the cohesiveness of the tribe.

He'd been working for several hours when the door quietly opened. He looked up and saw a short man in a tight black velveteen jacket and a natty homburg studying him intensely. The visitor removed the hat with a flourish. He was bald except for a few short sprigs of hair on top and his face was spattered with dark moles. There were pouches under his eyes flecked with peppery spots. He wore rings on every finger of both hands. He carried a briefcase in one hand and an ivory-tipped cane in the other. He made an asthmatic wheezing sound when he breathed.

"Mr. Tenbrook, I believe?" he said.

"I'm Tenbrook.. Can I be of service?" The man didn't answer. He was looking around the office from the ceiling to the floor as if inspecting it or memorizing its details.

"I've heard a great deal about you," the man finally said.

"That's probably not a good thing."

"I ought to introduce myself. I'm James Stafford." He recited some of Tenbrook's exploits on the football field and the basketball court.

"Bulldogs versus Wildcats, 1989. Game tied, three seconds left. Tenbrook takes the snap. People are still talking about that game."

"Only in Middleton," said Tenbrook.

"I'm a great admirer of athletic talent," Stafford said. "One of my great regrets is that I was born without it. Can you guess why?"

"You're kind of short," said Tenbrook.

"Good for you," he said. "Most people worry about sensitivities and pretend not to notice. Do you know what the definition of a midget is?"

"No," said Tenbrook, expecting a joke.

"I missed the cut by about three inches." The man took off his glasses, polished them with a handkerchief, and returned them to his nose. "You don't recognize me, do you?"

"I'm not sure," said Tenbrook.

"You used to know me as Roy Brainhardt. I was the fat little guy who ran the high school print shop. I was the ball boy and manager for the basketball and football teams. I was the source of amusement for you and Everett Pillars and the other jocks in the locker room." He made a gesturing of someone going back to throw a pass. "Go long, Roy."

He dribbled an imaginary basketball. "'Show us your dunk, Roy-bo…Fetch, Roy…Roll over, Roy.'"

"Of course, I remember you Roy. Or James. I feel terrible. I'm so sorry."

"Don't be. Funny thing is, I worshipped you guys. And you did me a favor. The abuse I suffered at the hands of you and the all the other high school heroes inspired me, motivated me. You determined me to succeed and I have. I've made a great deal of money. So I harbor no resentment. What's past is past. We're not the same people we once were, isn't that so?" He looked around the dingy office as if to make the point.

"One would have thought that with your heroic stature and pedigree you'd have been the one who'd have piled up bags of dough," he said. "But money's not everything. You have integrity. You have a reputation. Good reputations are hard to come by and easy to lose. Of course, they don't put any food on the table. But I see you're busy. I won't waste your time. I only wish to say that you and I have an interest in common and that I have a business proposition to make which could be beneficial to both of us. I won't go into details. It's all here in this envelope. All I ask is that you read it over and if you're interested, give me a call." He took a large envelope out of his briefcase and dropped it on Tenbrook's desk.

"You don't have to call me James," he said. "Call me Jimmy. That will remind us both where we came from." Without waiting for an answer, he tipped his hat, turned and left. Someone standing outside opened the door for him. And he was gone. Tenbrook got up and went to the door in time to see a familiar white limousine pulling away. He went back to his desk and opened the envelope.

"Jesus Christ," he said out loud. Inside was a sheaf of thousand dollar bills. Tenbrook counted ten of them. There was nothing else in the envelope. No business proposal, no name or phone number for contacting Jimmy. Tenbrook sat down and counted the money again. It occurred to him that he'd never seen or touched a thousand-dollar bill before.

Chapter 5

Middleton gets its name not from its location—which is in fact near the middle of the country—but from Amos Middleton, a Boston industrialist who made his fortune in a smelting operation which destroyed the lungs of countless immigrants hired at miserly wages. He atoned by becoming an abolitionist. He founded Middleton and waged war from a distance on the owners of slaves. Middleton lies on the Kansas-Missouri border where Free State Kansans and Slave State Missourians once routinely killed one another, often mistaking friends for foes in deadly skirmishes that opened the curtain on the Civil War. Industrious Germans settled on the Kansas side, bringing with them the hard red wheat that made Kansas the bread basket of the world. Shiftless, inbred Appalachian coon hunters and moonshiners settled on the Missouri side, according to the Kansas point of view.

But no one gets born on the wrong side of the tracks in Middleton. The Union Pacific and the Santa Fe run parallel to one another, north of town. Class division is marked by State Line, a two-lane road running north and south. West on the Kansas side are gated communities with names like Sherwood Forest and Fox Run, idyllic enclaves with swimming pools, golf courses, tennis courts and soccer fields, chemically treated lawns, fountains and statues of Greek gods and electronic surveillance signs. Tomahawk Lane, Indian Creek Boulevard and Shawnee Mission Parkway reveal Middleton's true origins.

Eastward towards the Missouri side, the neighborhoods grade down. Slate and shake roofs give way to asphalt shingles. Mediterranean and Tudor estates dwindle to ranch houses and split levels with bass boats and Winnebagos parked in the drives. Decaying downtown Middleton with its deserted civic center and boarded up multi-level department stores straddles State Line. Pigeons roost on the window ledges of defunct dime and drug stores where real estate was once valued by the front foot. Dark-skinned people wait there for the buses that convey them to the Kansas side, where the jobs are. The industrial bottoms extend north of downtown, along with the derelict stockyards, a warren of broken timber chutes and pens that once held carloads of cattle and hogs bound for Middleton's packing plants. Nearby stretch the railroad yards where ghostly bands of illegals slip out of boxcars and make their way to crowded dormitories, midway to the promised land.

It is a tale of two Middletons. East of downtown lies Middleton, Missouri, also known as Bottomtown, a ward of curbless streets, battered pickups, shotgun bungalows and double-wides. Disheveled, unzoned Bottomtown is home to thrift and pawn shops, storefront taverns and revivalist churches. Engine blocks hang from trees and pit bulls lunge at chain link fences. Mobile meat smokers and cabs of 18-wheelers stand parked in gravel drives.

Stabbings and shootings are not unusual on a Friday night in Bottomtown. One Sunday morning at 2 am, a fight broke out between two exotic dancers over the ownership of a pet ferret. Shots were exchanged between their common law husbands and one of them died. Black men drinking from bottles in paper sacks loiter outside Bottomtown's principal liquor stores, the Home Run, the Last Chance and the Bar None Bar. White men with ragged beards and wallets attached to heavy chains rev their Harleys in the night. Occasionally, a member of the Native American community falls asleep on the street and gets run over by a car returning from the Pistol Club or drowns in the Kansas River where it makes a bend on its way to meet the Missouri. A concrete teepee records the mark where the river crested in the flood of 1951, 32 feet above the street.

Middleton, urbs et orbis…Town of half-finished dreams, like the circumferential by-pass that was halted by environmentalists and the claims of Native American burial grounds. To its citizens, Middleton is the epicenter of the cosmos. Nuclear war might be breaking out in the Middle East, an asteroid might be moments away from colliding with the earth, but you'd have to read about it on the back pages of the *Middleton Reaper*. The front page is reserved for pet rescues, nursing home coronations, golden anniversaries, pothole reports. Headlines: "Uptick in Bedbugs," "Orange Cones Spread East on 6th Street." Person on the Street question: "What do you do on flag day?" Answer: "We usually put out a flag."

The editors of the *Reaper* believe that remote events won't pique the interest of local readership without a Middleton peg. So a recent fire in Pittsburgh, Pennsylvania, in which 17 people died was compared to the Middleton Fire of 1907, in which 21 perished. The election of a president named Bush was a footnote to an article noting that there were three citizens in Middleton with the same last name. An article in the *Reaper* reviewing the Middleton Symphony's performance of a composition by Dvorak, began by noting that, "The closest Dvorak ever got to Middleton was Omaha, Nebraska."

There is no middle ground in Middleton. It is a hive of polarities. You must take sides. Breast feeding in public—for or against? Global warming—yea or nay? Representational art versus abstract art, cowboy boots versus Birkenstocks, bean sprouts versus red meat, Right to bear arms—for or against? East Middleton Wildcats versus West Middleton Bulldogs. Working Moms versus Stay-at-Home Moms. Panchos' Tacos or the Tijuana Inn's?

***

When he left his office, Tenbrook turned on Paradise and followed the cratered road into Bottomtown. He passed a porn shop, a truck stop, a mobile home with a pink fortune teller's sign glowing in the window and two miniature concrete lions by the front door. A man in a red sweatsuit wearing socks for mittens walked in the street, his hands stretched out before him, groping his way like a blind man. Tenbrook passed a dilapidated two-story building whose façade displayed a crude mural of a man struggling in the tentacles of an octopus.

Tenbrook slowed down before the ruins of the Loma Vista Hotel, which he'd managed for Niestrom in the lean days after his divorce. He and Pillars had made a sortie to the hotel in high school. Pillars had tried out his negotiating skills on an amazon in knee-length vinyl boots. He'd haggled her down to five dollars but when he offered $2.50, she blew up and told them to get out to the country and find themselves some sheep.

As Tenbrook drove past the hotel's entry, a tall, regal hooker in golden toreador pants stepped out and beckoned with her finger. Policewomen dressed up as streetwalkers periodically caught upstanding Middleton citizens in that trap. Genuine whores, hauled off for a night in jail, were back on the street the next day. The girl walked toward Tenbrook's car with a broad smile. A gold front tooth gleamed in her mouth. She was one more trouble he didn't need. He waved her off and drove away and saw her giving him the finger in his rear-view mirror. Driving through that familiar wasteland he felt again like a man with a doubtful future on an errand he didn't understand. The cash-filled envelope that lay on the seat next to him seemed alive, trembling, about to emit smoke and burst into flames.

He slowed down at the outskirts of Bottomtown and stopped by Tenbrook Park, a small strip of land between two pot-holed roads. The park was strewn with refuse. The slide had been deprived of its ladder and the swings had lost their seats. A few junkies and homeless persons slept on benches and picnic tables. A couple of dangerous-looking boys with baggy pants hanging from their asses were dancing languidly to the music in their earphones, making occult signs with their fingers. On a small hill at the end of the park was a statue of Henry Tenbrook the Patriarch, surrounded by weeds.

A sense of shame came over him as he remembered homely little Roy Brainhardt and the way he and the others had treated him. That wasn't Tenbrook. Yet it must once have been. What other cruelties had he strewn on his path during his glory days? Things had come so easily to him back then. It wasn't that surprising that he succumbed to arrogance and adolescent meanness. But the thought filled him with disgust.

He drove to the end of Paradise, exited Bottomtown on 452 Road and headed east past the state line into Missouri. Where the blacktop ended the air changed, smelling of decomposing stubble and fermenting soil. Before him stretched miles of flood plain, a vast puzzle of cultivated rectangles, intermittently disfigured by toy-like, oddly-named hamlets—Foghorn, Peculiar, Ozone. At night for a couple of hours, the lights of those hamlets sparkled like fallen stars. He took the Coal Creek turnoff and felt the road beneath him rise to a congeries of hills. Sometimes fog filled the valley so that the hill tops looked like islands. From the top of the first hill he could spot the roof of his home, the Missouri Compromise, purchased in spite of Tenbrook's aversion to Missouri on account of the lower prices of real estate on the Missouri side. To the south, Troy Bilbrey's pasture rose to a hedgerow that jutted out like a Mohawk haircut, one of the few shelterbelts that hadn't been chain-hauled out by farmers obsessed with harvesting a few more bushels of corn. A little to the left of that hill was the brow of an esker, a relic of the last ice age, marking the point where the glaciers had stopped. The next hill was known as Conestoga Bluff for its resemblance to a prairie schooner. Perched on top of the bluff was an enormous house that had been under construction for several years, a bizarre presence in a neighborhood of clapboard farmhouses and trailers. Small planes landed and took off from the grass runway on the property, feeding rumors of drug trafficking. Beyond spread the unincorporated town of Erratum.

Tenbrook turned into his driveway and watched a feral cat dragging its dugs disappear into the weeds. Walnuts crunched under his tires. He stopped at the shed where he kept his tractor. It had been a dairy barn and was large enough to encourage the accumulation of equipment that was obsolete or beyond repair. Worn tires, broken cinderblocks, animal traps, ladders, empty tool boxes, an incubator, coiled hoses, utility carts, a wheel chair, a trailer, a tarnished trombone, two dollies, wine-making equipment, an air compressor, a miniature windmill, a twisted shortwave radio antenna, piles of fence posts. Tenbrook saved everything on the premise that someday he might find a use for the stuff. Organ pipe nests of mud daubers clung to some of the treasures. Lying in the middle of the shed like a farrowing sow was the fuselage of a float plane that Tenbrook had bought at a bargain price. He'd envisioned restoring it and becoming an Alaskan bush pilot, once he'd learned how gasoline engines work and how to fly.

The shed was a mausoleum of unfinished projects, a monument to enthusiasms that had flared up, then died. There were more projects than could be finished in the lifetime even of a man with focus and skills. Wasps drifted gracefully in and out of the darkness. Brushing off cobwebs, Tenbrook walked through the shed, stepping on piles of sawdust left by carpenter bees that were boring holes in the wooden beams. He thought of Kate and how he'd asked her to be a cheerleader for so many of his transitory dreams.

"Sailing without a rudder," she'd once said as she surveyed the clutter. In a corner of the shed he found what he was looking for, a plastic box filled with fishing reels and lures. He opened it and laid the envelope inside, first checking superstitiously to make sure the money was still there.

Chapter 6

Kate was on the phone when he walked in. Her bell-like laughter floated from the kitchen.

"You are so bad," she said with a gay laugh. "I can't believe you." She gave Tenbrook a flippant wave with her fingers without looking up. "Naughty boy," she said into the phone.

Tenbrook sat down in the living room and tried to tune out the conversation. Another gust of laughter struck his ears. How long had it been since he'd made her laugh like that? He picked up a piece of the wood duck house which he'd left partly assembled on the floor and tried to fit it into place. But Kate's conversation kept distracting him. He noticed a sherry glass on the card table by the couch.

"He was certainly entertaining you," said Tenbrook when she hung up and came looking for him.

"Who was?" said Kate.

"Father Ned."

"What makes you think it was Ned?"

"No one else excites you to such merriment," said Tenbrook. A frown passed over her face. She chased it off with a smile. "The telltale sherry glass suggests that he was recently here."

"Please, don't start in on that," Kate said. "Ned was here. He had his sherry. We talked business. He left. He just called me about his meeting with Florence. A great turf battle is brewing with the Altar Guild and Ned likes to stir the pot. But he's harmless. I'm not having an affair with him."

"Some people think he's having an affair with Gwen," said Tenbrook.

"You hear rumors about every minister in town," said Kate. "For some reason, people think ministers are all great Casanovas. By the way, we got the financing for the kitchen. Some anonymous donor gave us $20,000. I found a place that used to be a restaurant. It's all set up, ready to go. Tables, chairs, utensils, pots and pans, stoves and refrigerators. I got the owner down to $500 a month. I'm turning out to be a whiz at business. You should be proud of me."

"I am proud of you," said Tenbrook. "I worship you. Explain the concept to me again."

"Will you listen this time?"

"I listened last time. The homeless people need a place to get a free meal that's not like a soup kitchen."

"That's right."

"Ok. Go on."

"You're not laughing at me?"

"I'm not laughing. I promise. I'm interested."

"It would be nice if you could just support me," said Kate. "The idea is we'll give them a menu and choices. Volunteers from the church will act as waiters. They'll treat the homeless people like customers in a real restaurant."

"And this is supposed to help build their self-esteem?" said Tenbrook. "Have you thought about offering them omelets with truffles and crepes suzette?"

"You're being sarcastic," said Kate.

"No, I'm not," said Tenbrook, mustering a smile. "I'm all for anything that helps the homeless. I think it's great you've discovered this talent you didn't know you had. To be honest, I feel a little threatened by it. I'm not much of a business genius, as you may have noticed. If I hit the skids, I'll be your best customer at the Hosanna Kitchen, or whatever it's called." Kate scowled.

"Hallelujah Kitchen," she said. "I know it's hokey. That was Ned's idea. Let's talk about something else. How are the Pillars of society?"

"The Pillars of society send you their best. They are prospering. They are printing money. Everett bears his self-importance lightly."

"Has Gwendolyn gotten her new boobs?"

"She has. They're like the nose cones of guided missiles. The only piece of original equipment Gwen still possesses is her reddish-golden hair."

"You're naïve if you think her reddish-golden hair is natural."

"Gwen told me that if she had your looks and your body she wouldn't have to spend Everett's hard-earned money on face lifts, tummy tucks and boob jobs."

"Gwen is a dear."

"She was wearing a diamond ring the size of a jaw breaker."

"I've seen it," said Kate. "She kind of waves it in your face."

"Everett told me that she's found Jesus."

"Do you believe that?"

"She told me she was saved. I don't know. Maybe Jesus is just a smoke screen. Are you sure she's not getting it on with the rector?"

"It would serve Everett right if she did." It was a mistake to talk to Kate about the Pillars. The subtext was always money. Kate would make sarcastic comments about the Pillars' materialistic, philistine lives. Tenbrook would feel the undercurrent: "It must be nice." Then he'd try to defend their own existence.

"We wouldn't want to change places with the Pillars," he'd say.

"I'm sure the Pillars envy our quaint lifestyle," Kate would retort. "Gwen probably feels as if she's missing out on something by not doing her own housework." A little ritual would follow.

Tenbrook: "Hire a cleaning lady."

Kate: "We can't afford it."

Tenbrook: "I've got some new business. We can afford it. We're going to do it. Case closed." But they never did it. And they couldn't afford it.

Kate: "I don't need help. I don't want help…By the way, what did Everett want?"

"He wanted to inform me that he's moving ahead on the Griefmaker."

"And he wanted your blessing?"

"Actually, he doesn't care what I think. He was just trying out his case out on me. Everett doesn't take me very seriously."

"You don't take yourself seriously."

"In a few years the Griefmaker will be a sea of roof tops."

"You can't blame him for wanting to cash in."

"You really have become a capitalist," said Tenbrook. "Everett doesn't need the cash. It's an ego thing."

"What's it to you? You've got God's little forty acres right here."

Kate was looking at him as if from a distance, like the director of a play. Her gray eyes shone—with what? She was smiling, but it wasn't her spontaneous sunburst smile, the one that could suck the breath out of his lungs. It was an ironic, almost mocking smile. Her face was a mask.

Time had refined her lovely features, her fine mouth, her patrician cheek bones and nose. She could afford to be careless about her looks. She was beautiful with or without makeup. She rarely wore jewelry. Tenbrook loved the brusque way she attacked her hair with a comb, taming it with a rubber band and carelessly shoving it under a baseball cap. She didn't bother to hide the first few strands of gray. She defied her age, ignored fashion and that made her seem more beautiful, he thought. Compared to Gwen's hothouse, cosmetically enhanced beauty, her diamonds and bracelets, her anorexic figure secured by surgery and trips to the fat farm, Kate was natural beauty, the real thing.

"You don't need another project, Henry," she said. "Fighting Everett isn't going to make your life any more meaningful. And it's not going to help put Channy through college."

"Maybe I could sell him my soul," said Tenbrook. Kate wasn't amused. She was looking down at the floor. Suddenly the room seemed airless. He'd said something wrong. Kate sat rigidly, like a wooden idol.

"What's the matter?" said Tenbrook. Kate shook her head and looked down. Tenbrook stood up and walked over to her. He reached toward her, but she backed away.

"I'm not in love with you anymore," she said at last in a voice that was almost a whisper. Tenbrook looked at her. He wasn't stunned. Her words didn't crush him. They just lapped at him, like a caress. He almost welcomed them. He'd been expecting them any day for twenty years. Now the waiting was over. No need for explanations. Nothing left to fear. At last he had his answer. So it was time for a course correction. That was all. He'd just have to start over, invent the rest of his life. He'd done it once before, he could do it again. Without another word, without looking at her, he left the room, with acid corroding his gut.

Tenbrook climbed the bare wooden stairs to his study. The stairs creaked under his weight, a sound like some small animal in pain. The house seemed to have aged ten years since he last looked. The walls were covered with stains he hadn't noticed. They badly needed paint. The carpet was worn to the backing in spots. The knot holes in the room's pine paneling seemed like the eyes of deer, watching him in perfect indifference, safe in the knowledge that they were immune from danger, that he posed no threat, as if he wasn't real.

Tenbrook's office was a pack rat's cache of note pads, magazines, piles of half-read books, open in the middle. How weary Kate must have grown of all his unfinished business, his interminable disarray. He found his high school yearbook and thumbed through the pages. There were pictures: Tenbrook going back for a pass, Tenbrook kicking a field goal, Tenbrook running the high hurdles, Tenbrook diving for a loose ball. Big man on the campus with a square jaw and a victory grin. There were pictures of Roy Brainhardt, alias James Stafford, too: Roy carrying a sack of basketballs, Roy with his clipboard and giant ring of keys standing outside the huddle, Roy sitting proudly in his print shop domain. Tenbrook felt another wave of self-loathing.

Pinned to his cork bulletin board was a birthday card from Kate. It was a cartoon of two deer and a rabbit holding their noses at a skunk. "Hope your birthday doesn't stink," it read. Beneath the cartoon Kate had written in her child-like, almost illegible scrawl, "You're still as handsome as you were at 27…You still thrill me as much as you did with that first kiss. Thank you for making me so happy. For giving me the best years of my life. I'm so excited about our future."

He'd forgotten that card. It lifted him for a moment. But it had been written almost ten years before. The card was covered with dust. Once when they were first dating, he'd dropped to his knees to tie her shoestrings and said, "Tender is the knot." Kate had laughed and kissed him. Had he won her with that random flash of wit, tricked her into thinking that life with him would be just like that moment, an endless succession of good times and laughs?

Now she'd transformed herself into a business woman, a new Kate. A Kate who spoke like a deal-maker using expressions like "get-go," "slam dunk," "sounds like a plan," and "up to speed." Kate and the Reverend exchanging high fives in the kitchen when their deal went through. How many affairs had she had that he didn't know about? He couldn't blame her for trying other guys. He was calm. He'd prepared, already rehearsed his lines: "That's okay, Kate. You've been good to me. You've put up with me. You have the right to pursue your own life. I'm happy for you. Go." What a liberating show of power it would be to wish her well rather than collapsing in a heap of self-pity or exploding in a fit of rage.

Sweet, false music played in Tenbrook's ear: It would be better to be alone. He'd become too dependent on her. If he were alone, there would be no one to judge him. Draped beside the bulletin board was the fabric she'd woven for his birthday, two spiraling figures in vivid yellow and green intertwining against a background of sunset red. He remembered how she'd struggled with that pattern, her cheerful frustration expressed in the arcane language of warp and woof. "There's just not enough time," she'd said, as her deadline approached. "There's so much stuff…I'm so stingy with my warp that when I get to the end of a project, there's barely enough shed to get the shuttle through. It makes it hard to finish." But Kate did finish. And when she did she leaned back and studied her work. "The thing I like about weaving is there are boundaries," she said. "You're pounding against boundaries. I like freedom, but not too much freedom. You have to have boundaries and you have to pound against them." She was a pro. She was Penelope at her loom waiting for Odysseus to come home. But you are no Odysseus, Tenbrook said to himself. How many soft landings had she given him when his own passions waned and the thermals of enthusiasm stopped keeping him aloft? And now she was finished with him.

Suddenly, nothing seemed more precious to him than Kate, nothing more terrible than the thought of losing her. Fear of losing her had made it happen, precipitated it, called the demons of jealousy and insecurity into being. He'd sought her affirmation too often. A few times he'd made her cry, a way of obtaining reassurance. Why was she so free of this need? Money was the real problem. Every day he went to the mailbox with the irrational hope that a check had magically arrived that would bail them out. Maybe it wasn't too late for them to fly away in the De-Haviland and build a cabin in Alaska and live alone in the pristine wilderness before the last wild, uncorrupted things vanished from the face of the earth. No, Kate would scream if he evoked that dream again.

He thought of the Griefmaker. Virgin prairie, never plowed. Would Kate leave him if it still was Tenbrook land? A low flame of anger began to burn. What difference did it make if she weren't "in love" with him? Was he "in love" with her? No one had ever required her to pronounce those words. They weren't part of the marriage vows. What did they mean, after all? They belonged to the fleeting romantic stage of courtship when you were "falling" in love, the giddy free fall, the momentary loss of self in an ecstasy of self-absorption. The moment when you said endearing things like "tender is the knot." It was a matter of survival, of sanity to come out of that fall before you hit the rocks. At some point you had to return to the business of living. You had to graduate to the routine, the appreciation of companionship, the bond of partnership. That was normal. That was true of any marriage that had lasted twenty years. He didn't expect her to swoon when he walked into the room.

Now the formula "in love with you" would acquire a power over him, would haunt and obsess him. He would have to hear it every day, like a confession, a stamp of approval. If he couldn't win it, there would be a barrier between them. Whenever they were having a moment of spontaneous fun, it would come down on him like a guillotine. They were already divorced.

He showered and changed his clothes. When he came downstairs, Kate was gone. A note was waiting for him on the couch by the front door. He picked it up, sat down and read.

"Please, please, please, Henry, try to understand, since I don't understand. It just came out. I hadn't planned it. And I didn't mean I don't love you—I do. I always will. I know what you're thinking and I promise there isn't anyone else. Please don't leave me, don't fall silent on me like you do when you feel I'm neglecting you. I want to live with you forever. What I said—I don't think it meant anything. Maybe it has something to do with a kind of independence I need at this stage in my life. Maybe it's menopause. Don't let me ruin our wonderful life because I said something stupid, just words."

He wanted to ask her why women have some sort of biological need to blow things up when they're going smoothly. He'd lost her in the place where her unknowable female self dwelled, where half the secrets of life's purposes lay hidden like jeweled eggs or golden fleece. He would never be able to discover them. There was something belligerent, obstinate in Kate's declaration. It was a gauntlet thrown down, a gratuitous, trouble-making gesture. But she was on top. He would have to leave or ride it out. Part of her needed to be in that place that excluded him. That was all she was asking. She wasn't demanding that he change. He had to find a way of saving himself that didn't depend on her.

There was more: "I love our sex life. I want to keep having sex with you. I'm attracted to you. You're the best lover and the best husband anyone could have. I haven't fallen out of love with you. I love you, always, Kate."

Sadness settled down and folded its wings around him. Also, an unexpected quiver of expectation. Maybe it wasn't too late to start over. For an instant, he hated Kate. Somewhere he'd read about a prince who'd fallen so madly in love that he stabbed his lover to regain his spiritual freedom.

The door knob rattled. Suddenly Kate was there, framed in the doorway. The light of the setting sun glowed behind her. She looked apparitional. Without shutting the door, she started to undress, looking at him with a sad, inscrutable smile. She unbuttoned her shirt, slipped her arms through the sleeves and let it fall to the floor. Reaching with both hands behind her back, she undid her bra. She unzipped her jeans, pulled them down over her thighs, stepped out of them and walked towards him and in an instant they were together. His hand passed over her shoulder and back, met her hand as it played across his chest, followed the knobs of her spine down to the small of her back, over the swell of her buttocks, down along her legs, as if he were shaping her landscape and looking for the key that momentarily opens the secret exit from the world. Within the urgency, they found the movements they knew so well, coaxing one another to the finish line. But just then Kate's words came back, along with the image of Pillars looming over the Griefmaker and suddenly Tenbrook lost it. He tried desperate thrusting, but it was no go. He was finished. They lay there without speaking. A song passed through his mind about a maiden who wished she was a sparrow and that she had wings and could fly away.

"I'm sorry," he said. "I guess I was trying too hard." She patted him playfully on the rump. But he could feel the wetness of a tear on his shoulder.

"I've put you through a lot today," she said.

✳✳✳

He woke up in the middle of the night, startled by the crazy fear that mice had found the envelope and eaten the money. He got up, put on his shoes, and walked down to the shed with a flashlight. Coyotes started in, yipping like crazed hyenas. A dry wind shook the branches of a dead elm. He made his way through the crowded shed, found the box, opened the envelope and touched the sheaf of money and thought he must be going crazy. Back in the kitchen, he poured himself a glass of gin. He looked up. Kate was there in her robe.

"I heard voices," she said. "I got scared. I thought someone had broken in. Are you okay?"

"I'm okay," he said with an embarrassed grin. "I couldn't sleep. I was talking to myself."

"Are you sure something's not wrong?"

"Don't worry, Kate. I'm not crazy. When I start thinking that the person I'm talking to is real, you can start worrying about me."

Chapter 7

A $15,000 check from James Stafford made out to the church lay on Father Ned's desk. The vestry was divided on whether to bank it or send it back. Stafford was bad karma, probably a crook. He never came to church. What was he after? Ned's position was "Money is money. The Lord works in strange ways." He also thought it might be useful to wave the check in Pillars' face the next time he threatened to pull the plug on the church.

Sylvia, Ned's secretary, rang.

"Mr. Pillars to see you." Ned was expecting the visit, but he still stiffened. He looked forward to Pillars' visits the way a tenant who's behind on his rent looks forward to a visit from his landlord. Pillars burst into the room without knocking.

"May I come in?" he said with a curtsey and a grin.

"Make yourself at home," said Ned. Pillars sat down and leaned across the desk.

"I have a question," he said.

"That doesn't surprise me," said Father Ned. "Fire away."

"Just between us girls…Do you believe in this stuff?"

"What stuff?"

"Stuff like the Trinity, the resurrection, the 'brighter tomorrow,' you know what I mean."

"You know I don't talk about my own beliefs," said Ned. "Like everyone else, I'm searching."

"Funny, you seem so certain when you're up in the pulpit," said Pillars. "But I guess you have to play to your flock. You have to come across as all-knowing, tell them what they want to hear. They'd be shocked if they thought you were subject to doubts. Don't worry, I'm not going to tell on you. I don't believe in that stuff either. My guess is that when you die, the candle goes out—poof!"

"My guess is that even Jesus had doubts," said Ned.

"Why don't you come out and say you do too, if that's the case," said Pillars. "Didn't someone say that the truth will set you free? Seems to me that you ought to believe in what you preach."

"I didn't say I didn't believe."

"You wouldn't go to a surgeon if he said he wasn't sure about what he was doing, if he said he was 'searching.' But what do I know? I'm just a dirt man."

Father Ned glanced at Stafford's check. Now would be the moment to brandish it. Pillars had put up most of the money for his church, as well as the land. He seemed to think that entitled him to bully Ned. Whenever he visited Ned, there was a threatening undercurrent. If Ned didn't jump when Pillars said, "Jump," Pillars would start musing out loud about withdrawing his support for the church. He liked to question church expenses: "Why do you keep the temperature so low?" he'd say, looking over the monthly statement. "It's freezing in here. Air-conditioning costs money." "Five hundred dollars for flowers? Jesus Christ!" He'd let it drop that a minister in Wichita with a comparable parish was making twenty percent less salary than Ned.

"Isn't it about time for a sermon on stewardship?" he'd say. "I'm stretched to the bone. It would be nice if some of your pious worshippers would ante up a bit more. Tell them they're not going to get into heaven unless they open their pocketbooks. What was it Jesus said about tithing? Sometimes I think I ought to just pick up my marbles and join the neighborhood synagogue or mosque."

Ned had a tick in his eyelid, a little pulsing that showed up every time he had an encounter with Pillars. It had just showed up and Ned tried to cover it with his hand. Ned feared for his job. He feared for his church. But his greatest fear was that Pillars would confront him with the discovery that his relationship with Gwen was not altogether Platonic. Gwen was an emotional, unstable woman. It wouldn't be unthinkable for her to blurt out a confession someday.

His palms were sweating. He looked at them. What did he expect to see—the stigmata? Without Pillars' money, there would be no Hallelujah Kitchen. No costly vestry retreats. No gorgeous brocaded chasubles and Eucharistic stoles, no ornate communion chalices and censers—the accoutrements of office Ned was fond of. Anxious thoughts flew through his mind. The memory of the first time he and Gwen had kissed and ended up in a tangle on the carpet of his office. What were they thinking of? Had Sylvia heard them? Gwen had called it "The Kiss of Peace," but my God she stuck her tongue halfway down his throat. What was he supposed to do—resist? Ned recovered his composure and flashed his own good shepherd smile. He could tell that the ritual chastisements were over. Pillars face had changed. Now he wore his beseeching look.

"I need your help, Ned," he said.

"I never expected to hear you ask me for help, Ev," he said. "I'm the one who's always asking you for help."

"I need your support," said Pillars. "You know about my plans to develop the rest of this priceless land we're sitting on. You know there's some tree huggers in your congregation who are giving me a hard time about it. They think the Griefmaker belongs to them, that developing the virgin prairie would be a kind of rape, a sin, etcetera, bla, bla,

bla and flappa, flappa, flappa. You know what I'm talking about? It would help if you'd put a kind word in for me in one of your flowery sermons. Remind them of how much I've done for this church, remind them which side your bread—and theirs—is buttered on, however you want to put it. Threaten them with damnation. Tell them that the Lord commands us to make the land bring forth fruit. You can be eloquent. I've seen them gobble up holy platitudes like candy from your hand."

Pillars glowered. He slapped Ned's desk.

"Deal?" he said.

"I'll do my best," said Ned. Pillars gave him a thumbs up. Father Ned had a momentary impulse to give Pillars the finger, but he checked it and returned the thumbs up sign. Good to go. Anything to keep the gravy flowing. Nothing to rock the boat.

"That's my boy," said Pillars. "I knew I could count on you." Pillar got up, genuflected, made the sign of the cross, and lifted his gaze to heaven. Then he gave a rude laugh, shook his head and left, slamming the door behind him.

Ned felt a familiar twinge of impotence. He often sensed mistrust and even contempt for him among some of the men in his congregation. The women were his true believers, the heart and soul of his ministry. He flirted with them, listened to them, something not all of their husbands did. That was his secret. He knew women. He knew how to tease them, banter with them, how to make them feel as if he took them seriously. He looked out the window and watched Pillars get into his car and drive away. He felt ashamed, craven. Ned was not without pride. He wanted to strike back. He was no nature boy. He wasn't moved by all the virgin prairie talk. But as he resented Pillars bullying him, he felt a faint sense of protective allegiance to the Griefmaker. And the first words of a sermon he might deliver condemning Pillars' plans to develop it came to his mind: "The Bible says, 'Cursed is the ground for man having passed over it.'" Then he thought about Gwen again and fell to his knees behind the closed door and prayed for the first time in years to a God that didn't exist.

Chapter 8

Pillars stepped from the limousine and walked to the house, slapping the rolled-up plans against his thigh. Folded into the roll was the document that secured the bridge loan he needed. It was a strange way of doing business, a few sentences scribbled on a sheet of yellow paper. But the little man had promised that the money would be in Pillars' bank account the next day, money that would furnish the required equity. Now he had breathing room. He could start lining up tenants. He didn't like doing business with an ugly little troll who had an unsavory reputation. But the man had money and in business, you had to do what you had to do. Survival first, success thereafter. Let T stand for Time and P for Profit.

He stopped at the wrecked Mercedes. An "Expose Exxon" sticker had been affixed to the bumper, not for the first time. He went to the house, slammed the door, threw the plans down on the marble-top table in the foyer and headed up the corkscrew staircase in the turret.

For once, he felt foolish. Tenbrook's great-grandfather had modeled his mansion after some castle he'd seen in Scotland and had stones and stone masons shipped from the Hebrides to build it. The poor bastard had had a heart attack and died before the monument was finished, before he'd assumed the mantle of Lord of the Manor, before he'd had the chance to climb to the top of the turret and survey his domain. Now Pillars felt like his caricature, Everett the Bold. His footsteps echoed in the stone column. He stood at the door of Tod's room. Thundering bass notes shook the walls. Pasted to the door was a picture of a demonic figure with horns, rampant facing the dexter side, brandishing a pitchfork and displaying a huge tongue the color of Pepto Bismol. Behind the demon were flaming crosses. What the hell was that supposed to mean? Pillars knocked on the door. No answer. He pounded. After a minute, the music fell to a dull throb. The door opened slowly and there was Tod, rubbing his eyes, white acne medicine spotting his face. He was dressed in black jeans, a black turtle neck and black military boots.

"I'd like to have a word with you," said Pillars.

"Whatever." Tod shrugged, disappeared into his den and turned the music back up. Pillars entered, stepping over piles of socks and underwear, dirty dishes, half-empty sacks of chips, scattered magazines and comic books, tangles of wire leading to a bank of amplifiers. The walls were covered with posters, including one of Hitler giving the Nazi salute and the one depicting Che Guevara with a crown of thorns, along with the message, "Meek, Mild…As If!" A musky odor of incense permeated the room. In one corner was a pyramid of beer cans from defunct breweries—Schmidt's, Griesedick, Potosi, Namar, Frankenmuth—collector's items that Tod had accumulated when he was a kid.

"Would you mind turning that racket down?" said Pillars. "When I was your age, music had a tune. I've asked you not to light fires in your room."

"It didn't light a fire," said Tod. "It lit a match."

"Something's burning. And stop calling yourself 'It.'"

"It's incense, Pater."

"It smells."

"Duh. That's what it's supposed to do. Covers up other odors." Tod made little quotation marks with his fingers.

"If you want to destroy your brain, that's your business. But my home insurance doesn't cover incense fires."

"Incense instills insights."

"Such as?"

"That which is not forbidden is mandatory."

"Christ, what's that supposed to mean?" said Pillars.

"Just trying to raise your consciousness, Father," said Tod.

"I'd like to raise your consciousness a little," said Pillars. "You took the Mercedes without permission. You wrecked it. But you didn't just wreck it. You drove it over about $5,000 worth of sod. It was a deliberate act of vandalism."

"A mere hiccup in the great scheme of things."

"More of a fuck-up than a hiccup."

"More of a political act of protest."

"What were you protesting?"

"Development."

"What do you think pays the bills around here?"

"I'm also against degradation of nature," said Tod. "Covering the planet with asphalt. It's a good thing that the Mercedes got wrecked, because the gasoline engine is doomed."

"The Mercedes didn't 'get' wrecked. You wrecked it. Cause and effect. It's an issue of responsibility."

"It's an issue of self-expression. Responsibility is a code word for repression."

"At least you owe me an apology," said Pillars.

"Owe," said Tod. "I love that word. You can't think of relationships in any terms other than owing. Debtor and creditor. I owe everything to you."

It was maddening. Tod dealt in nonsequiturs. That was his secret. Pillars couldn't win an argument with his son because Tod ignored the rules of logic. But like a moth to the flame, Pillars couldn't resist getting sucked into these futile discussions. He knew he was in the right. He was being reasonable. He held all the cards. Tod was unjustified, incorrigible, a fake rebel dependent on his father's largesse. Nevertheless, Tod always won. Pillars always folded. This never happened to him in business. He walked all over the opposition. What was the source of the power his feckless son had over him?

He had tried threats. But he couldn't find one that cowed his son. He couldn't wrest even a minimal concession from him. When Pillars unsheathed his anger, Tod just laughed: "Boring, boring." Pillars scripted his arguments, but Tod always threw some devious retort back at him. Pillars came away from their confrontations feeling defeated and secretly impressed.

"You're not living up to your part of the bargain," he said. Tod jumped on the word.

"Always bargaining—right, Pater?" Pillars felt trapped in the role of the cheapskate, the haggler, the exploiter.

"Sometimes, I swear, I don't understand where you came from," said Pillars.

"Maybe you're not my real father," said Tod.

"I've thought about that," said Pillars. And he had. The genes had run out, that much he knew. Tod had no drive, no ambition. He didn't care about anything. His interests were transitory and diffuse, like Tenbrook's. Neither of them had the instinct for pursuit, for connecting the dots. Take the connection between the quarry and the landfill. Pillars had intuited it. One enterprise complemented the other. Mining the rock had created a pit for rubbish. A stream of cash flowed between the two. When the bulldozers weren't busy at the quarry, he transferred them to a construction site or leased them out for county road work. Nothing was idle, nothing went to waste. The right hand always knew what the left hand was doing and if you practiced hard, there was no limit to how many balls you could keep in the air. Making money out of other people's trash and garbage—that was sweet. A kind of art. He liked to stand on one of his hills when they were crushing gravel and watch the dozers push mounds of trash around while seagulls wheeled overhead. He didn't mind the stench. It was the odor of profit. He was a workhorse, that was all. Everett Pillars, without liability for deficiency judgment. He had his deals. The vanity plate on his silver Humvee read "Entreprnr." Enterprise. Creativity. Those were the key words. What would Tod and his anarchist friends ever create? They were all hat and no cattle. Wrecking a Mercedes represented the height of their capabilities and ambitions.

Pillars didn't tell Tod that he and Tenbrook had driven his father's Cadillac flat out on a joy ride across the Middleton Country Club golf course when they were kids. The difference was, when they got caught, they had to work it off, an entire summer spent haying the Griefmaker under the July and August sun, eighty-pound bales by the hundreds, shirts and pants soaked with sweat, gallons of water gulped, utter exhaustion, entire days without a thought except for rest, the sleep of the dead at night and then up at six in the morning for another go'round. The thought of Tod haying was laughable. He wouldn't last 15 minutes. He'd be writhing on the ground gasping about his asthma, "I can't breathe," calling for his mommy. And Gwen would come running to her precious.

"About this 'material thing' you wrecked last night," said Pillars. Tod rolled his eyes and picked up a cigarette roller. "If you want to renounce your material possessions, fine. But that doesn't give you the right to destroy mine. Would you be so cavalier about the Mercedes if you'd bought it with your own money? If you had to pay to have it repaired?"

His sarcasm sounded sophomoric. He ought to be making assertions rather than rhetorical questions. He knew that Tod knew that there would be no consequences.

"Property is theft," said Tod.

"What about your stuff? That guitar—that cost one thousand dollars and that you never play—that's just a material thing? That's property. But it wasn't stolen. I paid for it." Pillars paused, thinking he'd landed a blow.

"Isn't this where you tell me that when you were my age, your first car was a VW Beetle that didn't even have a gas gauge and that cost less than the guitar cost?"

"That beer can collection that meant so much to you when you were a kid?" said Pillars, plunging on. "You had to have it. You begged. How much money did I shell out for those cans? Isn't that collection just a material thing? If I came into your room and started stomping on them, wouldn't you object?"

Tod twirled the handle of the cigarette roller. His frown turned to a sly grin. Slowly, he got up and walked over the pile of cans and kicked it over.

"Watch," he said. Then he stomped down on one of the cans.

"You have a great aptitude for destroying things," said Pillars.

"Isn't that what capitalism is all about—creative destruction?" said Tod. "For everything to stay the same, everything must change."

"What did I pay for that can? Five bucks? Ten bucks?"

"It's worth a hundred today," said Tod. He fished another can out of the pile with his foot and deftly nudged it upright. He raised his foot high like a drum major's and brought it down smartly on the can. Pillars watched, spellbound. Tod wasn't just trampling on beer cans. He was trampling on respect for authority, private property rights, free enterprise, the fruits of one's labor, everything Pillars believed in. Stomp! Tod crushed another can.

"And when this is over, I'll get the blame," said Pillars. Stomp! "You won't even have to clean up the mess. Mary will do it for you." Stomp!

"Some of my best friends are Jews," said Tod. "Make the homeless work for their handouts. Build more prisons." Suddenly Pillars felt strangely hooked by the orgy. He walked over to the pile of cans, bent down, righted one and then flattened it with a stomp. He did another. Then Tod did one. They had a kind of rhythm going. Comment-Stomp. Rejoinder-Stomp. They kept it up. It was almost as if they were working together.

"As long as you're living under my roof and on my payroll…" said Pillars, stomping on a can.

"Trite argument Number One," said Tod with another stomp.

"Don't expect any more handouts until you come up with a plan to repay me." Stomp.

"Aren't you going to tell me about the two thousand tackles you made your senior year?" Stomp.

Pillars' anger returned. He stopped and watched Tod methodically flattening the remaining cans. The next time the little punk came to him for a handout, he'd tell him to go get the recycling money for the cans.

"Someday you're going to pay," said Pillars.

"You'll be hearing from my lawyers." Stomp.

Pillars left the room without another word. He took the stairs in the tower two at a time, slipping once and losing his balance and by the time he was out the front door, he was raging. Bess, his favorite pointing bitch, chose that moment to trot past. Pillars sent her sprawling with a kick to her flank. The dog yelped and slunk away from her master with a sullen look and her tail between her legs. It was a perfectly executed kick, but the sudden motion of it pulled a muscle in Pillars's buttock, a muscle he didn't even know he had. And he walked off limping, looking for something to break.

Chapter 9

Tenbrook was at the breakfast table reading an article in the *Middleton Reaper* about the Girls of Middleton University Swimsuit Calendar: "They will break your heart, they will kick your butt."

"When did the word 'butt' become acceptable parlance?" he asked.

"It's not my favorite word," said Kate. "There's an outfit on TV that promises 'the butt you've always dreamed of.'"

"One of the girls said she prayed before she posed. 'I think God wanted me to do it,'" she said.

"Isn't it amazing how God gets involved in everything?" said Kate.

"The girls had to submit photos of a seductive look, a pouty look and a look of their choice. What would be good for a third look? One with the mouth shaped for a blow job?"

"Tenbrook!" said Kate. "What if Channy heard?"

"She's heard worse," said Tenbrook. "Remember when she asked you about oral sex?"

"'Oral sex: Is that when you talk about it?'"

"She was what, when she said that—seven years old?"

"Speaking of your precocious daughter, Channy has requested an audience with you," said Kate.

"If I'm not back in 24 hours call the highway patrol." Tenbrook walked up the stairs and stood outside Channy's door. From within, Ani diFranco was singing: "Welcome to the freak show, here we go." Tenbrook tapped on the door.

"Enter," Channy yelled. She was standing before the mirror, holding up the Rainbow Brite Halloween costume Kate had made for her years before.

"I just wanted to see if I could still get into it," she said.

"Aren't you a little young to be worried about your weight?"

"Dad, I gained two pounds this week."

"Horrors. My daughter turning into a blimp before my eyes. Beware of anorexia, Channy. My first girlfriend died of it."

"You wouldn't like me if I was morbidly obese," she said. "I have to keep tabs on my figure. Sit down, Dad."

"There's no place to sit." She pointed to the open bathroom door.

"Sit on the toilet seat," she said.

"That doesn't seem very dignified," Tenbrook said. He stepped into Channy's bathroom, taking care to avoid the hair curlers scattered across the floor. He looked at the shelves holding tubes and vials of potions designed to transmute mortal flesh into immortal beauty.

"This place looks like an alchemist's lab," he said. "Almond and aloe foaming bath gel…tango-mango body butter…frizz-ease moisture barrier…mint energy alpha hydroxyl foot scrub…invisible concealer."

"Now you know what it takes to be a woman these days," said Channy. A yellow doll was lying spread-eagled on the toilet seat, its red-threaded mouth frozen in a dopey grin. Tenbrook picked it up and placed it on the floor.

"Dotty's been around," he said. He sat down.

"All over the planet," said Channy. Tossed on her bed were a hair dryer, a guitar, a radio, a laptop computer, bras and panties, roller blades, a tennis racquet.

"Where do you sleep?" said Tenbrook. It seemed as if a wand had passed over the room and swept away all vestiges of her childhood, except for the yellow doll, a life-sized cardboard cutout of a Star Wars robot, Channy's collection of birds' nests and a fish tank that had once been home for a lizard named Cilantro and still contained his desiccated remains.

"It looks as if Hurricane Channy hit this room," he said.

"You should talk, Dad."

"Touché."

"Did Mom tell you what this was about?"

"Something about getting birth control pills for pimples?" said Tenbrook.

"I think you know we're not really talking about pimples."

"You mean there's a subtext to this conversation?"

"You don't want me to get pregnant, do you?"

Tenbrook didn't answer. He looked at the picture of the lizard. "Remember when you and Cilantro got married?"

"Of course. You gave the bride away and Jennifer was the maid of honor."

"Does your boyfriend know you were married to a lizard? That you're technically a widow?"

"He knows everything and I'm pretty sure he still loves me."

"He'd better. Tell me about him."

"He's 23. He's in college."

"That's too old, Channy."

"Not really. He's very immature."

"Now that's reassuring."

"He doesn't even shave."

"He's robbing the cradle. You're too young. A fifteen-year-old ought to be selling Girl Scout cookies and reading 'The Little House on the Prairie.'"

"I'm sixteen, Dad. I got my period when I was thirteen."

"I guess we're both old enough to talk about this sort of thing," said Tenbrook.

"I shouldn't have to ask your permission."

"What happened to my little girl, the one who tried to sniff flowers in picture books, who used to dress up as a fairy and go around knocking on doors offering to grant the neighbors all reasonable wishes?"

"The one who stuffed tennis balls in her t-shirt when she was seven?"

"Okay, Channy. We're locking you up in a convent. We'll let you out when you're 21."

"At least give him a chance, Dad. Wait until you meet him. He's smart and funny. He's obscenely cute." The boyfriend's name was Toby. He worked at the coffee shop Channy had been frequenting. She volunteered that she'd been sneaking out of the house for late night rendezvous with the young man.

"You ought to appreciate that I'm being honest," she said.

"Listen, Channy. I'm not in a position to offer you advice about how to live your life. You're an intelligent girl. You're a woman."

"Dad. There are girls in my class who come to school wearing t-shirts that say, 'Baby Inside.' Some of my classmates are sort of amateur prostitutes. We had to watch a video that showed dance moves that wouldn't be acceptable at the homecoming dance. It featured Freddy, our big bird mascot demonstrating no-no dirty dancing moves to Nelly's 'Shake Ya Tail Feathers.'" Channy laughed, gave out a 'Bock-bock-bock' and did a little rear end wiggle. "You should trust me, Dad. I'm responsible. I'm not promiscuous."

"When I was a kid our principal said that ballroom dancing was the only acceptable form of physical contact between men and women prior to marriage."

"Isn't this when you tell me about the sonogram?"

"Yeah. I guess it is. We could see your tiny heart beating. That's when they told us you were going to be a girl. Your backbone wasn't any bigger than a splinter. The idea was to make sure it was straight, that you wouldn't be deformed."

"What would you have done if my backbone wasn't straight?"

"Don't even ask that question," said Tenbrook. The image of his daughter, suspended in amniotic fluid, seemed fragile like the skeleton of a bird. The hollow eyes had a ghostly glow at the edges, a skull's or a mummy's eyes. "I'm very grateful that you're alive. That you're my daughter."

"So will you sign off on my pills, Dad?"

✱✱✱

"How did you come out?" said Kate when he came back downstairs.

"I bombed."

"That was predictable."

"I told her she was too young. She told me she was 16 and it was high time her soul was charred. I know this sounds kind of Victorian, but the idea of her having sex gives me vertigo."

"I'm afraid you're kind of naïve," said Kate. "She probably thinks you don't care about her since you didn't go ballistic."

"And if I'd gone ballistic, she would have hated me for that. I guess the days of Dotty are over. Dotty no longer suffices as her paramour. By the way, I think Dotty is due for a visit to Kate's Doll Hospital."

"I'm working on Heart Balloon right now. Heart Balloon needs a new pair of diapers."

"How many transplants and skin grafts have you performed on Channy's dolls?"

"I don't want her to grow up either."

"Why are little girls so anxious to experience woe?"

"Don't worry, Ten. She'll marry someone just like you."

Chapter 10

Tenbrook had once gone antelope hunting in Wyoming's Red Hills. The experience hadn't awakened any archetypal Iron John memories of communal hunts, of a time when a man had to slay wild beasts to survive, when to return heroically to the village with meat was to earn a masculine sense of purpose and pride. It was more like shooting cattle in a barnyard: Stop the rented Jeep, jump out, aim, fire. Tenbrook shot a female. The doe fell, stood up and walked slowly, drunkenly away to a stony culvert where it lay down as if to rest. A regal buck appeared, herded the rest of his harem off to a safe distance and then returned, regardless of Tenbrook and his high-powered rifle. He came around behind the doe and butted her gently to her feet. She walked a few steps, swaying and stumbling and then fell back down. The buck turned and faced Tenbrook who was not fifty yards away. They actually made eye contact, the buck's black eyes boring into Tenbrook's. It was like looking into the eyes of another human being, a male rival, full of hate. He thought it might be about to charge. The buck tried once more to get the doe to her feet but it was no go. He gave Tenbrook a final parting look as if to memorize his features, then trotted back to his other does, leaving Tenbrook feeling ashamed and rebuked. When he field-dressed the doe, a trickle of milk flowed over the viscera. She was nursing. He'd left her unborn offspring motherless.

"Got yourself a Susie-girl?" said the butcher, when Tenbrook brought the carcass in for processing.

***

On his way to the doctor's, Tenbrook passed a young man sitting cross-legged on a bench, holding up a cardboard placard with a crudely written message soliciting alms. Other shadowy figures with signs and receptacles for donations were camped on both sides of Free State Street. Middleton, which had acquired a reputation for being friendly to the homeless, had become overwhelmed by them, provoking a backlash. Citizens complained about vagrants sleeping on the sidewalks and urinating in public. Shopkeepers claimed that panhandlers were driving shoppers away and tarnishing Downtown's image. The city council had passed new ordinances: No aggressive panhandling, no physical contact with shoppers, no panhandling within twenty feet of an ATM machine.

"Good evening, sir," the young man said in a musical, ingratiating voice. He didn't look destitute. His shirt and pants were frayed, but might have once been Joe College apparel. Tenbrook returned the greeting curtly, quickened his pace and focused on an invisible point in the distance.

"Sir, could you spare a smile?" the man called after him, his voice changed to an unctuous whine. A retort didn't come to Tenbrook until he reached the corner: "Sorry, but my wife died this morning and I just can't find much to smile about." But he kept it to himself.

Dr. Hubbard's office was in an old three-story building whose facade had been dressed up with an ornamental metallic screen. It had once served as the Selective Service office, a waystation for young men destined to go to Vietnam. "Headquarters" was the only word still legible on the weathered rooftop billboard, an appropriate address for a shrink, Tenbrook thought.

He entered the musty building and climbed the stairs to the second floor. He walked down a dimly lit hall past a weight loss clinic, a travel agent specializing in senior citizen bus trips and a broker of poultry processing equipment. At the end of the hall he came to a door with the lettering, "Dr. Blaine Hubbard, Slayer of Demons."

The waiting room was empty. A clipboard with forms for patients to fill out lay on the sill of the receptionist's window, but there was no receptionist. Posters of Tuscany, the Greek Isles and other iconic getaways decorated the walls. A few captain's chairs and a small table covered with old *Popular Mechanics* and celebrity magazines were the only furnishings.

Tenbrook had found Hubbard in the yellow pages among various counselors offering treatments for anxiety, depression, addiction, grief, obesity, bulimia, co-dependence, anger—a laundry list of contemporary ailments. He noted that the listings shared the same page with psychics and fortune tellers. "Lasting Solutions to Repetitive Patterns and Tenacious Symptoms" read one ad. Dr. Hubbard's was the only one that made specific reference to sexual dysfunction.

Tenbrook sat down and thumbed through some old issues of *People* magazine that chronicled the trials of Brad and Angelina, Jennifer and Vince: "Jen is in love! Sweet, down-to-earth Vince is just what she needs—the anti-Brad." "Angelina: 'Brad and I are going to adopt a lot more babies!'" "Watch out, Jen! Playboy Vince will break your heart." "Angelina's fears: Brad will cheat." From the next room, he heard murmurs, then sobs. After a long silence, an interior door opened and closed. Then the door to the waiting room opened. Dr. Hubbard appeared in the doorway. He was frail-looking, with sloping shoulders, ice blue eyes, pale skin, a few strands of silver hair. He wore a white physician's jacket spotted with coffee stains. Steel-framed glasses perched on the bridge of his nose. He gave Tenbrook a myopic, puzzled look as if surprised to see someone in the room.

"Ah, Mr. Tenbrook?" he said at last. He gestured to the other room. Tenbrook followed him and sat down on a worn armchair. Faint background sounds floated through the room—a waterfall, loon calls, frogs chirping to the accompaniment of a flute. On the wall behind the desk were a few aboriginal masks, several diplomas and a picture of Sigmund Freud bending over a patient stretched out on a couch. A bookshelf held volumes: *Tantric Sex, The Multiple-Orgasmic Couple, Sex With Your Ex, The Bedside Orgasm Book, The Idiot's Guide to Oral Sex, The Rebel Cock.* The doctor watched Tenbrook.

"In this business, you have to try everything," he said. "Family therapy, group therapy, cognitive behavioral therapy, rational emotive therapy, acceptance and commitment therapy, interoceptive exposure therapy, Kinner-child therapy, supportive-expressive therapy, massage therapy." He paused to catch his breath and gave a faint chuckle. "Energy systems therapy, internal family systems therapy, meditation, role-playing, acupuncture, prayer, hypnotism, eye-movement desensitizing and reprocessing. Have I left anything out? There's a smorgasbord of drugs: Thorazine, Nardil, Prozac, Paxil, Wellbutrin, Valium, Librium, Xanax, Klonopin. I've cured some patients by suddenly leaping out of my chair and letting out a scream."

He handed Tenbrook a form and asked him to fill it out. The document was identified as "Depression Checklist."

There were fifteen items with boxes to check, from "Never" to "A lot." Questions about sadness, feelings of discouragement, low self-esteem, inferiority, guilt: "Have you been feeling sad or down in the dumps?" "Does the future look hopeless?" "Do you feel worthless or think of yourself as a failure?" "Have you lost interest in your career, your hobbies, your family or your friends?" "Do you get self-critical and blame yourself for everything?" "Do you think you're looking old or unattractive?" Tenbrook held his pencil poised without making a mark.

"Doesn't everyone feel sad, worthless, inferior and unattractive?" he said.

"That's right," said Hubbard. "I applaud your perspicuity. Misery is normal. As Freud said, the job of therapy is to transform hysterical misery into common unhappiness. People who say they're happy are the crazy ones. By the way, do you ever have suicidal thoughts?"

"Doesn't everyone?"

"Right again. How close have you come?"

"I stand at the door to the basement every day and consider jumping."

"What keeps you back?" Tenbrook thought for a moment.

"I hear two voices," he said. "One says, 'You're worthless, you don't deserve to live.' The other says, 'Don't take yourself so seriously.'"

"That's a sign of mental health!" cried Dr. Hubbard. "Congratulations. You're not crazy. But the phone message you left suggested that you do have a real problem. So, speak. Begin at the beginning." Tenbrook looked at his hands as if the answer might be written there.

"I've had failures in bed recently," he said. "I had a dream about a woman I used to love.

I see her all the time in Middleton. I never feel any attraction to her. But in the dream, Gwen and I were rolling around in the grass again and the old feelings came back, vivid and intense. When I woke up, I felt as if I'd betrayed Kate, committed adultery in my imagination. I thought that if she and I made love, everything would be okay. But after a little foreplay, I lost my erection. I haven't been able to maintain one since."

"You wanted to re-establish intimacy," said Dr. Hubbard. "You wanted to atone. But your sense of guilt opened the door to an ogre. It was a creature of your imagination, but you gave it power. Still, haven't you experienced desire for other women before without it leading to sexual failure with your wife? What made this different?"

"I don't know…Kate had just said that she loved me but wasn't 'in' love with me anymore. I don't expect her to be madly infatuated with me after twenty years. But this 'in love' declaration hurt somehow. It stirred up more anxieties. It put another barrier between us. It sounded like discontent, a prelude to divorce…We'd had an argument about where to put a dresser. Afterwards, I noticed that we'd managed to put it with the drawers against the wall. That seemed to say it all. I went looking for her, hoping we could share a laugh about it, but when I found her she was in tears. I was afraid we'd crossed some kind of threshold."

There were other ogres. The mortgage was coming due on his house. His business was drying up. There was Jimmy and the thousand-dollar bills, Pillars' plans to develop the Griefmaker, Kate's involvement with Father Ned and the Hallelujah Kitchen.

"Also, I feel age creeping up," Tenbrook said. "I look at my friends, the people I started out with in school, and they seem to have made better choices. They've passed me by. I feel as if I've lost my medicine bundle."

"Quite a laundry list," said Dr. Hubbard.

"That's just for starters," said Tenbrook. "I'm down on myself. I feel as if I have nothing to say. I feel some vague sense of guilt. I feel like a cuckold."

"Do you suspect your wife of cheating?"

"Not really. I mean cuckold in an existential sense."

"Perhaps you depend too much on your wife for your sense of well-being?"

"If you saw her you'd understand why," said Tenbrook.

"So you live in constant fear of losing her," said Dr. Hubbard. "And that makes it all the more likely that you will."

"That's what I'm afraid of."

Dr. Hubbard asked Tenbrook for a brief summary of his sexual history. Tenbrook conjured up a parade of girls from his adolescence. Peggy, Bonnie, Debbie, Linda, Patty. Their names still had a magical ring, like passwords to a world of secret desires. Everything changed when one of them entered a room. They turned the boys into clowns. They seemed wonderfully exotic—their braids, their bangs and barrettes, even their braces. Suddenly they'd go into a pout, and you couldn't understand why. You'd ask them what was the matter and they'd burst out laughing at you.

Tenbrook recalled his first date.

"At the movie theater, I put my arm across the back of her seat. Halfway through the show I touched her shoulder. I thought I'd scored. I bragged about it at school the next day. Word got back to Leslie and she was furious. She demoted me to number three in her hierarchy of boyfriends."

"You felt rejection," said Dr. Hubbard. "You experienced desire and disappointment of desire. Frustration. The awakening of self-doubt. Let's move on to the loss of your virginity."

Tenbrook told the doctor about the pilgrimage he and Everett Pillars made to the Cozy Rooms in Topeka, where Middleton High boys went to shed their virginity. It was July in Kansas, the usual inferno. They drove to a part of town that looked as if it had been passed over by time. Stubby black cars that looked to be 30s vintage. Old brick tenements with fire escapes hanging from the walls. Gauzy curtains in open windows. Rooms lit by bare bulbs. They climbed a wooden staircase in a rooming house that smelled of urine and fried onions and stopped at an open door where a gaunt man in a sleeveless t-shirt sat smoking in front of a fan.

"You boys looking for girls?" he said with a grin that showed decayed and tobacco-stained teeth. He took them to the window and pointed out a clapboard house. They crossed the street and pressed a buzzer beside a metal door with a frosted window. A woman in a filmy, flowered dress, her hair done up in a turban, answered. She ushered them into a waiting room, took their $20 bills, disappeared and returned with two women wearing bathing suits with modesty skirts, introducing them as Jasmine and Frankie. They presented themselves like runway models, pirouetting, showing off their goods front and rear. Pillars took the peroxide blonde, leaving Tenbrook the dowdy brunette. She led him to a dimly lit room with an odor of mildew. Patches of water-stained paper hung from the walls. A mangy teddy bear lay on a faded spread covering the mattress of a tubular metal-framed bed.

Jasmine slipped out of her bathing suit, squatted on the floor above a pan and slopped water against her crotch. Tenbrook felt desire slipping away. She dried herself off with a terry cloth towel, stretched out on the bed and beckoned him with a weary look. Tenbrook lay down beside her, still wearing his white socks. The bed springs groaned and the mattress sagged in the middle. She stroked him, and made a little moan, but nothing happened.

"Try to think of something sexy," she said. Tenbrook marched wanton images through his mind. They might as well have been circus animals or farm implements. "Are you cherry?" she asked. "You should have brought more money. I could have given you a half-and-half."

A rapping at the door signaled that time was up. The woman rolled off the bed and slipped back into her bathing suit.

"That was a pretty good deal for you," Tenbrook said. "Twenty dollars is a lot of money."

"I'd rather have a good screw," she said.

"Try to think of something sexy," snorted Dr. Hubbard. "Trying is what kills desire. Fantasies separate us from our sensations. Hmm. I asked you to tell me about losing your virginity, and you tell me a story about not losing it. That's interesting."

"My friend boasted that he'd finished in sixty seconds," said Tenbrook. "He said his girl called him a 'rabbit.'"

"So there was competition between you two?"

"Still is," said Tenbrook. "Isn't that the way it usually works between friends?"

"All is tangled in a web," said the doctor.

"I did finally manage to get the job done," said Tenbrook. "I met a girl at a college mixer one night, took her to my room and in about five minutes the great event was over."

"And you felt?"

"Just relieved. I just wanted to get it over with. It wasn't very sexy. Actually, it was kind of sad. She referred to sex as 'amor' and wanted to know if I 'liked' her."

"Yes, sex and sadness seem often to go together," said Dr. Hubbard. "And since then?"

Tenbrook told the doctor that his first marriage ended in divorce. In the brief window between sexual liberation and the age of AIDS, he'd had a number of short-term partners.

"Any dysfunction in those days?"

"I always had trouble the first time."

"But then you met your true love, the goddess, Kate."

"We were sitting in a cafeteria. I think we were having a conversation about 'Ohio' and 'Iowa,' how they're made up mostly of vowels. All of a sudden, she gave me a funny look. We'd just met, but I told her I knew what she was thinking. She asked me what. I said, 'You're thinking that it's time we kissed.' She said that was right. We got up from the table and went outside and we had a long, unforgettable kiss, the best I've ever had. A fairy tale kiss. Whenever I think of it, I think that for once I got something right."

"Isn't it wonderful that love and destiny can spring out of a discussion of Ohio and Iowa?" said Dr. Hubbard. "And that a frog can turn into a prince." He leaned back in his chair, looked up at the ceiling and began to expound.

"We evolved in an environment where survival often depended on making the right choice between fighting and fleeing," he said. "When a lion charged, it provoked a rush of adrenaline. That gave us the power to fight—or run away. Fear constricted the blood vessels. A good thing. If we got injured, we'd be less likely to bleed to death. The beasts we encounter today are mostly phantoms. But the chemistry persists. In the presence of fear, the flow of blood that gives you an erection is diverted to help you face the illusory beast. A voice whispers: 'You're going to lose it.' Your muscles tense and you peter out. How to master fear, how to defuse that physiological reaction? That's the question."

"Okay. How?"

"Your problem can be addressed by drugs."

"Drugs scare me," said Tenbrook. "And I think that this

problem relates to my other issues. If I dealt with it without drugs, it might help me in other ways."

"Bravo," said Dr. Hubbard. "Most people take the easy way out. Drugs may get your sex life back, but you'll never find out how you got lost in the labyrinth to begin with. You'll miss an opportunity to follow the thread that leads to freedom."

The time was almost up. Hubbard looked at Tenbrook above the rim of his glasses, like a scientist studying a specimen.

"You're not impotent," he said. "You suffer from 'performance anxiety.' The first step is to stop approaching sex as a performance. The secret to that is in not caring."

"How can you not care about something you want?"

"When you learn that secret, you'll have conquered the beast," said Dr. Hubbard. "You're given to catastrophic thinking. Your wife develops a new interest, a new relationship, and you imagine the worst—infidelity, divorce. Fear is a magnet. It draws all sorts of irrelevant evidence to back it up."

"But not all my fears are imaginary."

"That may be true. And I can't change reality for you. But I can suggest ways to help you wrestle with phantoms. You have to learn how to turn the thinking off. When the 'got-to' thought arrives—you've 'got to' keep your erection, you've 'got to' make your partner have an orgasm—let it flow past. Guide awareness back to the present and the palette of sensations. If the doubt message comes, hit the Error key. Clear the screen and refocus on breathing. When you feel an attack of insecurity coming on, draw a picture of your body and an arrow to the place where the feeling is. Turn the survival response off. Slow down, meditate, take deep, oval breaths. After a while, your body will say, 'Okay, it's not a tiger.'"

"I'm cutting and pasting all the time," said Tenbrook. "I keep thinking that if I could just hit one home run."

"And if you did, you'd think: If I could just hit one more," said Hubbard. "As long as you keep thinking in terms of success and acquittal, you'll never be free. You may be in prison, but the prison is a fiction. Anytime you wish, you can step outside. Who do you think Jacob was wrestling with? The angel was Jacob himself."

"There's nothing unreal about my mortgage," said Tenbrook.

"What I've said might be written off as mumbo jumbo," said Dr. Hubbard. "It only works if you believe it works. I offer a kind of exorcism. But I advise skepticism in all matters." He gestured to the masks on the wall. "We witch doctors shake many different rattles. Some promise peace of mind and some promise salvation."

"I could have gotten that from Father Ned," said Tenbrook.

"Don't dismiss that brand of magic. The idea of Original Sin explains many things. But I can't minister to your soul."

"Do you think we have one?" said Tenbrook.

"I've never seen one. But then I've never seen an ego, either. Maybe the soul will make a comeback. Just remember that the ultimate magic resides here." Dr. Hubbard tapped his head. "And not in some medical textbook or sacred text. Only you can redeem yourself. By the way, I was a great fan of yours. Bulldogs versus Wildcats, 28-21."

On his way out, Tenbrook glanced at the posters on the wall. They reminded him of his adolescent obsession about running away. If he could just get away from Middleton where everyone knew him, he could start over and reinvent himself. In time he figured out that it wouldn't work. You carried yourself along wherever you went. But wasn't the self a phantom too? And wasn't the idea of self-worth as illusory as the values he assigned to real estate? And would he ever outrun that football game?

It was dark outside. A few ragged clouds sailed above the treetops. Through the branches, Tenbrook saw fragments of the moon. He heard a sound like the shuffling of papers. He looked up and saw a small deltoid kite tacking and darting in the breeze. The string was tied to a parking meter. Someone had left it—for whom or what? It seemed like a gesture of perfect, anonymous generosity, like firewood left for the next camper.

"You went looking for a cure and found a witch doctor who didn't believe in his own medicine," he thought. But maybe magic was what he needed. Not some chemical cooked up by scientists in the labs of Pfizer that reduced sex to a dilation of blood vessels, but some enchantment that would transform him into another kind of creature.

Across the street some sort of carnival was in progress. Calliope sounds floated up. The usual features were there—Ferris Wheel, Octopus, Tilt-A-Whirl. Above the treetops loomed a crane illuminated with bright lights. A figure like a rag doll tethered to an orange cord plunged from the top. Was it a dummy—or was he witnessing a suicide? The cord squirmed like a snake in the garish light and when it reached the limit, the figure recoiled and danced above the ground like a lure at the end of a fishing line. At first, Tenbrook was puzzled. Then he understood. It was a bungee jump. The figure wasn't a dummy but a thrill-seeking human being. It seemed like a parody of suicide.

A throb of bongos came from unlit portals down the street. Under a streetlamp a man was juggling tennis balls. A voice spoke out of the shadows: "Sens, sens…Something for the head, my man?" A waif-like fiddler sat on the sidewalk with her instrument case open, displaying a few crumpled bills. The man who'd solicited a smile was still in his niche.

"What would you rather have," Tenbrook said as he passed the young man. "That smile or a dollar?"

"Give me the fucking dollar," he said.

Chapter 11

The Missouri Compromise was Tenbrook's miniature Griefmaker, a surrogate of his lost legacy. He liked to roam his postage stamp prairie, looking for deer sheds, owl and hawk castings, morel mushrooms. He'd fall to his knees to watch a beetle rolling a ball of dung, like a tiny Sisyphus. He was certain that a shallow depression where the grass didn't grow was a buffalo wallow. And he imagined herds of the majestic beasts which once numbered in the millions. Purposeless wanderings brought temporary peace. Until he'd wake up and recognize that it was a form of escapism. Money was owed, business was down.

He dug in the creekbank beneath a limestone overhang and found charcoal mixed in the sandy soil, remnants of pre-historic fires. He discovered a knobby bone that a university paleontologist identified as part of an extinct camel. He found a beautiful pestle that another professor attributed to the Clovis people who pursued mammoths in Kansas, ten thousand years before Kansas became a state. Tenbrook was always finding stuff. But it was unlikely he ever found what he was really looking for. Who does? He probably would have been happier living in a cave, gathering nuts and berries and wearing an animal skin. One thing for sure: He was crazy about that little patch of land...

Always at the back of his mind was the imaginary graph that showed the downward trajectory from his peak in high school, and Pillars' line of ascent in the after years. The iconic Griefmaker cedar appeared there too, bent northward from the force of the prevailing wind, gnarled branches flailing at the air.

A weather-beaten Mercury with a moth-eaten fabric top cruised by from time to time. Sometimes it parked a little way down the road like a blowzy feral cat, tinted glass obscuring the occupants. When he approached, the car sped off. Sometimes he saw the white limo parked like an apparition in front of the unfinished mansion on Conestoga Bluff.

A few weeks before he and his family moved to the Missouri Compromise, Tenbrook had been out cutting hedge trees, having "pioneer daydreams." Clearing the land, taming the wilderness. Mind on vacation. When he turned off the chain saw, he heard the faint thread of a sound that didn't belong. He couldn't identify it, or where it came from, but he was sure it was alien. It wasn't any of nature's sounds. He listened and followed the thread. The sound became more distinct. Someone was playing music, country music, hard luck, lost love, truck driver music. It was coming from the shed next to his neighbor's house.

He heard a hammer blow, then the whine of a saw, then more twanging, lamenting, nasal crooning. Someone walked from the barn. Apparently, his neighbor listened to the radio when he worked outside and played it loud enough for the rest of the neighborhood to hear. Tenbrook uttered a curse. He was moving to the country for peace and quiet. He wanted to get away from leafblowers, boomboxes, car alarms. But in town, noises mingle and cancel one another out. You get used to them. You don't even hear them. In the country, you can hear a screendoor slam half a mile away. Voices in the distance are amplified. Tenbrook feared his dream of solitude was going to be violated by cornpone music.

He lapsed into catastrophic thinking. He'd have to pay his neighbor a visit and beg him to turn the music down. He'd have to start wearing earphones. He'd counsel his neighbor about the virtues of silence. He might even offer to pay him to keep quiet. But then he realized that any confrontation with the man about his unfortunate taste in music and lack of appreciation for the joys of stillness would only antagonize him. People move to the country to do as they please, and they have conflicting ideas of what's pleasing. So there would have to be war. Tenbrook imagined an on-going duel between him and his neighbor—Tenbrook blasting the "Ride of the Valkyries" against his neighbor's Willie Nelson. He began to wonder if moving to the country was going to save him after all.

On New Year's Day, just after they'd moved to the country, Kate and Tenbrook sat on the farmhouse porch, sipping left-over champagne. Channy was setting off left-over fireworks on the driveway south of the barn. She was already complaining about the move to the country—she hated the isolation, felt cut off from her friends. Her parents suggested she set off some explosives to assuage her boredom. In daylight, the brilliant colors promised by the label on the rockets were invisible, but the dainty parachutes they launched were easy to spot. The Tenbrooks watched them rise above the treetops, where the breeze caught them and flung them north toward the house like thistledown. They were busy trying to keep Max from getting into the champagne cups when they heard Channy cry, "Fire!" A parachute had caught fire and landed in the dry grass. In an instant black smoke curled up and a wall of flames headed toward the barn.

Tenbrook grabbed a bucket and ran. By the time he reached the barn the flames were only a couple of hundred yards away and roaring. He opened the barn door, hoping to find a hose. Then he realized that the yard hydrant was too far away for all the hoses they owned to reach. Channy ran up to him shouting incoherently.

"Idiot!" yelled Tenbrook. Channy had tears in her eyes and gave him a radiant, anguished, "Gone with the Wind" look.

"I didn't know, dad," Channy cried. Tenbrook felt a pang of remorse.

"I know you didn't," he said, hugging her. "I'm sorry. You're not an idiot. I'm an idiot." Channy ran to the hydrant and hosed herself down. She took her shirt off and ran towards the flames.

"What the hell are you doing?" cried Tenbrook.

"I'm going in there," said Channy.

"The devil you are," yelled Tenbrook. "Get back here or I'll shoot you. You can't put that fire out with your shirt. And I'm not having you go up in flames." Channy walked back, dejected. Tenbrook put an arm around her shoulder. The two of them stood like statues, mesmerized by the raging fire. It didn't occur to Tenbrook to call the fire department. He didn't even know if there was a fire department that served the county's rural areas.

A row of cedars along the driveway burst into flame with a crackling like bedlam laughter. Fanned by the wind, the fire leaped up in malevolent spirals and raced toward the barn. A torpor came over Tenbrook. The barn was lost. There was nothing to do but to watch the conflagration. It would be an advertisement to his neighbors of incompetence and failure. The barn had to be a hundred years old. It had a manger, a milking room, tracks and pulleys on the second floor for hauling up bales of hay. It was a sturdy, post-and-beam construction, built by artisans without power tools, a communal project, part of the history of the place, a tribute to tradition. He was supposed to be the steward and he was presiding over its ruin.

A contrary sensation possessed him, a perverse excitement in the approach of fire. For a moment, he welcomed it like a purifying force that would sweep away the past, the dead thatch, the barn, the fenceposts, the chicken coop, the farrow pen. The prospect of a fresh start.

Then he heard the faint whine of a siren. A toy-like red truck appeared at the end of the driveway. It hesitated, then sped to the barn and came to a rocking stop. Figures in yellow slickers leaped from the truck, unrolled a thick hose. A pump chugged to life. The hose writhed like a python. The firemen fed it over the fence. A broad spray of water shot forth, fanning showers over the burning grass. Within minutes, the fire was subdued, reduced to a sputtering, hissing cloud of acrid smoke. The firefighters stalked around the barnyard and the pasture with rakes, chain saws and axes, hacking down fire-gutted fence posts, snuffing out burning embers. Other volunteers had followed the fire engine in pickup trucks. Tenbrook walked among them, introducing himself and babbling apologies for disrupting their New Year's Day. They were old and young, including a couple of teenage girls.

"We were setting off firecrackers," he explained. "It happened so suddenly. We weren't thinking. You were probably watching football games." The workers waved off his comments with smiles and all-in-a-day's-work shrugs, assured him that it was no problem, there was nothing they enjoyed more than getting the call and waging war against fires. A burly man in a rain suit blackened with soot introduced himself as Ralph, the township's volunteer fire captain.

"Just doin' our job," he said. "You was lucky. We was out answering a false alarm nearby when we got the call from Troy."

"Who's Troy?"

"You haven't met Troy? Where the hell is Troy? Tell Troy to get over here. You got to meet Troy. He's your next-door neighbor." A man with short-cropped white hair and baggy overalls approached, walking with a slight limp.

"Troy Bilbrey," he said, holding out his hand. "Howdy, neighbor." The sleeves of his blue workshirt were rolled back, revealing massive forearms. His ruddy face was pocked and mottled like a windfall apple.

"I been meaning to come over here and introduce myself, and you just hurried me up." He turned his head and spat a thick wad of tobacco juice, wiped his mouth and looked at Tenbrook with blue, mirthful eyes.

"This isn't the way I would have chosen to meet my neighbors," Tenbrook said. "I feel like a complete idiot."

"I saw smoke," said Bilbrey. "I didn't think you'd mind if I went ahead and called the kids. Fires don't give you much time for dilly-dallying or shilly-shallying. And these boys and girls got nothing better to do. They're all firebugs anyway."

"I can't believe all these people showed up," said Tenbrook.

"These here all live close by," said Bilbrey. "And they like to work. The county don't look out for us. Everything is volunteers. I like it that way. Helluva lot better than dealing with a lot of pig-headed bureaucrats."

"Get ready, Mr. Tenbrook," said Ralph. "Joke a-comin'."

"County agent was crying at his desk," said Bilbrey.

"'What you crying 'bout?' said the agent at the next desk. Crying agent says: 'My farmer died.'"

"Ain't that the truth," someone said. "One bureaucrat for each and every one of us."

"He'll joke you to death if you don't look out," said Ralph.

"Man comes into a café," said Bilbrey. "Says, 'I'll have coffee. But hold the cream.' Waitress says, 'We're out of cream, so you'll have to take it without milk.'"

"You need some new material," said Ralph. "I've heard that one a few hunert times."

The firefighters gathered up their equipment. After the last truck had left, Tenbrook walked with Kate and Channy around the barn and pasture. The scorched ground exposed a network of rat holes, smoldering sunflower stalks, spines of blackened shattercane and the remains of accumulated tinder. Buzzards had showed up and were flying low, back and forth, looking for roasted rodents and snakes. The barn stood like an abandoned cathedral surrounded by ashes.

"Happy New Year," said Kate.

"I guess that's enough excitement for today," said Channy.

"I'm sorry I blew up at you," said Tenbrook. "I shouldn't have let you set those things off. That grass was bone dry. It might as well be gasoline. I should have known."

"It was a learning experience," said Kate.

"I've got a lot to learn," said Tenbrook,

That night, Tenbrook woke up. He saw headlights in the barnyard. He got out of bed.

"What's the matter?" asked Kate.

"Someone's out there." Tenbrook got dressed and walked down to the barn. When he approached, he found Bilbrey on his four-wheeler, spraying a still-burning fence post.

"Them railroad ties burn forever," he said. "It's that creosote they got in them." Bilbrey stopped spraying. "You think that sucker's done?"

"I have no idea," said Tenbrook. "As you might have guessed, my knowledge of these matters is somewhat limited. I need someone like you to follow me around and put out my fires. I tend to set a lot of things on fire, literally and figuratively."

"Literally and figuratively, huh?" said Bilbrey. "Well, I got a lot to learn too." Tenbrook felt foolish once again, sure he was coming across as some kind of citified egghead. Bilbrey gave him a reassuring grin. "Barn looks like it might be ready for a coat of paint, if you don't mind me saying," he said.

Tenbrook woke Kate up when he came back. He told her about his encounter with Bilbrey.

"It's kind of amazing," he said. "That old guy out in the middle of the night worrying about our barn. I think I'm going to like it out there. I like the idea of a volunteer fire department. It's old-fashioned, 19th Century stuff. Pioneers helping one another, that kind of thing."

"You know what you are?" said Kate. "You're a romantic. You're a dreamer. You're a little boy. That's one of the things I like about you. I can just see you out there with your farmer friends, branding cattle, baling hay, tossing your lariat."

"I've got to work on the talk. I heard a lot of 'howdies' and 'hecky darns' today. One thing I'm glad about is that I didn't make the trip to tell Mr. Bilbrey to turn his music down. It'll be a long time before I find a bone to pick with him."

Chapter 12

Troy Bilbrey had invited Tenbrook to meet some neighbors. Bilbrey's yard was crowded with dust-covered pickups when Tenbrook showed up. Troy met him at the door.

"Welcome to the Posse Comitatus," he said.

"Stop that nonsense, Troy Bilbrey," said a tiny, gray-haired woman with an incipient Parkinson's nod. "I'm Retta Lou," she said. "That one's wife. Don't pay no never mind to him."

Tenbrook looked into the room. A gallery of square-jawed faces looked back. Some he recognized as members of the fire-fighting crew that had saved his barn. The room was furnished with camouflage-upholstered chairs and couches and cluttered with country collectibles—blue plates decorated with farming themes, cowboy figurines, framed photos of John Deere implements, a mounted jackalope and a plastic largemouth bass that said "Howdy" when you passed by. At the far end was a table covered with Dale Earnhardt memorabilia: Dale Earnhardt dolls, shot glasses, lacquered victory plaques, a Dale Earnhardt Wheaties box, a Dale Earnhardt chrome hubcap, a teddy bear wearing a jacket with "Number 3," a photo of the racecar driver with his arms raised in victory and a motto: "PERSEVERANCE… To remain steadfast against all odds."

Retta Lou handed Tenbrook a jelly glass filled with lemonade. Bilbrey introduced the men: Virgil, Verlyn, Donnie, Chester, Lou, Clyde, Tommy, Buster. They responded to the roll call with a nod or a lifted finger. They paid homage to the Tenbrook name and the legends of Henry Tenbrook's athletic prowess. They groused about the government and Middleton city politics. They bemoaned the transformation of the rural countryside.

"City folks takin' over…Men wearin' earrings and women covered with tattoos. Most of 'em wouldn't know a shoat from a boar or a combine from a cuckoo's ass."

"Watch your language, Donnie," said Retta Lou.

"I don't even like to go into that damn town," someone said. "They's so many panhandlers on the streets and they won't take no for an answer."

"One of them Middleton bureaucrats was out here the other day with a clipboard and a camera. Said he was looking for 'view sheds.' You know what a view shed is? Those are scenic views the county wants to preserve. You watch: They'll be coming out and saying you can't build a tool shed 'cause it would block a view shed."

"The boys are kind of at war with Middleton," said Retta Lou. "They's always threatnin' to make a raid on Middleton with their pitchforks and hoes."

"Where do you stand on this, Mr. Tenbrook?" someone said.

"I don't know," said Tenbrook. "There are people in Middleton who think we'd be better off in caves or teepees and living off roots and grubs. It's pretty easy to be against development if you don't own any land."

"Good answer," said one of the men. "Everything depends on which side of the table you sit."

A man at the back of the room tapped his cane loudly on the floor in agreement. Retta Lou passed a plate of sugar cookies and poured more lemonade. The men talked about Middleton football, the price of fertilizer, their health problems. They joked about their prostates. After a round of ceremonial pronouncements, Bilbrey abruptly announced it was time for the visitors to go home and get some sleep. Retta Lou chided him for rudeness at the same time she went about the room collecting glasses and plates. The men lined up and shook Tenbrook's hand. The gathering broke up. Retta Lou excused herself to clean up in the kitchen.

"How'd I do?" said Tenbrook.

"Jury's still out," said Bilbrey. "Ask me forty or fifty years from now. Sometimes it takes a couple of generations to get legitimized." They stopped at the Dale Earnhardt display. "This here shrine is Retta Lou's," he said. "And I actually do think she does pray to Dale Earnhardt. I believe she adopted him in her mind after our boys grew up and moved away. We raised three boys in one room in this house and all three has left the farm. My, how the fur used to fly in that room. Like three catamounts in a rain barrel. But they was sure fun. You pray much?"

"Not so much anymore. Do you?"

"I pray to the rain god. He don't very often answer my prayers. Let's go outside and find us a beer."

Tenbrook followed Bilbrey out to the barn. He took two beers out of an ancient refrigerator and handed one to Tenbrook.

"Retta Lou won't let me drink in the house," he said. "Can't hardly do anything with that woman watching you." They opened the beers and sipped in silence. Coyotes started up, some far off, some close at hand. They howled and wailed, forlorn calls and wailings that sounded like hungry babies.

"That's quite a chorus," said Tenbrook.

"Lots of pups this season," said Bilbrey. "Hear 'em yip? 'Can't hardly's' not proper, is it?"

"They call it a double negative."

"I should of knowed that," said Bilbrey. "Miss Grady taught me that in seventh grade and I plumb forgot it. 'Plumb' is wrong too, isn't it?"

"I'm not sure it's wrong. Country vernacular, I'd say."

"Redneck talk?

"I didn't say that."

"Vernacular? I like the sound of that word. I'm gonna tell my friends I'm fixin' to hitch up my vernacular. Oh, well. Rednecks knows one sort of stuff and city folks knows another."

✳✳✳

When Tenbrook returned home, Kate asked for a full report.

"It went pretty well," he said. "They quizzed me. I think I passed the test. I told them that there ought to be a bounty on communists, that the earth was created in seven days and that Roy Rogers was my favorite singer. Troy kind of adopted me. Told me he was going to teach me how to work a grease gun and build a fence."

"You're going to turn into a born-again farm boy," said Kate.

"It wasn't all farm talk," said Tenbrook. "We got into a lively discussion about figurative and literal speech."

"You're going to start saying 'shucks.' You're going to start dipping snuff."

"It was a kind of initiation. When it was all over, we held hands and sang 'God Bless America.' I ought to tell you that I'm now Brother Tenbrook of the Sword, the Covenant and the Arm of the Lord. By the way, Troy offered us a deal on boarding a horse."

"We don't' have a horse."

"We might get one—for Channy."

"We can't afford a horse."

"Actually, he offered us three deals. One hundred dollars a month to board the horse and we get to keep the manure. Eighty dollars to board the horse and we get half the manure. Fifty dollars to board the horse...and there won't be any manure."

"Hilarious," said Kate. "So that passes for humor in the country?"

"Get used to it, darlin'. We've got to learn to split our sides over jokes like that or we're not going to fit in out here. And we must split our infinitives too."

"Retta Lou," said Kate. "Goll darn it, I do declare that's the cutest name I ever done heard."

"It's purest country," said Tenbrook.

"If we're going to make it out here I gonna have to change my name to Dottie Belle Sue."

"Soo-Wee!" cried Tenbrook.

"Hee-Haw," said Kate. "Camptown racetrack five miles long..."

"Do-dah, do-dah," sang Tenbrook.

"Roll 'em up and twist 'em up a high tuck-a-haw," sang Kate. She gave him a gentle elbow to the ribs. Tenbrook would remember it as one of the rare moments when he was almost at peace. That was early in the days of the Missouri Compromise, when things were looking up.

***

Sometimes when they're out driving, chatting away, Kate falls silent, tunes out, and Tenbrook fears he's boring her or that he's said the wrong thing. She reassures him, tells him she's not bored or angry. And she smiles that smile that reminds him of Leonardo da Vinci's women, smiling with some secret, other-world knowledge. He wants to know her secret.

"I was thinking that I have seven weft colors, but only four shuttles. I don't want to buy three more shuttles—they cost twenty dollars apiece. I'm wondering if I can do two bobbins on one shuttle."

He has no idea what she's talking about but it's at such times he loves her the most and feels as if he knows her the least. She really does seem like some goddess or a character in a Greek myth uttering a riddle: "Seven weft colors, but only four shuttles." Of course, it means more than it reveals. He'll never know. When they get home, she goes straight to her loom and he can hear the click of the thrown bobbin and the shudder when she beats the weft. And he feels alone, like a prisoner in an enchanted castle, like a lotus eater.

All her life she's been told how beautiful she is and there was a time in her adolescence when she tried to make herself look homely, because she wanted to be valued for her intrinsic worth, loved for herself alone, much as Tenbrook came to almost resent the athletic gift that won him so much praise, just because it was a gift that he'd done nothing to earn. Part of Kate's obsession with weaving was the desire to create something beautiful that was distinct from her own beauty. But her attempts to play down her good looks only seemed to make her more gorgeous.

Men were forever trying their luck, making gallant passes at her. It was something Tenbrook had to live with. When they pranced for her, they didn't really expect to seduce her. They wanted to amuse her, to see if they could coax out her famous smile. They wanted to feel that they'd aroused a flicker of interest. It had driven Tenbrook to the depths of jealousy at first, but in time he enjoyed watching how the suitors wilted when she cast her frigid spell.

Chapter 13

Cosmopolitans like to quote wide-eyed Dorothy when she entered the Land of Oz: "We're not in Kansas anymore." The implication is that the real world is a lot more complex and ambiguous than simple-minded Kansans suppose, that Kansas is a four-square wasteland of mind-numbing normality, a hatchery of rubes. But if they knew Kansas, they'd be surprised to discover that it is a strange and enigmatic state, a hive of aberrations and oddities rivaling any sophisticated metropolis. Kansas of the Grasshopper Army law, Kansas of Dr. Brinkley's monkey gland operation, Kansas of Wichita's "Bind, Torture and Kill" murderer, Kansas of the man-eating Nonesuch of Ozakie, of the Laughing Toadstool of Neodasha, of the Virgin Creeper of Yessir and the Devious Straightman of Potbelly. Take heed, ye worldly-wise, lest you be conned by Kansas, where a mountebank posing as a wizard hides behind every door…You sophisticated city dwellers have much to learn about the mysterious Heartland and the rimless state of boundless circumstance.

Visitors were few, but noteworthy. An itinerant painter from Tennessee who called himself Hopscotch appeared in a truck that sagged under a massive contraption of pipes and vats like the guts of a tramp steamer. He offered to spray-paint Tenbrook's barn.

"Two coats, five hundred dollars," he said. It sounded too good to be true, and it was. Hopscotch showed up the next day with a crew of savages who swarmed over the barn with a mess of tubes like hookahs that spewed red paint. The two-coat concept turned out to be one sweep of the spray gun from left to right, followed by a sweep from right to left. They were through in two hours. Within a month, the paint was peeling off in shaggy strips.

Every couple of months a Fed Ex guy delivered yarn for Kate's loom. When he got out, he disappeared behind the truck and then reappeared.

"I never walk in front of a vehicle," he explained. "I got hit that way when I was a kid. They said I would never walk again. They were going to amputate both my legs. But I walked out of that hospital after four days. They call that 'true grit.' I'm a Medical Miracle. They're still writing stories about me in the *Middleton Reaper*."

An emaciated woman in a frayed dress came to the door one day. She said she was Mandy and claimed she'd had sex with Tenbrook when they were in college, borne him a son and wanted child support. Tenbrook shooed her away.

"I never knew anyone named Mandy," he said.

"Who was that?" called Kate.

"Jehovah's Witness," answered Tenbrook. True enough, the men in black suits showed up from time to time to talk about the Bible. Tenbrook always said he was busy. They thanked him kindly and said maybe some other time. Tenbrook sometimes regretted that he hadn't invited them in and asked them the secret of their faith.

On weekends when the weather was mild, an ultra-light aircraft flew over the house. It roared like a giant leaf blower, but looked delicate as a damselfly. Back and forth it went without an apparent destination. Tenbrook wondered about those solitary flights. Did they signify freedom, or escape? Sometimes he suspected he was being watched. One day he read in the paper that the pilot had died when a gust of wind blew him into a power line.

During deer season, the neighborhood was overrun with road hunters. Trucks prowled along the edges of woods and fields where deer fed at twilight. Poachers worked at night with searchlights and often took only the back strap, leaving the rest of the carcass for coyotes and buzzards. Tenbrook found leftovers on his land—skulls, backbones, ribs, shin bones. One bright morning, the peace was shattered by the boom of a high-powered rifle just outside the house. Tenbrook ran outside. A man dressed head to foot in blaze orange was standing beside his truck in the front yard.

"I got one, but he ran into the trees," he said. A rifle barrel projected from the open window of the truck.

"It would have been nice if you'd asked permission," said Tenbrook. The man gave him a contrite look.

"You're right, I'm sorry. I got excited. I'll never do it again."

"And I don't think you're supposed to shoot from the truck," said Tenbrook.

"I can," said the man. "I'm handicapped." He pointed out the card with a wheelchair icon hanging from the truck's rearview mirror.

"You'd better drive over to the woods and see if you can find him," said Tenbrook.

"That's ok, I can just walk in."

"I thought you were handicapped," Tenbrook said.

Roscoe Wedin jogged past once or twice a week and left Tenbrook with some nugget to chew on.

"What's the good word, Roscoe?" Tenbrook once asked.

"Futility."

"What's so good about that?"

"That is the mystery. Seek and ye shall find. Have you been saved?"

"Not yet." Roscoe claimed to have ridden with Yellow Knife and Sitting Bull. He'd seen buffalo herds that stretched to the horizon. He was there when Geronimo prophesied that the buffalo would disappear and with them the soul of the nation.

"Then what?" Tenbrook asked.

"The streams will dry up and the grasses will wither."

"What should I do?"

"Have you any idea of the temperature of hell, sir? The flames melt steel ingots like sticks of butter. Define your terms. Take care of your immortal soul lest you burn. Have you read the book of time? You are living in excrement. Sackcloth and ashes, hell and damnation, farewell to flesh, repent, repent." Roscoe's eyes rolled so that only the whites showed. He crouched and moved his hand in a level sweep above the road.

"The CIA has a secret compound under a mountain in Alaska," he murmured. "The shadow government meets there. It will convene when Armageddon comes. They have a spaceship waiting to take them and their families to Mars. They're digging mass graves and building huge concentration camps for the rest of us. Their agents are flying crop dusters all across the country spraying a powder that sterilizes human beings. The United States is not a country, my friend. It is a foreign corporation that has invaded our land. Its agents have implanted identification chips in our butts while we slept and they will force us to choose between God's law and man's law."

Troy Bilbrey dropped by from time to time, rescuing

Tenbrook from frequent mishaps. He stopped when he saw Tenbrook stranded on the roof of his barn, "treed like a coon." The wind had blown Tenbrook's ladder down. He fished Tenbrook out when he got his truck stuck in a ditch.

"Why can't I get this plow to work?" Tenbrook asked one day.

"Plow's on backwards, Pilgrim," said Troy. He reached over, pulled Tenbrook's collar down and examined his neck.

"What do you see?" said Tenbrook.

"Comin' along," said Bilbrey. "Getting' redder every day." Tenbook liked the way Bilbrey pronounced "barrel"—"barl." And "bell"—"bayl" and said "day-ud" for "dead." Troy enjoyed mimicking Tenbrook's esoteric city vocabulary. He named an ornery sow "Nemesis," after he'd heard Tenbrook use that word. He referred to his overweight boar as "laconic," after he heard Tenbrook observe that most farmers are laconic.

"That boar's gotten so laconic he can't muster the energy to mount a sow," said Troy.

"I'd call that 'lethargic,'" said Tenbrook.

"All right then. From now on I'll call him lethargic."

One day Tenbrook was mowing when the front end of the tractor began to rise. When he let up on the throttle, the tractor settled back down to earth. When he gave it some gas, the machine began to rise again.

"What the hell's going on?" he said when Troy showed up.

"Looks to me like one of your goll-darn conundrums," said Troy. "Get down from there before you get electrocuted." Tenbrook eased the tractor down and got off. The front tires were straddling the guy wire of a utility pole. When the tractor moved forward, the front began to ride the wire up.

"I couldn't see that wire," said Tenbrook. "It's almost invisible."

"It looked like you was riding a bucking bronco," Troy said.

"I thought I was levitating," said Tenbrook. "I thought it was the rapture."

"Literally or figuratively?"

***

In those encounters Tenbrook felt a twinge of happiness. They were solving little, manageable problems. Mundane projects distracted him from his official job, offering the satisfaction of completion, the illusion that things added up. He'd say to himself, "God, I love this place." Losing it would be a kind of death.

He and Troy burned the pasture. Bilbrey walked along the edge of the field with his drip torch, lighting backfires. Tenbrook followed with a manure shovel to beat down maverick flames. When they were finished burning protective strips, Bilbrey lit the south property line. A wall of fire leapt up and ran before the wind. Flames rose 20 feet high, singeing the upper leaves of nearby trees. The fire raced over Tenbrook's 40 acres in minutes. A cloud of black smoke rose up in a perfect rectangle, a template of the field itself. It held its shape for a while. Then it drifted away to the north, finally blurring into an amorphous mass.

Tenbrook acquired a few skills, but nothing to put money in the bank. He went to the office less and less.

***

Sometimes, he sits in his old deer stand, surrounded by trees that seem like the masts of ships, a crow's nest watchman, listening to the stream of his thoughts. He thinks of places he's been and places he's never been, books he's read and ones he ought to read, girls he slept with, some without love, and ones he's only dreamed of, never known, glimpsed on a street or in a magazine. Sometimes he thinks about sailing away.

He remembers moments of selfless joy and long droughts of loneliness, and he wonders what the point of it is, not despairing that there might be no point, he finds that easy to accept, but stubbornly asking that question, as if it was a duty to ask. Like the fisherman who goes day after day without a strike, he still can't help imagining something beneath the surface that might be giving his bait a look. He keeps watching his line, waiting for a tug. The wind ruffles the few leaves still clinging to the branches, a druid whispering, and suddenly he feels as if the deer stand itself is moving, that his seat is not secure, is giving away, the feeling you have of going backwards when the train on the next track moves forward, leaving the station. It makes him queasy. He reaches out as if to grasp something solid in the air and then he realizes that he really is moving, that the giant hackberry his deer stand is attached to is waving gently, bending in the breeze, leaning against Tenbrook's back as if seeking support from him.

Waves of Canada geese fly overhead, yelping and honking, pandemonium in the sky, thousands of them a mile high, flying south to outrun an arctic front. A flight of speckle bellies passes over, cackling wildly. The vast convoy of clouds comes to a sudden stop, as if the great stage manager is considering his next move: gale force winds, hailstorm, or a tranquil segue into night? A rift opens in the western sky and a raft of light passes through. The setting sun drenches the woods with golden bars. Shadows of giant cottonwoods stretch across the ground. A range of bruise-blue clouds on the horizon reminds him that peace doesn't last long in

Kansas. High winds are on the way. Then darkness falls and sudden cold. Above the treetops, more tattered clouds fly past beneath the shoreless sky.

***

Tenbrook calls Troy for more help. The tractor won't start. Troy gives him a searching look and spits into his plastic cup.

"You remember to turn the ignition on?"

"Of course," says Tenbrook.

"Will it turn over?" Tenbrook turns the key. The engine answers with a series of groans and coughs.

"Sure it's got gas?"

"Of course it's got gas."

"Let's have a look-see." Bilbrey opens the gas cap and peers inside.

"Bone dry, huh?" says Tenbrook. "I knew it was going to be something stupid like this. Hecky darn, I just filled it up the other day."

"You keep it greased?" says Bilbrey. "Ford built a good tractor back in the day. It'll last forever, if you oil it and keep it greased." He takes a can of snuff from his hip pocket and puts a pinch in his lower lip.

"I greased it the other day," says Tenbrook. "A whole wad of grease shot out of that gun like it was alive. Squirming like a snake all over the shed. It was like a carpet of banana peels on the ground."

"Grease is alive," says Bilbrey, chuckling. "It don't like be'in told what to do." Troy wipes his eyes and blows his nose on a tattered rag. Tenbrook notices it's covered with blood. They sit down on a bench in front of the shed.

"You know, I kinda like getting these calls from you."

"It gives you stories to tell," says Tenbrook.

"You like it out here?" says Troy.

"I do."

"I like it too. Can't imagine living anywhere else. When you breathe out here, the air tastes like it's never been breathed before. Course the place has changed. And it's a-changing."

A small bus comes rumbling down the road. Troy and Tenbrook watch it pass. Displayed on its side are three posters of naked women, colossal bosoms and bottoms, and the words, Booty Bus.

"What the hell is that?" said Tenbrook.

"That's your neighbor's mobile lap dance facility," says Troy. "Fat little toad with a big head, always dressed up like he's going to a wedding or a funeral." He points to the unfinished mansion on the bluff. "Notice that every six months or so there's a flurry of work done up there? That's when Jimmy gets a big payoff. Then after he's spent a hundred thousand or so the work shuts down until the next windfall.'"

"I don't get it," said Tenbrook. "If he's into prostitution and drugs, why would he operate out of such a conspicuous spot? Wouldn't it be easy for the police to check it out?"

"Unless the police was in on the business."

"You're kidding."

"You're innocent, son. Stay clear of that man." Tenbrook wondered if Troy knew he was already involved with that man. The sun came out and struck Troy's weathered face and suddenly he looked ten years older. There was a hint of weariness that Tenbrook hadn't seen before.

"Gwan gadeen," said Bilbrey to Sam, his blue-tick dog. "Time to go." He opened the truck door and Sam jumped in.

"Gwan gadeen?" said Tenbrook. "That sounds like Farsi. What's it mean?"

"Go on, get in."

Chapter 14

The Mercury comes roaring up the driveway in a billow of dust. Tenbrook watches from the kitchen window. Two men get out, one short and muscular with a thick neck and a bullet head, the other tall and thin with a ragged goatee and a face like a pair of needle nose pliers. They pound on the door. Tenbrook opens. They brush past him and start to look around.

"Can I help you?" asks Tenbrook.

"Methinks he's the one who's in need of help," says the short guy with a grin that shows only the eye teeth remaining of his uppers.

"Hush, Roland," says the other man. "Thou minimus of hindering knot grass made." His name is Benny. He's wearing a plaid jacket and a porkpie hat made out of some synthetic straw-like material. He has a tic of recurrent squinting. Roland wears a tight-fitting, powder-blue warm-up outfit that shows off his muscles. "We're here to check your papers. Let's have a look at your license."

"My license?" Tenbrook laughs.

"Bright boy don't have no license," says Roland.

"That's my line," says Benny.

"You don't own it," says Roland.

"Technically, that line belongs to Ernest Hemingway. Plus, you've got the accent all wrong. Think Edward G. Robinson."

"Tell you what," said Tenbrook. "While you guys work on your lines, I've got some chores to do, if you'll excuse me." Benny's bony hand lashes out and strikes Tenbrook on the mouth. Tenbrook tastes blood.

"That's a message from Jimmy," says Benny.

"Jimmy who?"

"Jimmy who gave you ten thousand dollars."

"I didn't ask for that money," says Tenbrook. "Tell Jimmy to take his money back."

"Don't no one tells Jimmy what to do," says Benny.

"Jimmy owns you," says Roland.

"Shut up, Roland," says Benny. "Speak when you're spoken to."

"I've heard you say the same thing a thousand times," says Roland. He sits down on the sofa, crosses his leg over the armrest and begins to swing it. Then he suddenly jumps up and approaches Tenbrook.

"We started off small time," he says. "Car jackings, dope peddling, bush-league shit. Then we met Jimmy."

"Will you shut the fuck up?" says Benny languidly. Their accents change from Shakespearean to gangster. Their faces seem to be made of plastic. Their facial expressions change from sinister to cartoon masks.

"Bright boy needs to know who he's up against," says Roland. He pulls back the sleeves of his warm-up suit and begins to massage his forearms, which are defaced with a swarm of dragon and gargoyle tattoos.

"So Jimmy promoted you?" says Tenbrook.

"Jimmy's got class," says Benny. He opens his jacket to show a pistol tucked under his belt.

"Enough said," says Roland.

"I'll say when enough's been said," says Benny. "Keep your eyes on me. Don't let your mind wander." He picks up a broom and wields it like a rapier. "En garde…touché… Jimmy's got work for you."

"I don't want work," says Tenbrook. "Tell Jimmy to take his money back."

"Fine," said Benny. "Let's have the money."

"Well said, true-penny," says Roland.

"It'll take me a few days."

"You don't have a few days," says Benny. "My guess is you don't have the money. 'Tis true, 'tis pity, 'tis pity, 'tis true. Now, serve Jimmy and you won't have to pay the money back. This is easy work. Any idiot could do it."

"Much more so a bright boy," says Roland. Benny shoves a package covered with duct tape in Tenbrook's face. "All you have to do is deliver this."

"From now on we call him 'Delivery Boy,'" says Roland. Benny hands Tenbrook a scrap of paper. "Here's the address. Memorize it and throw it away. Remember, you're a delivery boy. All you do is deliver. Don't answer questions. Don't snoop. Just show Jimmy you can deliver. Then you'll get more jobs."

"I don't want more jobs," says Tenbrook.

"That's where you're wrong," says Benny, caressing his pistol. "More jobs is just what you want. Without jobs you're just another dickhead. One of Jimmy's dead-end dickheads." He grins. Flecks of saliva gather at the corners of his mouth. He laughs. "Which would you rather be—a man or a woman?"

"I haven't thought about it," says Tenbrook.

"Delivery Boy hasn't thought about it," said Roland.

"And you, my dear Roland—what would your preference be?"

"I'd like to be both a man and a woman," says Roland. "Like one of those fish that mates with itself."

"Fuck the fish," says Benny. "We're here on business."

"We're professionals, don't you see?" says Roland.

Tenbrook concludes that the two men are crazy or high on drugs. There's a chemical odor about them. Tenbrook wonders if they're the ones who'd been cooking meth in his field.

"Jimmy's all business," says Benny. "He takes aim and fires. Never misses. Don't even have to look and point." He takes out his pistol and starts aiming it around the room, saying, "Pow…Pow…Pow." Then he puts the barrel of the pistol against Tenbrook's nose. "To Jimmy, an AK-47 is like a pea-shooter," he says. "It takes an RPG to fan his interest. Taking out your house here would be like blowing out a candle to him. So watch your step. That's my advice. Jimmy would take a look at you and say: 'Shoo, fly.' Now you see it, now you don't. Remember, this ain't your house anyway. It belongs to Jimmy. You belong to Jimmy. That ten grand was an investment—in you. All Jimmy wants is a fair return. But don't nickle and dime him. Jimmy hates to be nickled and dimed." Benny takes one more turn around the living room. "This place could use a spruce-up," he says.

"You got anything against spruce-ups?" says Roland.

"Shut up, Roland," says Benny. "You got some rotten boards in his house need replacing.'

"Something's rotten in the state of Denmark," says Roland.

"Okay, Roland. Enough. Let's got out of here. Vamanos." He bows, takes off his hat with a courtly flourish. "Pleased to meet you, Delivery Boy." And they take their leave with raucous laughter and a chorus of obscenities on the theme of having intercourse with one's mother.

After his visitors leave, Tenbrook goes to the shed. His calculation was correct: There are only five $1,000 bills left. Little by little, he's returned to the well to keep his little ship afloat. Now it's sinking. He's been sucked in.

Chapter 15

Pillars was aroused. He paced. He flung his arms. His mood swung from aggravation to anger to anxiety. He felt besieged, as if a tribe of pygmies had tied him to the ground with ten thousand strings. The Friends of the Prairie and the tree huggers were on the march, vowing to foil his plans to develop the Griefmaker. There had been vigils and wakes, prayer meetings and poetry readings, press conferences, protests, voices crying in the wilderness. They claimed the Griefmaker as their own, pronounced it "sacred," a patrimony belonging to future generations that must be preserved. Leaders of Middleton's Native American community claimed that it had been a burial ground of their ancestors. Pillars had been cast as "The Antichrist."

"I'm not interested in winning a popularity contest," he told his wife.

"You don't want to be public enemy number one, either," said Gwen.

"They crucified Jesus and he ended up being a hero."

"You're not Jesus."

"Excuse me, Gwen, but to hell with Jesus." Gwen closed her eyes and shuddered.

"God forgive you, Everett," she whispered.

"Do you think God gives a damn what I do with my

land?" Pillars stood glaring at her for a moment, waiting for an answer. But she was somewhere else.

"Have mercy upon us," she said. As Pillars turned and left the room, he reached for the handle on the leaded glass door. He wanted to slam it, but that might break the glass, and it was a valuable door. In the soft light of the hallway, he saw a small porcelain crucifix his wife had recently placed on an antique table where pictures of Tod were displayed. He was about to reach for it, but stopped himself and let it go. He re-channeled his anger. There was work to do. If the work went according to plan, there would be no virgin prairie to preserve.

It was Sunday evening. The next morning the Friends of the Prairie were going to file some sort of petition. That would mean publicity. The next thing would be a restraining order, environmental impact studies, archaeologists digging for pottery shards and bones. Pillars feared that his development might be held up in court. That thought impacted him physically. He owed big money and interest was accumulating. He felt a constriction in his chest. But he was going to beat the pygmies to the punch.

He walked out of the house and strode across the lawn. Good: it was clear, a full moon rising. Jenkins was already in the implement shed, the big tractor humming. The sweet aroma of machine oil mingled with the machine's exhaust. The plow hung in readiness from the three-point hitch. Jenkins had a wrench in his hand, his ear to the engine, a faint smile on his face. The sight of the huge rotund man, in overalls large enough to envelop a refrigerator, cheered Pillars.

"How's it running?" he said.

"She had a little indigestion. Maybe a drop of water in the fuel? Anyway, she's perking up, feeling better now." He tapped the tractor with his wrench. "I had to tweak the carburetor. And I replaced the ignition coil. Pack rats ate clean through it. When rats gets bored they has to chew."

"Put out some bait, Jenkins. I don't want vermin in my shed."

"Dogs might get into it. You don't want that."

"Well, get rid of the rats. I don't care how it's done."

Jenkins had a magic way with machinery. He could listen to an engine and tell what ailed it just by the sound. He managed tools as if they were extensions of his massive hands. And he was strong. Pillars had seen him lift the back end of a pickup truck to move it from a muddy rut. At times, Pillars almost envied Jenkins—his simplicity, his four-square existence, his freedom from bottom lines, creditors, competition. Jenkins slept alone in a three-room bungalow. Other than tools, all his possessions were contained in those four walls: an ancient stove and refrigerator, a black and white television, the linoleum-topped table where he ate his meals, the armchair patched with duct tape. No worries about cholesterol. Beef and potatoes for dinner, biscuits and gravy for breakfast, a six pack every night, in bed by nine, up by five, a routine dictated by the seasons, no one to argue with or impress, no health insurance, no fear of failure or death, self-possessed, his moon-like face the image of contentment. Though not a simpleton. Pillars bounced ideas off him not just to hear how they sounded but to hear Jenkins respond. Jenkins possessed country logic. He wasn't afraid of Pillars and he spoke his mind.

"Ready for battle?" said Pillars.

"Aye, aye."

"They'll be troublemakers."

"Educated fools. Wouldn't know a whiffletree from an ox goad."

"You're full of wisdom tonight, Jenkins. Don't you think it's a sin to break the virgin soil?" Jenkins ran a hand over his beard, smiled and shook his head.

"People been plowing up Kansas since the day they got here. Sodbusters was heroes. If it's a sin to break ground, there's been lots of sinners in the state of Kansas. A time to sow and a time to reap, ain't that right, Gov'ner? And a time to plow"

"Tell that to Mrs. Pillars."

"I'll leave that to you. I've never been much for lecturing females."

"You've got it made, Jenkins. You're married to a tractor. And it doesn't talk back to you."

"Oh, it talks back. But you're right. I do love this machine. It just don't always love me back."

"Love is overrated, Jenkins. So is sex, for all the trouble it costs. Say, is it true what I've heard about rural folk having sex with sheep? I wonder if anyone's ever tried to mate with a tractor." Jenkins snorted.

"This tractor's almost pretty enough."

"It ought to be for a hundred and fifty grand," said Pillars. "The only thing it lacks is a hot tub."

"Tractors have come a long way since John Deere made his first plow," said Jenkins. Pillars surveyed the implements arrayed in his shed—chisel, disc, harrow, planter, sprayer, arranged in the order of their seasonal uses. Sacks of fertilizer and seed stacked in neat rows. Plastic jugs of herbicide—Crossbow, Remedy, Lasso—some more costly than wine. Racks of trophy bucks he'd shot. Branding irons, including a miniature one Pillars used to mark steaks when he staged one of his lavish cookouts. No one belly-ached about his money and his greed when they were chowing down on his food and guzzling his booze.

In the shed he felt solidity of purpose. Let people scorn him for being a shrewd and ruthless businessman. He was a descendent of pioneers. It was his land, his birthright, his duty to cultivate the soil. What business did hippies and agitators have to question what he did with his land?

Buoyed by his own rhetoric, Pillars clapped his hands. The metal shed amplified the idling tractor's sound to a thrilling rumble.

"I'll drive," he said to Jenkins. "You follow in the four-wheeler. And bring a shotgun."

Jenkins pulled a wool cap down over his ears. He plucked a 12-gauge shotgun from a wall rack. The ATV sagged when he mounted it. He pressed the starter and it sputtered to life.

"Come on, darlin'," he said. "You and I goin' down a path we never been down before." He touched a button on a post above the kerosene heater. The metal garage door rose, opening to the night.

Pillars stepped on the tractor tire and boosted himself up to the cab. He slid in and sat down on the swivel seat. It was like a cockpit inside. There were computer control panels and digital gauges, buttons for adjusting tilt and depth and the angle of draft. There was a cigar lighter, a CD player, even a dial to vary the windshield wiper speed.

He ran his hand over a maze of levers. He raised the plow higher above the concrete floor and put the engine in gear. The tractor lumbered from the shed. The great tires made a sound like rushing water on the driveway's gravel. They passed the pen where Pillars' champion bull, Echo Ridge Experiment, slept on a bed of Astroturf and the horse barn where his Morgan horses were coddled and groomed.

The trees in the orchard leapt up like dancers in the sweep of the tractor's light. Their limbs had been uniformly pruned. The gardens, organized with rigid symmetry, and the tidy outbuildings spoke of order and control. Beyond the compound lay terraced fields fenced and bounded with rows of stumps, vestiges of hedge rows which had been cut down to gain a fraction more of productive land, a few more bushels of grain. Pillars drove over the concrete low-water crossing of a creek he'd straightened and entered the first pasture.

The land was more unruly there, cut by swales and knotted with hillocks. His mind began churning projects. To the north was a cedar shelterbelt. What purpose did it serve? It should be cut down. And that dried out pond, perhaps dammed by the original settler. It should be bulldozed out and the dam reformed. The bottom land along the creek ought to be cultivated. It was money down the drain to have it in grass.

The air was crisp. The moon floated on a tissue of clouds. The sky was like a field sown with gem-bright stars. They stopped at the top of a hill overlooking the site of the proposed highway interchange. Jenkins opened a gate and Pillars drove the tractor over a cattle guard. He lowered the plow—a dozen daggers to the hearts of the eco-mystics. The tractor bucked once as the plow heads dug into the soil. It lunged forward as Pillar gave it some gas. Then it settled in. Pillars felt a satisfying tug as the steel bit into the soft earth, folding back the fabric of sod, opening fresh furrows to the pale light of the moon. Jenkins drove alongside, like the pilot fish of a shark.

Breaking new ground, thought Pillars. Wasn't there a hymn? "We plow the fields and scatter the good grain on the land, but it is fed and watered by God's almighty hand." There it was in gospel black and white: Make the land bear fruit. God favors the farmer. The land is ours.

He plowed along the fence line down to the road, then back up the hillside. He plowed for an hour in a peaceful hiatus, listening to Frank Sinatra on the CD player: "Somewhere there's music, how high the moon…" They don't write songs like that anymore and they don't sing them like that. Pillars had finished about twenty acres when he saw the lights of the first cars, a cortege probing the night mist like a glowworm, slowing down and stopping on the shoulder of the road. More followed, a procession of headlights. Pillar idled the tractor. Jenkins drove up beside him.

"Here come the self-righteous bastards in their holier-than-thou Priuses," said Pillars. "Here they come to rage against the machine. Fire away, Jenkins. But don't shoot to kill."

"It's not loaded. I don't want to go to jail any more than you do."

Pillars opened his cell phone and punched the numbers in. The sheriff answered.

"We got company, Tom," said Pillars.

Cars were lining up on the road to the south, horns honking in unison. A motley band of pilgrims crossed the road and marched toward the tractor, waving flashlights, chanting, blowing shrill whistles. They carried signs with words like "Shame" and "Greed." Some were dressed in pioneer attire, women in long dresses and bonnets, men in overalls wielding pitchforks, some folks wrapped in Indian blankets, some with their hair in dreadlocks. A few wore sweatshirts stamped with the Griefmaker's iconic, wind-bent tree.

"What do these people do for a living?" Pillars asked. "Any of them ever do an honest day's work?" As the mob approached, he suddenly spotted his son Tod, looking back at him with a defiant smirk. It must have been Tod who'd sounded the alarm.

Two men hoisted a straw-stuffed effigy in a tattered thrift-shop suit. They hung it on a fence post and set it on fire. A frail-looking lady with a bundle of white hair walked with a cane, gesturing with it angrily in Pillars' direction. The protesters raised a carnival din, but their faces were masks of tragedy and outrage. They marched up a small incline, struggling to keep their footing on the plowed ground, shielding their eyes from the glare of the tractor's headlights. A truck from one of the news stations, with a satellite dish mounted on the roof, arrived and set up flood-lights. A man with his hair in a ponytail wearing a feath-ered headdress stood on a wooden box and started making a speech into a bullhorn about the curse of private property and the sanctity of community.

Others took turns at the bullhorn. They spoke in rhap-sodies of the miraculous grasses that flourished in the harsh, dry Kansas soil, mementos of unrecoverable time, of purple coneflower and prairie larkspur, gayfeather and beebalm.

"No compromise in defense of Mother Earth!"

"Pillars: You can't eat money!"

A woman who identified herself as "Prairiefire" recit-ed a poem that played on the theme of "grief" in Grief-maker, juxtaposing it to the theme of greed. Highways of blood and grief, innocent grass mowed down by the sickle of profit, wounds in the womb of Mother Earth, orisons of meadow mouse and prairie vole and the lost sanctuaries of solitude, land smothered beneath lava flows of asphalt, devouring hordes of consumers.

"Where have the buffalo gone?" she cried. "Where are the teepees, the ponies, the braves? Beware the beast that stands on two legs, the predator, the destroyer." With her hands raised, she evoked the specter of an interchange with hordes of gas-guzzling vehicles spewing out noxious fumes. The crowd cried back: "No, never…Stop the destroyer." She introduced two children, Freedom and Justice, who read statements about protecting the planet for future generations. A woman wearing a serape passed out grass seeds and urged people to sow them in the furrows so that the sacred grasses would return. The crowd moved towards the tractor, holding hands and singing "We Shall Overcome." Pillars put the machine in gear and drove around them with his plow still engaged. A man in a Halloween skeleton costume ran ahead and lay down in the path of the tractor. Pillars put the tractor in neutral and gunned it.

The crowd pressed close. Jenkins drove his four-wheeler between them and the tractor and showed his shotgun. From the road came the sound of sirens and the hectic flashing of blue and red lights. Squad cars bounced up the hillside, raising clouds of dust. Policemen jumped out and jogged in the direction of the tractor, ordering the trespassers to disperse. The man lying in the tractor's path hadn't budged. Two cops pulled him up off the ground and stood him up, but his legs went limp. They hoisted him up again, held him by the arm pits above the ground then stood him down again. His legs collapsed like a marionette's.

"We are not trespassing here," someone cried. "The earth belongs to all. Earth is bleeding, save the Earth."

Someone climbed up to the cab of the tractor. It was Father Ned.

"Look back, Everett!" he cried. "While there's time."

"Get the fuck off my tractor," Pillars yelled. Policemen pulled Ned off and threw him to the ground. Pillars seethed. But he didn't look back. He forged ahead.

A tall, gaunt woman with raven-black hair wearing a shiny black cape and a black beret stepped out of the shadows, waving a kind of scepter at the tractor. She bobbed up and down like a heron, moving her head with strange feints, her face contorted with deranged ecstasy.

"Prairie chicken, qu'est-ce que c'est," she sang. "Spider smile, business feaster, history eater, die on poisoned seed." She chanted in an eerie, cracking voice. ``Paw-paw-paw-paw-paw. Paw-paw-paw-paw-paw. You better run, run, run, run away." Pillars stared at the apparition as she uttered strings of incomprehensible words, punctuated with odd "Yips." For an instant he was rattled. The woman's eyes were outlined in thick circles of black make-up. She kept shaking her scepter at him, witch-like, laughing and yipping. For a second he imagined she was Gwen. One of the policemen grabbed her by the elbow and led her away. She kept up her crazy chanting, and looked back at Pillars, sticking out her tongue.

"All that you love will wither and die," she cried. "Wither and die."

The protesters filed away, herded by the police. Pillars was in a sweat. He felt drained. He called to Jenkins for a drink. Jenkins held a half pint of peppermint schnapps up to him and Pillar took a few swigs. The protesters reconvened at the roadside. Soon they had a small fire going. Pillars watched them through binoculars. He caught a glimpse of the white limousine. Emerging from the shadows, it slowed as it passed the crowd, briefly lit by the flashing lights of the squad cars, then glided away.

The crowd turned inward. The protesters seemed to abandon their outrage. They hugged, they danced, some in whirling circles. They waved their arms, they bowed down and rose back up, opening and closing like jack knives. Tom Stives showed up with his bagpipe wearing an ill-fitting kilt and played "Amazing Grace," the single tune in his repertoire, distinguished by numerous painful squeaks. A prophet of doom in a hairshirt bore a cross made of four-by-fours resting on a pair of bicycle tires. A group of cheerleaders from Middleton High appeared in short skirts waving pom-poms. They gave an incoherent cheer for planet earth while they scanned the assembly for handsome boys. Jugs of wine passed from hand to hand. The scene began to look more like a bacchanalian fertility rite or Halloween orgy than a funeral for the Griefmaker.

Late arrivals showed up costumed as animals: a wooly bison, a grizzly bear, an antelope. There was a Mad Hatter, a Zeus with cardboard lightning bolt, a skeleton, a pirate in a purple wig. A man towed a wagon occupied by his child wrapped in a blanket, busily playing a video game. An apparitional figure bobbed and leaped on stilts fashioned from the shanks of deer. His costume was covered with pheasant and peacock feathers, turtle shells, skulls of sharp-toothed rodents, his belt studded with chicken bones. He brandished a feather-tipped lance as if casting out demons. Some pole dancers from the Pistol Club were amusing the audience with a partial striptease. Food trucks pulled up. Two men got into a shoving match. Father Ned came running and pulled them apart. A young man who'd had too much wine threw up. Someone lit a portable grill and began cooking brats.

Pillars plowed on. His tractor plunged westward into the night. The twin beams of its headlights probed into the darkness, momentarily illuminating shapes of startled deer and cattle and other nocturnal animals. He transferred his anger to the earth itself, attacked it, and felt a brutal satisfaction as the passive soil gave way. And as he plowed he began to feel a kind of exaltation. He had won.

He plowed into morning and at the first light of dawn he laid open the last furrow. The Griefmaker was now cropland for the time being. But it was destined to be a suburban complex, a hive of commerce. Tatters of fog rose from the warm earth in the cool morning air. Deer scattered as the tractor climbed a hill and a coyote, out hunting early, crossed the path, giving Pillars and Jenkins a casual glance. A pair of owls exchanged interrogative hoots. A blade of orange light lay over the city to the east.

Pillars was drowsy but as he approached the shed something snapped him alert. Pheasants were loose in the yard. The door of the bird pen was open. Pheasants everywhere. The dogs raised a chorus of plaintive howls.

"My pheasants!" Pillars shouted. "They let my pheasants out." Jenkins had already driven to the shed and returned with a net in his hand. He chased the birds, but he was slow and they were excited and eluded him with an outcry of cackles. Pillars raised the birds for his annual pheasant hunt, to which he invited Middleton's top businessmen, politicians, small-town celebrities and civic leaders.

"Get the dogs, Jenkins," he shouted. "Get some shells and another gun. If we don't shoot those birds now, the hawks will have all their heads off by noon."

Jenkins loosed the dogs from their kennel and they began hunting in the yard, frenzied by the surfeit of scent. Pheasants flushed from under the patio furniture and the stone-lined tree wells in the backyard garden. They ran from beneath the Pillars' cars parked on the circular drive in front of the house. Pillars and Jenkins fired without pausing, shot after shot, reloading on the run as the birds sprung up in twos and threes, the dogs quartering back and forth, pointing and flushing. They left the dead birds in piles and moved on in a tumult of barking and shots.

"I got a triple, Jenkins," Pillars roared. "`Haven't missed yet." Then, remembering his outrage, he bellowed, "My goddamn birds!" They followed the dogs out of the compound, stopping to fire. He grabbed the birds from the mouths of the retrieving dogs and then marched on.

"More shells, Jenkins. I'm out." Jenkins fumbled in his overalls and out came several boxes of shells. Pillars stopped for a moment. He surveyed the land. He envisioned an exit ramp of the Middleton Loop 200 yards to the south of where he stood. It gave him a momentary lift.

The sun was up, warming the air. They followed the route of the tractor to the freshly plowed prairie. But with the cover gone, they found fewer and fewer pheasants. The birds that had gotten that far had kept flying, probably across the road and into the city park where they couldn't shoot. But Pillars kept hunting. Jenkins stopped to catch his breath. He watched Pillars disappear over the top of a rise.

"My birds! My birds!"

PART TWO

COMING HOME

"It was Ulysses and it was not...

that kept coming constantly so near."

—*Wallace Stevens*

Chapter 16

The ferry wove in and out of the mangrove islands, surging forward in deep water, throttling back in the shallows. Startled egrets and spoonbills flew up, fluttered and settled down again on the dying wake. Ospreys glared from their nests on the tops of buoys. Overhead, a frigate bird hung motionless, like a black hole in the sky.

Tenbrook was traveling as a bachelor. Kate had stayed home to be with Channy, who was competing in a soccer tournament. He'd been invited, along with the rest of the Pillars' other Middleton friends—the Yosts, the Curtains, the Foresters, the Tellers—to the Pillars' vacation home on Jacamar, an island in the Gulf of Mexico.

The boat emerged from the mangrove maze and sped toward a thread of white beach, beyond which loomed a row of grandiose houses that reflected the sunlight, crowding the shoreline like colossal mirrors. Tenbrook returned from the cockpit. He'd been talking to the captain, who was dressed like a pirate with a striped jersey, a bandana cap and an earring in the shape of a cutlass.

"What did you learn?" said Ridley Tellers.

"Calls himself Captain Pete," said Tenbrook. "Born and raised on the island. Father homesteaded forty acres back in the Depression. Be a millionaire today if his pappy hadn't sold out to the first pickpocket that came along. Sees himself as being in the entertainment business. Wanted to know if they still sell drinks on airplanes. Used to take his own booze on board because you had to wait too long for the drinks cart. 'Feel pretty good by the time you get to Mobile,' he said. Give that guy a pegleg, an eye patch and put a parrot on his shoulder and he'd pass for Long John Silver."

The ferry made a lazy curve. The captain reversed his engines, producing a throaty rumble that rattled the gunwales. The boat slowed and floated gracefully to the dock. The guests paid the fare, stepped out and rolled their luggage over the planks, making a syncopated clatter. The sun was already beating down at ten o'clock and a veil of humidity hung in the air.

Gwen was at the end of the dock in a golf cart, shouting at a rental boat that had just motored up. "No! No! No! That's our slip." The guests dropped their bags in her cart and exchanged hugs.

"This is not a public dock," said Gwen, smiling sweetly with mock indignation. She drove down a pebble path, past a huge banyan tree with sprawling limbs and roots like the drippings of immense gray candles. Majestic live oaks presided over the grounds along with royal palms that looked like the columns of pharaonic temples. Swarms of poinsettias, hibiscus, oleander covered manicured yards. Mountains of bougainvillea blossoms spilled over the gardens like cascades of purple water. Nests of orchids hung on the trees, giving off waves of cloying perfume. The sun burned down through openings in the vegetation.

"This is the Garden of Eden, Gwen," said Charlie Curtains. Small dark-skinned men worked with pruning shears, snapping off dead flowers. They smiled, showing their fine white teeth, as the cart glided by. In the front yard of one of the homes was a white-haired man in a wheelchair, his head thrown back, his mouth wide open. Flowers with blossoms like puckered lips spilled out of huge urns and crowded the borders of raised beds. Beneath the fragrance floated a whiff of septic odor.

"Just leave your stuff and José will unload it," said Gwen. "Come see Mariposa Cottage."

The "cottage" was actually a sprawling villa, painted bright white with turquoise, orange and yellow trim. A veranda surrounded the first floor. Balconies jutted out from the rooms above. A widow's walk surmounted the rooftop. A deck with twin gazebos protruded from one side. It was dark as a funeral parlor inside. Other guests, holding drinks carved out of pineapples greeted the newcomers with cries of recognition, as if they hadn't seen one another in years. Everyone was wearing flamboyant Hawaiian shirts with the Pillars logo on the pocket. The room was cluttered with nautical objects and seaside knickknacks— model ships, glass buoys, a rust-encrusted anchor, seashell picture frames, tortoise shells, shark teeth, a harpoon. The fireplace was filled like a cornucopia with seashells spilling out on the floor.

Gwen led her guests around the house, then sat them down and launched into a bit of history. A famous pirate had used Jacamar for a hideout. According to legend, his treasure was buried on the island. Children of the home-owners spent hours digging with their plastic shovels in hopes of discovering the hoard. Archeologists had dug up remains of aboriginals who inhabited the island before the Spanish arrived.

After the tour, the guests picked their room assignments out of a straw hat. Each bedroom had a name: Pelican, Wahoo, Sand Dollar, Mango, Hurricane. The bathrooms were furnished with Jacuzzis and gold fixtures in the form of dolphins. Terry cloth bathrobes with the "EP" monogram were spread on the beds along with fruit baskets and bottles of champagne. After a little time for unpacking, a ship's bell summoned them.

"This place is a disaster area," said Gwen. "A pigpen." The women protested. The cottage was perfectly stunning. The decor would make Martha Stewart weep. Gwen enlisted Tenbrook to make daiquiris.

"This is going to be catch as catch can," she said, serving hors d'oeuvres. "I'm short of help. It's impossible to get help on this island."

"I have some skills," said Curtains. "I'm slow, but dependable. I'll work for food."

The building boom had turned the locals into prima donnas, said Gwen. You had to bow and scrape to get them to lift a finger. The Pillars were already thinking about selling and finding a more unspoiled place. After he'd poured the drinks, Tenbrook walked around the room. The walls were covered with photos of Pillars holding up trophy fish. Tenbrook remembered trying to teach his friend how to cast. Pillars had gotten tangled up in his line, thrown a tantrum and broken his thousand-dollar bamboo rod across his knee. You had to give him credit for perseverance. Now he was a pro.

Gwen ordered her guests to bring her up to date. Gossip time. They sat on cushioned bamboo chairs and settled into the easy chatter of lifelong friends, trading stories about the successes of their children, the declining health of their parents, the misfortunes of others in their social circle. No one said a word about Pillars' rape of the Griefmaker.

Curtains leaned over to Tenbrook and said, "Friends are the mirrors in which we seek ourselves." Curtains had gone through bankruptcy, spent a short term in a white-collar prison for some financial shenanigans and had come out looking younger, refreshed rather than crushed or shamed. He was a ruddy bantam-rooster man and before his downfall he'd been a blowhard who could out-boast Pillars. Now he had an aura of serenity, a look of quiet amusement, as if he were in on a joke the others didn't yet get. He made it look as if losing your fortune and getting sent to the slammer was a stroke of good luck.

"Oh, I still belong to a lot of exclusive clubs," he said. "The Hen House Salad Club, the Book of the Month Club..." He and Tenbrook moved on to the front porch and stood close to the screen. A squadron of pelicans flew by a foot above the glassy water.

"What do you think this place cost?" Curtains said.

"Everett said he'd bought a thirty-foot lot on the mainland for $100,000 just to have a place to dock his boat," said Tenbrook. "Do you envy him?"

"No. I'm happy for him. I rejoice in his success. Let him worry about roof leaks, shower mold, rust on the doorknobs. Let him wheel and deal and wrestle with the undependable help. We're lucky. We don't have the worries and we get to stay here for free."

A flats boat appeared in the distance. It shot up to the dock raising a fan of sparkling water. Its single occupant stood up and tossed a line to a man who was whitewashing the pilings.

"Look," said Tenbrook. "It's Pillars." Pillars looked gigantic in the toy-like boat. He jumped out and stalked down the dock, clutching fly rods in both hands like spears. He was sunburned and unshaved. He grinned when he saw Tenbrook and Curtains on the porch.

"I had a tarpon hooked big as Moby Dick," he said. "Fought him for two hours. Had him beat. Then he goes on a run, jumps twenty feet in the air and throws my fly." He gave out hearty handshakes, stood back, looked his guests over.

"We're your real trophies," said Curtains.

"He's going to have us mounted on the wall."

"You know you've gone off the deep end when you'd rather go fishing than have sex," said Pillars, laying his rods carefully in a green-velvet lined case. "What's the point of getting and spending, when all you really want to do is fish? You don't need a fortune. All you need is a can of worms, a pole, some line and a hook."

"Somehow I suspect that you wouldn't be happy fishing for crappie from a bridge in the Ozarks," said Tenbrook. Pillars laughed.

"You're right," he said. "I've gone from Patagonia to Russia to feed my habit. It's ridiculous. You had a good flight? Gotten settled? How do you like my shack?"

"It's charming," said Tenbrook.

"You should have bought a lot down here when I told you to," said Pillars. "Property's been doubling every three to four years."

✳ ✳ ✳

"The prodigal fisherman returns," said Gwen when Pillars barged into the room. He went around, patted his guests, apologized for neglecting them and expressed his satisfaction with "my little friends." He poured a tumbler full of dark rum, tossed in a few ice cubes and drank it all in a few swallows. "Real men don't drink daiquiris," he said, making his fingers do a girlish dance. He led the men around the room, pointing out mounted salmon, trout, bonefish he'd caught. He had an anecdote for every trophy—the permit he almost lost in the Keys when his guide passed out, the brown trout he jumped into a freezing Chilean stream to retrieve. He showed his collection of antique reels and a box of flies he'd tied: Anderson's McCrab, Crazy Charlie, Popocic's Surf Candy.

"Charlie, Ridley, Ten, you guys are going to fish with Donnie Kestler tomorrow," he said. "He just has a nose for where the fish are going to be. He and I won the tarpon tournament here two years ago. Hundred-thousand-dollar purse. Sounds like a lot, but it cost five thousand to enter. We gave it all to charity."

Gwen called them to dinner. They lined up and covered their banana-leaf shaped plates with food. There were shrimp the size of small lobsters, meaty crab claws, raw oysters, garlic grits, corn on the cob, everything dripping with melted butter like molten gold. They sat down at a long yellow-lacquered table. A drone of appreciations for the feast rose up. Gwen had outdone herself, the ladies said. They begged her for recipes.

"Good heavens, I didn't do anything," she said. "Estelle cooked ten pounds of shrimp in four pounds of butter and two bottles of Louisiana hot sauce. She calls it Heart-Attack Shrimp."

"This is going to take a year off my life," said Curtains.

Pillars began making pronouncements. His plans to develop the Griefmaker would produce a tax windfall for Middleton, he said. The tree-huggers who were trying to stop the development didn't know squat about nature.

"I don't have any respect for our so-called environmentalists," he said. "Most of them are afraid to go into the woods for fear of ticks. I'm ready to do battle with them. I don't have first-strike capability. But I won't back down. When I get into a fight, I want to inflict pain. I want war, not a series of skirmishes." He laughed at his own outrageousness. He tore off a hunk from a baguette and started chewing it. Then he took on the welfare state: Handouts fostered dependency and irresponsibility. America was becoming a country of victims. The Chinese were going to eat our lunch. It was vintage Pillars. They'd heard it all before.

The Pillars Creed: We believe in private property, in tax shelters, in the profit motive, in the rule of law. God so loved the world that he gave it free enterprise, compound interest, comparative advantage. I did this, I bought that, I doubled down, I ante'd up. My plate is only half-full.

"Let someone else get a word in," said Gwen.

"This is my party," said Pillars. "I paid for the microphone." He ate and drank and talked with brutal gusto. How many tree-huggers own their own homes? The government needs to get out of the way and let the free market flourish. The power to tax is the power to destroy. The American standard of living is not negotiable. He paused to see if he was driving his points home. The women at the other end of the table started talking quietly again.

"Some freeloaders in this country think success is a crime," said Pillars. "They think people get rich by stealing from others."

"Do you think you'd be rich today if you'd grown up in an east Middleton housing project?" said Tenbrook.

"I've said the same kind of stuff you just said," said Tenbrook. "It just sounds silly when I hear someone else say it. It's funny to hear a bunch of country club boys spout off about the evils of welfare and affirmative action, as if we'd started off with nothing and clawed our way to the top."

"Tenbrook doesn't want me to develop the Griefmaker," said Pillars. "He thinks it still belongs to him." Pillars paused. Then he said, "At least he won't be able to say, 'Virgin prairie, never plowed' again." He gave a nasty laugh.

Tense silence hovered over the table. Then Pillars muttered, "There was a time when every wheat and cornfield in Kansas was virgin prairie."

"I think that's quite enough, you two," said Gwen. "You're spoiling my party."

"Don't worry, dear," said Pillars. "It's a game. Tenbrook likes to needle me and I like to bully him. Conflict makes the world go 'round. You don't get fire without friction." Pillars was beaming. He gestured with his glass toward Tenbrook. Someone toasted the host and hostess. The moment passed and the swashbuckling din of silverware against the plates filled the room. The guests heaped more praise on Gwen for the dinner. Later, in private, they'd condemn the whole performance for its excess, over the top, like everything the Pillars did. They'd heap scorn on Mariposa "cottage" for the hackneyed décor, the conspicuous opulence. The wives would make sardonic comments about Gwen's ambition to establish a Middleton debutante ball, while they feared that their daughters might not make the cut. Anxious souls cowering inside each feathered ego.

After dinner, Gwen passed out tiny gift-wrapped packages to the men.

"Surprise!" she said. The men opened their party favors with a show of childish excitement. Inside were peanut-sized, penis-shaped figures wearing sombreros. Curtains wound his up and set it down. It skipped and hopped over the table in circles, provoking whoops of laughter.

"That's about the size of it," he said. After dinner, the men went out on the porch to smoke cigars and drink brandy while the women played bridge. When they finished their cigars, Pillars announced a six o'clock wake-up call. The party broke up. At the hallway that led to the bedrooms, Pillars stopped Tenbrook and shook his hand.

"I have a wager to offer you," he said. "Do your best tomorrow."

✳ ✳ ✳

They met on the dock after breakfast. Tenbrook, Curtains and Tellers found their guide, Donnie, a sun-bronzed, bearded young man who was busy checking his tackle, moving nimbly around his boat, cigarette hanging from his lips.

"I don't know what Everett told you, but fishing's been lousy," he said. "We got Red Tide, big time."

"I don't care if we catch anything," said Curtains. "It's the fellowship that counts." They loaded two coolers into the boat, freed the lines and took off, skipping over the waves. The water was choppy and they got showered when the boat slapped down on the troughs.

"That'll keep you awake," yelled Donnie. It felt good to be on the water. For a moment Tenbrook forgot his demons and allowed himself the illusion that he was starting over, that adventure lay ahead. Donnie pointed out a school of black rays tacking on the surface of the waves and some porpoises swimming past.

"Look," he exclaimed, pointing to large black shape knifing through the water, dodging and darting with astonishing speed, a frantic tarpon leaping before it.

"Hammerhead," yelled Donnie. "Tarpon doesn't stand a chance. Don't dangle your toes in the water here."

Donnie stopped the boat at the wreckage of an abandoned concrete dock. He stood up in the bow and cast a line rigged with tiny jeweled hooks. The rod trembled and Donnie reeled in. The line danced with small herring-like "thread" fish. Donnie took them off the hooks, tossed them in the live well and cast again. Another black shape glided through the murky water close to the boat.

"Cobia," yelled Donnie. He called for a rod, baited it with a thread fish and tossed the line in front of the snaking shape. It struck at once. Donnie handed the rod to Tellers.

"Don't let him get too close to the pilings, or we'll lose him," said Donnie. "He won't fight much but you'll have to horse him in." Tellers reeled and pulled on the rod. The cobia chugged away. It was like being hooked on a tire. The fish made a few last frenzied sprints, then gave up and lay exhausted on the surface.

"That's a good cobia," Donnie said, hauling it aboard. He drew a knife from under the console and with a few deft slices filleted the fish, tossing the guts to a pelican that had swooped down and landed by the boat with a splash. He put the filets in a plastic bag and tossed it in the cooler. He took a blue net of woven plastic filament out of a hatch and went to the bow. He studied the surface of the water, which was puckered with darting fish. Balancing himself on the prow, he cast the net. It fanned out like a curtain of lace and sank. He paused for a few beats, then hauled the net back in. It was sagging with fish.

"That's easier than fishing for 'em, but it doesn't always work," he said. The tiny fish tumbled like silver coins from the net into the live well.

"We'll fish the Trough first," he said. "It's a demolition derby. Something you have to see."

The Trough was an opening in an undersea shelf between the islands and the Gulf. Tide waters, compressed into the narrows, carried masses of crabs through the gap. All the tarpon had to do was open their mouths. They gathered there in numbers. And so did the fishermen.

A carousel of boats was milling in circles, bobbing and jockeying for position, swerving to avoid collision. Shouts and horn blasts filled the air. Ragged flocks of seagulls flew above the boats, diving to retrieve discarded bait.

"Mobs of tarpon down there," said Donnie. "Problem is, most of them have been caught a dozen times. They get selective. And there's a rat's nest of lines down there. Hook a tarpon and you'll get fouled in a rat's nest too."

A man on a nearby boat was reeling furiously, bent over his rod. Cheers went up when the tarpon broke through the surface. Donnie motored slowly through the maze. Some girls in bikinis called out to him.

"You're a celebrity," said Curtains.

"Bow bitches," said Donnie.

"I'd be testing those waters if I were in your shoes," said Tellers.

"There's not a guide out here who hasn't," said Donnie.

Between the sounds of muttering engines and bleating horns, they could hear Jimmy Buffett singing about his lost jigger of salt. Boats passed by and passed back again, all equipped with spotting towers, radar bowls, rods with gleaming reels pointing skyward above the blue biminis. Exhaust fumes mingled with the salty, seaweed odor of the water. Fishermen watched the other fishermen watching them, the brief exchange of glances, sleek bodies, tanned and oiled, passing like dreams across the agitated water, like children on painted horses, riding the waves.

"Let's get out of here," said Donnie. They plowed away from the Trough and headed out to sea, changing course several times, slowing down while Donnie studied the water. Two miles out, he cut the engine. Hurriedly, he baited hooks, cast and handed out rods.

"What's going on?" said Curtains.

"Tarpon everywhere," whispered Donnie. At first, they saw nothing. Then the silver torpedoes came into focus, ripping through water around the boat. One rolled twenty feet away, showing a glistening eye.

"I got a strike," said Tenbrook. "Should I set the hook?"

"That's just nervous bait," said Donnie. "Something's chasing it, though. Don't do anything."

"Doing nothing," said Curtains. "That's my kind of fishing."

"I can't believe a little four-inch fish is tugging this hard," said Tenbrook. Then he felt a true jolt and the line began to sing.

"Rod tip up," yelled Donnie. "Back off the drag. Let him run. When he stops, pull up, then lower down and reel." Tenbrook reeled hard but the fish didn't stop. It drove away with brute power, drawing out line with a thin, thrilling whine. "Rod up, high as you can," Donnie cried. "Act like you're trying to break it. If it doesn't hurt, you're not wearing him out." Tenbrook pulled back on the rod with both hands, lowered it quickly and reeled. He put the end of the rod under his leg for leverage and felt it gouge into his thigh. A hundred yards from the boat, the fish jumped, twisting in the air to shake the hook.

"Point your rod at him quick," shouted Donnie. The fish hung for a moment, quivering, shedding silver drops. Then it fell back into the water with a slap. "Now reel." Tenbrook reeled. The line came in freely. "He's coming. Bring it in, bring it in. Don't let him get under the boat." And there he was, close enough that they could see his button-like eye. Then the fish turned and bolted away. In a few seconds he'd drawn off another city block of line.

Donnie handed Tenbrook a belt with a cup to hold the butt end of the rod.

"That'll save your gonads," he said. "He's a good one, hundred eighty pounds at least. You're in for a fight. Don't forget to point your rod at him if he jumps again. He'll jerk your line when he falls and if you don't give some slack it'll snap." Tenbrook braced his feet, leaned back, pulled on the rod, then bowed forward, reeling hard. Every time it looked like the fish was giving up, it made a run. Through the taut line he could feel the frenzied creature fighting back. His shoulders and forearms began to ache.

"Why am I doing this?" he said out loud.

"I can answer no question that begins with 'Why?'" said Curtains, laughing quietly as he stretched back on a cushion and covered his eyes with a towel. Twice more the tarpon jumped, walking over the water once with his beating tail. Tenbrook thought its runs were getting weaker.

"You've got him now," said Donnie. The fish made a few more spurts, and then hung like a snagged log. Tenbrook reeled in. Donnie kneeled down and grabbed the fish by the mouth and lifted it halfway out of the water. "Get down here," he said. "Someone take a picture." Tenbrook kneeled and leaned over the boat so that his head was near the fish's. Curtains took a couple of pictures. Donnie weighed the fish, then let it slide back into the water. The fish lay still for a moment. Then with a single sweep of its tail, it was gone.

"That's it?" said Tenbrook.

"We don't keep 'em. They're not good eating."

"Tenbrook's disappointed," said Curtains. "He wanted a trophy."

"The days of the skin mounts are over," said Donnie. "You can go to the taxidermist and pick out a fiberglass form that's the size of the fish you caught. He presses a copy out of the mold."

"Why not just go to the taxidermist and buy a plastic fish in the first place?" said Tenbrook.

"You wouldn't be happy," said Curtains. "You must go mano-a-mano with the great fish."

"I'll tell you what," said Donnie. "That was a hell of a fish. Ol' Everett'll be sore. He hasn't got anything over a hundred and forty pounds this year." They anchored off a beach littered with driftwood and brightly colored trash. Donnie opened a cooler and tossed them sandwiches wrapped in foil.

"We were lucky to catch that fish," Donnie said. "When I started, twenty years ago, it was nothing to catch a dozen tarpon a day. This year, a four-inch snapper won the ladies' tournament. Caught by an eight-year-old. That was the only fish anyone caught all day. Red fish, mullet, snook. They're all way down. Used to be dozens of holes. You'd catch so many fish you'd get tired of it. See if you can find one of them old holes without at least dozen boats fishing it today."

Donnie apologized for his negativity. His girlfriend of seven years had moved out a couple of months before. She'd wanted to get married, Donnie had balked, and the next thing he knew she was gone. He lit a cigarette and looked out to the horizon, where shrimp boats were cruising back and forth.

"Used to see wild pigs on that beach," he said. "Then somebody decided they were destroying the native plants. So they rounded up the pigs and shot 'em."

"Was that good or bad?" said Tenbrook.

"Seems like they could have left them alone. They'd been there five hundred years."

A low drone in the distance built to a thunderous roar as a fleet of sleek boats flew by, tossing up great tails of spray.

"Tampa boats," said Donnie, tossing his cigarette into the water. "Half a million bucks apiece. They'll go sixty miles an hour. Good for running drugs." A corpulent man with a flowing mane of silver hair stood at the helm of one of them, surrounded by nubile girls.

"With one of them boats, an old guy can get three or four pit lizards," said Donnie. "Girls love them boats." They were competing in a kind of game of poker, he said, stopping in ports on the way from Tampa and picking a card at each stop.

"Sometimes you see them anchored, they'll be 20 pit lizards swimming naked for the old guys."

"Sea nymphs frolicking in the spume," said Curtains.

"Pussy does strange things to men," said Donnie.

"A man's mind doesn't venture very far therefrom," said Curtains. "But how do those old goats do it? My testosterone level has been going down and my estrogen level is going up. I'll probably die of breast cancer."

A flats boat came towards them, leaping over the speedboats' wakes. It was Pillars. He slowed as he neared them and came along side. Donnie cleated a line and tossed it. Pillars caught it and held on.

"I got into a gang of 'em," he said. "They were daisy-chaining near the Ink Spot. Made a perfect cast, Then, 'Shazam!' They were gone. Haven't seen a thing since."

"Tenbrook here caught a damn fine tarpon, hundred eighty pounds," said Donnie.

"Moby Tarpon," Curtains said.

"On a jig or on bait?" snapped Pillars. He didn't wait for an answer. He tossed the line back to Donnie, slipped on his way back to the console, kicked a plastic bucket, and cursed. Then he revved his engine and sped away.

"Watch and see if he doesn't break something," Curtains said.

"He doesn't like it when someone else catches a bigger fish," said Donnie. Pillars disappeared into the setting sun, swallowed up by the trail of orange light that lay quaking on the water. The sun fell between a pair of billowing clouds that squatted on the horizon like two Buddhas. Tenbrook opened a can of beer.

"What's eating Everett?" Curtains said.

"We've got a little wager going on," said Tenbrook.

"Gentlemen?" said Donnie, looking at his watch. "Reel in."

***

Gwen had invited her island neighbors for a cocktail party that evening. She asked her Middleton guests, in joking fashion, not to embarrass her.

"You mean no flatearth Kansas talk?" said Tenbrook.

"Is it okay to say that abortion stops a beating heart?" said Curtains.

"You know what I mean," said Gwen. "Don't say 'Howdy.'"

As the islanders flowed in, Gwen fluttered around the room, introducing them with little resumes. A din arose, bird calls and yelps fading into magpie chatter. The women were costumed like tropical flowers. They wore heavy gold bracelets and pugnacious diamond rings. The islanders talked vacation-home-owner talk. Something had to be done about the iguanas that were eating flowers and turtle eggs and leaving their droppings on the decks. The power kept going out. Newcomers were ruining the ambiance of the island.

"The billionaires are driving the millionaires out," someone said.

A man with a toad-like face and enormous horn-rimmed glasses button-holed Tenbrook. He was fishing for details about Pillars' background and the source of his wealth. He told Tenbrook that his own fortune derived from a formula his grandfather had invented for a laxative. He was a staunch opponent of inheritance taxes.

"A man's office ought to be equidistant from his club and his home," he said. He'd had a triple bypass. He'd shot a tiger in India.

"When my father was on his death bed, I told him I loved him," he said. "I was worried about him cutting me off. Dad looked at me, I thought fondly at first. Slowly, his hand snuck out like a claw from his hospital gown.

He raised it as if to give me his blessing. And he gave me the finger! That was his idea of a benediction." He erupted with a cackling laugh. His mother had given him and his siblings enemas when they went on trips so they wouldn't have to use public bathrooms. That was the source of his psychological ills.

"I married a good housekeeper," he said. "When we got divorced, she kept the house." He unleashed another barrage of barking laughter then took a gulp of wine. "Someone needs to tell our hosts that they're not in Kansas anymore," he said. He looked away, scanned the room for other prospects. Then he wheeled away to the bar for a refill of the Pillars' nouveau riche hooch.

"I will make you a fisher of men," said Curtains, who'd appeared beside Tenbrook.

The next day Gwen herded her guests to the island's one-room museum. A woman with voluminous bosoms and snow-white hair in a tight bun, gave them a lecture about the Paleo People who'd inhabited the island ten thousand years ago.

"They came here for fresh water and defense," she said in a high-pitched, slightly hysterical voice. Archaeologists had found hammers, fish gorges, scrapers, knives, dippers and net gauges made of shells. The Jacamar Maritime Kingdom had reigned for over eight hundred years before Columbus came to the New World. The Jacamars believed they had three souls. One was their reflection in water, one was their shadow, one was in the pupil of their eye. One soul vanished at death. One entered an animal. One lived with the body throughout eternity.

A few years before, the archaeologists had discovered the remains of a three thousand-year-old man and woman during the construction of an island home. They were buried in a sitting position in a mound of shells and their bodies were perfectly preserved. The day after they were discovered, three eagles appeared and flew around the island three times.

"The wife of the man who was building the house got cancer and died."

After the lecture, the ladies reported to the island's workout room for massages. The men returned to headquarters to shoot clay pigeons and smoke more of Pillars' Cuban cigars. Tenbrook told Curtains about Pillars' wager.

"He said if I caught a bigger tarpon than he did, he wouldn't develop the Griefmaker."

That afternoon, after lunch, they poled john boats through a lagoon on the inside of the Gulf shore dunes. They entered a tunnel which the Indians supposedly had cut through the mangroves before the white man came. The day was warm but it was cool in the tunnel and their voices made muffled echoes in the dark. They poled out into the dazzling light and stepped onto the burning sand.

While the others walked on the beach looking for shells, Tenbrook stretched out beside the narrow shadow of a driftwood log, closed his eyes and dozed. He daydreamed of a woman made of sand whose image slowly dissolved in the surf. He listened to the wind ticking in the palmettos. And he remembered lying on a beach when he was young, feeling the sun beat down on his chest, forcing winter from his lungs, transporting him beyond the reef to the open sea.

He woke up with a stinging sensation. Red ants swarmed over his arms and chest. He slapped them off and got to his feet. He looked out to sea. The water danced with facets of light. Sun-polished pieces of driftwood lay strewn like tusks across the sand. Just this side of the horizon, a cormorant fell out of the sky and settled on the penciled waves. Tenbrook brushed the sand from his legs and walked to the edge of the beach.

When he found the others they were wading. The tide had gone out and their boats had gotten stuck. Gwen was on her cell phone and before long Pillars, who'd spent the morning fishing, appeared in his flats boat in a channel that led to open water.

"Immigration officer," he yelled. "Let's see your green cards, please." He jumped out, swam to one of the john boats and grabbed the painter. Then he swam back and towed the boat to deeper water. Curtains climbed into the other boat and attempted to pole it out.

"I gets weary and sick of trying," he sang. "I'm tired of living and skeered of dying."

When they got back to the dock, Pillars called Tenbrook over to one of the piers. He pulled on a line and hauled up an enormous tarpon.

"Caught him on a fly," he said. "Donnie said it was the biggest tarpon he'd seen in a couple of years. Two hundred five pounds, avoirdupois."

✳✳✳

The houseguests gathered on the dock for departure. They showered thanks upon the Pillars. The ferry pulled up, piloted by the same captain who'd delivered them to the island two days before. They piled in and the boat slowly pulled away. Behind them on the dock, the Pillars exchanged high fives in mock celebration for deliverance from their friends. The wives were planning a return trip to Jacamar in February for bridge.

"The bow bitches can't wait to get back here without us," said Curtains. "They'll be out on some old guy's speedboat wearing thongs."

While the rest of the company took shelter from the sun under the ferry's canopy, Tenbrook stood with Curtains on the foredeck. He reached into his pocket, pulled out his wind-up penis toy and tossed it overboard with a faint grin.

"Rod tip up," Curtains said.

If Tenbrook was depressed about losing the bet with Pillars, he didn't show it. "It wasn't really a bet," he said. "It was more of a taunt."

"He probably had that tarpon in one of his gilded bathtubs overnight," Curtains said.

"I wouldn't put it past him."

"My fish is bigger than your fish, huh? Classic Pillars."

The captain opened the engine and the boat leapt forward. When they came out of the mangroves and entered the bay, bulldozers were working on a gaping hole beside the marina. Cranes lowered steel beams for the frameworks of condos. Cascades of concrete poured from cement mixers into the foundation forms. Big-bellied men paraded on the marina docks in front of their sport fishing boats.

"Look at them strut," said Curtains.

"Pussy does strange things to men," said Tenbrook. He was thinking about his three souls—the one he'd left behind in Middleton, the one he had with him on board, and that one that was just starting down the path of the future. He felt free—and empty. Buzzards spiraled upward beyond the domesticated paddock. High above a jet passed over like a silver needle. I came, I saw, I sailed away. Ready, about. Homeward bound.

Chapter 17

After he got back from his fishing expedition, Tenbrook got a call from Jimmy.

"It is I," he said in a gravelly voice. "James, also known as Jimmy. Come for a ride, my friend. I've got something to show you." Tenbrook looked outside. The white limousine was in the drive. Tenbrook considered: if this was a visit from the bill collector, so be it. Sooner or later, the bill would be due. He went outside.

"How was your fishing trip?" said Jimmy when Tenbrook got in the car.

"How'd you know I was on a fishing trip?"

"I was one of those fat old farts zipping past in my Cigarette, playing water-borne poker. Perhaps you saw me, surrounded by nymphs. I won $75,000 that day, by the way."

"You're everywhere, Jimmy" said Tenbrook.

"I keep up with my friends."

"You've become a playboy."

"I like spending as well as getting. You can't take it with you, I'm told."

"If you don't have it, that's not a worry," said Tenbrook. Jimmy gave Tenbrook a look of sympathy.

"What are friends for?" he said. "I hope you appreciated the lovely bills I gave you. They stopped printing those thousand dollar bills years ago, but they're still legal tender.

In fact, they're collector's items, worth more than their face value." He gave a lecherous wink. "So don't be in a hurry to spend them."

They drove up a long, paved driveway to the top of Conestoga Bluff.

"Welcome to Excalibur," said Jimmy. "Or Valhalla. Or whatever. Go ahead and smile. I know it's foolish, this mania for castle-building. But I can't help it. It's human nature. Perhaps I'm driven by the same furies that drove your ancestor, Tenbrook, the Patriarch. Anyway, you can't imagine the pleasure it gives me to take off from work and drive out here and see this monstrosity taking shape. I like to stand on the top of my hill and proclaim: 'Little Jimmy built this.' I hope it's never finished. What the hell will I do with it when it's done? I can promise you this—it's a money-eating beast."

Workmen were putting up stones on the cinderblock wall that surrounded the estate, crawling over scaffolds with nail guns, installing windows, doors. Jimmy stopped in front of an iron gate. The gate slowly opened.

"Open sesame," he said. "Ah, peace and joy. What do you think?"

"It's impressive," said Tenbrook.

"Perhaps you think I picked this spot just to keep an eye on you," said Jimmy with a laugh. "But the real reason is that I like being king of the mountain. Who doesn't? This is the highest point in Middleton County. I may be a little fellow, but up here I'm Goliath. And I ask you: If I was engaged in illegal activities, why would I build such an open and notorious edifice?"

"Who said anything about illegal activities?" said Tenbrook. Jimmy shrugged, put a finger to his lips and winked. He parked, got out of the limo and motioned Tenbrook to follow. Workers waved at him as they walked along. Jimmy tipped his hat and fenced at the air with his cane. Behind the house were three large metal buildings. Jimmy stopped in front of one of them.

"My, my," he said. "Don't these structures look suspicious?" he said. "Surely, this must be where that scofflaw Stafford stores his marijuana and processes his methamphetamines. The police have raided this place a dozen times and this is what they find." He opened a metal door. Inside was a wood-working shop where men were busy assembling and spray-painting cabinets.

"One of my businesses," said Jimmy. "Stafford Products. Look it up in Dun and Bradstreet. How sinister can you get? I get a big kick out of watching the cops scurry about the premises with their drug-sniffing dogs looking for telltale clues. I welcome them. I offer them refreshments. I make contributions to their fraternal orders. My hands are clean. I am a model citizen. Come along."

As they walked, a small plane approached low from the south, circled the bluff, settled down and landed on the grass runway. Jimmy stopped, watched it turn at the end of the runway and taxi back.

"What's this?" said Jimmy. "Must be a shipment of heroin. Excuse me for a second." Jimmy went back into the shop. After a few minutes he returned with a smile and pointed his cane.

"All is well," he said. "Ten cases of Veuve Clicquot. We do a lot of toasting around here. People pay a thousand dollars to get into one of my parties. They act like children, getting drunk and jumping around naked, losing pots of dough at my poker table, pinching my girls' asses. It's pathetic, but harmless. I laugh at them. Only in America. Forward march. Start and stop, stop and start, that's the way things go around here. When the money pours in, things start hopping. When the kitty dries up, things grind to a halt." The second building housed a metal-working operation.

"Sheet metal, welding," said Jimmy. "We can make and repair anything. Custom auto and truck work." A man wearing a welder's mask was attaching an over-sized fuel tank to a truck. A bright green racing car with an enormous engine and a gash in one side perched on a hydraulic lift.

"Stafford's Siren," said Jimmy. "It was in the lead at Riverside the other day when it ran into a wall. Che sara." The third building was a storage shed for machinery: a backhoe, a skid loader, various tractors, a drilling rig, air compressors.

"I collect equipment," Jimmy said. "I am a connoisseur of machines. These gadgets are my children, my loved ones." He walked around tapping at them with his cane. They walked back outside. The compound was a hive of feverish, apparently directionless activity: Flat-bed pickups delivered loads of lumber, forklifts bore pallets of bagged concrete. From time to time there was a crash of rubble dumped from a frontloader. Warning bells of vehicles backing up rang out, the clatter of pneumatic tools and hammer blows, the whining of saws.

"Listen to the music," said Jimmy, gesturing like a conductor with his cane. The bare earth was imprinted with tractor tracks and covered with spidery swarms of electrical cables. A burning trash heap emitted sullen yellow smoke. Tenbrook felt his usual sense of discomfort and involuntary awe in the presence of a hustler. Where did their energy come from? What purpose, other than the promise of money, did it serve? What was Jimmy's agenda in bringing him to his headquarters and showing off his stuff? Was he just trying to impress Tenbrook? Was he trying to convince him that he was a legitimate businessman? Or was it part of settling an old score?

Several girls in bikinis lounged around the pool at the side of the house. One wore a t-shirt that said, "Fuck more, bitch less." A young woman in shorts and a halter top opened the front door. Jimmy took off his hat and she kissed him on top of his warty head.

"Sasha, this is my friend Henry Tenbrook," he said. "We grew up together." Sasha smiled and held out her hand. Tenbrook shook her hand, but when he tried to withdraw his own hand, she wouldn't let go. She pressed her long fingernails playfully into his wrist.

"Tut, tut, Sasha," said Jimmy. "Enough of that. Henry is a happily married man. He's a business partner, not a customer." He turned to Tenbrook. "Sasha can't help herself. She's so affectionate. All the girls who work for me are. That's the first thing I look for. Warmth and empathy first, beauty and sex appeal second." Sasha let go of Tenbrook's hand but she kept eyeing him with a bold, wanton look. "Go ahead, precious," said Jimmy. "Stop trying to seduce this poor man. Make yourself scarce. I'm going to show Mr. Tenbrook around."

Jimmy led the way from the entry. They passed an exercise room with the treadmills and weightlifting apparatus still in their plastic wrapping. Jimmy opened a door to reveal a movie theatre with plush armchairs. They passed a commercial-scale kitchen with gleaming appliances.

"All the bells and whistles," said Jimmy. "Croesus must feed his minions." He led Tenbrook up a wide staircase to the second floor. They walked down a hall with rooms on either side decorated in neo-bordello style: gaudy satin curtains opening on circular and heart-shaped beds, mirrors on the ceilings, pictures of copulating animals and human beings.

"Beautiful, aren't they?" said Jimmy.

"I'm not a judge of art," said Tenbrook. "Someone told me that people no longer speak of beauty but of presence."

"You can't deny that these works have presence," said Jimmy.

"It's hard not to look at them." Jimmy showed Tenbrook into one of the rooms. He shut the door behind them. A wall-mounted television big as a bath tub was showing a tangle of naked bodies, women bouncing on top of men, women with their faces in the crotches of other women, all of whose limited vocabulary seemed to consist of incessant, repetitious moanings: "Oh, yea, oh my God, oh yea." Tenbrook sat in a velvet upholstered chair that almost swallowed him up. The air was scented. A priapic fountain splashed water in a tiled pool. Jimmy picked up the remote and turned the television off. He took out a handkerchief, wiped his forehead and sighed.

"Remember how you and Everett and the other guys used to amuse yourselves?" he said. "I was the goat. You made me pick up your jockstraps and wear them like a nose guard. You'd throw a basketball at me when I wasn't looking. You'd mock me and chastise me when it hit me in the head. Remember how you got me to steal cigarettes for you? I did it to win favor. You used to put a naked lightbulb in my face and make me confess to unnamed crimes? Oh, what fun you guys had. Remember the time you borrowed my car and bawled me out when it got a flat tire?"

"What we did was disgraceful," said Tenbrook. "It was cruel. I'm ashamed. All I can do is to say I'm sorry."

"Hush. All is forgiven. In fact, I owe you an apology. I apologize for sending Benny and Roland to visit you. People think I'm some kind of gangster, so I send those two clowns as a kind of joke: See, here are my hit men. Those two couldn't hurt a flea. Forgive my sense of humor. But they screw up. They talk too much. They go too far. They think life is a theatre and that they're starring on a stage. Anyway, you won't be hearing from them again. I am not a gangster, by the way. I'm a professional. I'm not that different from our friend, Everett Pillars."

Jimmy started telling Tenbrook the story of his life. After high school, his family moved away from Middleton. They were a pitiful bunch. His mother had Alzheimers, his father was an alcoholic who couldn't keep a job.

"Back when we were in school, I had to work nights to make money to keep us alive. I sacked groceries. I worked in a convenience store, a dry cleaner. I was working for an auto parts store when a customer noticed that I had a good mind for numbers. I could multiply four, five figures in my head. This customer needed someone to keep his books. He had a fleet of panel trucks and said he was in transportation. I never saw what it was he transported, but it involved sacks of cash. He had a strange system of accounting. I had to work with notes and figures and names scribbled on scraps of paper. I was supposed to translate them into some kind of respectable accounting, to keep track of credits and debts. I was good at it and I was making some money. One night when we were busy counting, armed men broke into our trailer and shot my boss, more times than necessary. I sat at the desk, surrounded by money, and tried to make my peace with the Lord. But they didn't shoot me straightaway. They sat down and finished the pizza we'd been eating and made jokes about how they were going to finish me off. I knew the boss kept a pistol in the drawer of the desk where I was working. I'd seen him clean it. The image of that pistol presented itself in my brain. It was the only thing between me and death. I had an epiphany: I didn't have to die. I had a choice. I'd never shot a gun. The last thing I had ever thought of was killing another human being. But I knew I must learn, and very quickly. I discovered that all it takes is a little imagination and you can become someone else in a flash. So while those wretched curs were stuffing their faces with pizza, I quietly slid the righthand drawer of the desk open. I felt for the gun, running my hand over it, turning it until I found the barrel and the trigger guard. There were three of them. I realized that I would have to shoot fast and true. This I did. I shall never forget the astonished looks on their faces.

"As you remember, I was not just physically short, I was short of self-esteem. I was an ugly little troll, as our friend Pillars liked to say. But as I sat there in the room with those bodies on the floor and that hot, smoking pistol in my hand, I felt as if I was ten feet tall and handsome as Gary Cooper. I was a gunslinger. I scooped up all the cash, stuffed it in a duffel bag and took off, whistling 'Zippity, do-dah.' I was free. I was rich. I was ready to conquer the world.

"My mother and father died. I was alone. I had nothing to do but study how to invest my bundle. I bought a small apartment building. I fixed it up, raised the rents, sold it and bought another, bigger one. I did this several times, each time taking a little larger step. I found I had a knack for business and I prospered. I didn't drink, I didn't smoke. I wasn't really interested in sex. My only vice was ambition. Call it greed if you wish. To be sure, I've cut some corners, but I have never broken the law. I have great respect for the law. I couldn't have climbed the human anthill without the law. For a man to prosper there must be laws—isn't that what Pillars the Great likes to say? And so you see me now. A new man. You'll have to admit I've done well. I've dreamed of this day for a long time, Henry. I dreamed that I'd come back some day and have something to show you."

"I'm impressed, Jimmy," said Tenbrook. "And I can't blame you if you want to get back."

"I don't want to get back," said Jimmy. "I don't want revenge. What good would that do me? What I want is cooperation, teamwork. I want to help you and I want you to help me. A business relationship is all I'm asking for. One that would be good for both of us. I envision a partnership: Stafford-Tenbrook, LLC. If you feel so bad about the way you treated me, this would offer you a means of absolution."

"You don't want to be in business with me," said Tenbrook. "I'm a lousy businessman. I can't afford to be in business with you—or anyone else. It's taking all the time and energy I have to keep my head above water."

"I can help you," said Jimmy. "The greatest favor you can do me is to accept my help. If there's a score to settle, that would settle the score."

"Jimmy, I appreciate your offer," said Tenbrook.

"What are you afraid of? Do you think I'm a crook?"

"This has nothing to do with who or what you are."

"If you won't accept my offer for assistance, it will cause me great pain. I will feel rejected. My feelings will be hurt. That might reopen old wounds. Anger and resentment might rear their ugly heads. Who knows what I might do? I might be forced to call your loan. Can you pay me back?"

"It will take some doing, a little time, but I will get it done."

"I have no time. I have no patience. If you can't pay back your debt, then our relationship will change. I understand: You don't want to be involved. But you need to be involved. Opportunity knocks. Seize the day. You have no choice. All I ask is that you deliver various packages as per instructions. Then we will be square. Your debts will be forgiven. You're a Christian man. This will be your penance. You will be free."

Chapter 18

Tenbrook drove north along a broken street in Bottomtown. The address on the package, 517 Kidrow, sounded familiar. It was a neighborhood he'd once known in his days managing derelict properties for Sylvester Niestrom. Many of the old buildings had been boarded up or razed. The neighborhood looked as if an apocalyptic wind had roared through. Entire blocks were vacant except for vestiges of foundations. Weedy spaces were littered with trash bags and abandoned shopping carts. The area had been known for drive-by shootings and pickup games that turned suddenly into gang wars. But now it was almost safe. The drug trade had moved south. There was no turf to fight over. Nothing left worth stealing. A few trees hung on, but they looked defeated, as if they'd succumbed to boredom or despair.

Tenbrook stopped at a two-story brick fourplex covered with graffiti. In front of the building was a pile of appliances stripped of salvageable metal. A couple of boys rode bicycles in aimless circles. Two elderly black men sat on a rotting orange sofa in the front yard. They gave Tenbrook wary, hostile looks. White faces were a rarity in the neighborhood. Middleton, for all of its abolitionist heritage, was radically segregated. Kidrow, which had been the finest address in the early days of Middleton, had become part of the ghetto. The gentry, who had promenaded there on

Sundays in horse-drawn carriages, had fled to the Kansas side, ceding Kidrow to the blacks.

Tenbrook stepped up to the entryway. The concrete stoop was scattered with fragments of glass that crunched like ice under his shoes. There were no names on the buzzers, so Tenbrook rang them all. One door was battered in splinters. Four massive padlocks hung on another. There was no response from within. He knocked on the one door that looked functional. An operatic female voice answered. The handle rattled. The door flew open. A woman in a voluminous turquoise muumuu with her hair done in elaborate cornrows stood in the doorway with a gigantic revolver in her hand. She studied him for a moment and then burst out laughing. Her face lit up. Then she frowned.

"Land of Goshen," she cried. "Look what the wind blew in. Henry Tenbrook. What kind of trouble you in?" She gave an impatient gesture for him to enter and with an apologetic look set the pistol down on a table. "You're lucky I didn't shoot you. We don't get many friendly social calls here these days. We usually do our communicating with guns." She laughed and kissed him on the cheek. "And don't say one word about my girlish figure. I know I'm fat. But I just joined Weight Watchers and the pounds are melting away."

"You look good, Evie," said Tenbrook. "It's been a long time."

The air inside smelled of incense. A large plastic Buddha illumined from within glowed before the fireplace. Above it hung pictures of Jesus and Martin Luther King. A neon Budweiser sign blinked on one wall. A vase in one corner was filled with peacock feathers. A mangy yellow cat lounged like a dirigible on a bed of newspapers, regarding Tenbrook with a single listless eye. A sharp odor of cat urine cut through the incense. On the floor was a heap of overstuffed pillows upholstered in fragments of carpet along with scattered burger wrappers and pizza boxes. A three-foot-tall bong pipe squatted on a glass-topped table. Trophies and sports photos were displayed around the room, including one of two young men, one white and one black, holding up a football above the caption: "State Champs 1989." Bob Marley was singing in the background, "No woman, no cry."

"Cupid," Evie bellowed. "You got company." She started picking up trash. Sounds of coughing and stomping came from another room. A tall, thin man wearing Bermuda shorts and a Kansas City Chiefs t-shirt appeared in the doorway rubbing his eyes. He looked emaciated, deflated. His eyes had a look of blank exhaustion. He stared at Tenbrook for a second, then grinned and put out his fist for a bump.

"Gunslinger," he said. "I was afraid you were gonna show up. Your name's been in the air. Sit down, mo-fo. You want something to drink or smoke? What you got there?" He pointed at Tenbrook's package. "Don't let me guess."

"I'm supposed to deliver this to you."

"Oh, I know," said Cupid. "I know. Listen, I had nothing to do with this. Jimmy started asking questions about you. I told him we were out of touch. He said that was a shame. We should all get together, celebrate a reunion. He'd like to have us all out to his big house, sort of thing. Then he got on this jag of going into business with you, helping you. I swear to God. I told the little man to leave you out of this. I told him to forget the past. I told him you were the last man on earth who'd want to get into business with him. God knows I didn't mean to get you involved in this bidness."

"What the hell bidness are we talking about, Winston?"

"The less you know the better."

"What the hell's in this package?"

"Oh, you can guess. You're not that naïve. There's proba-bly about $50,000 worth of craziness in there, is my guess." Tenbrook shook his head.

"The little man," he said.

"Our little Roy," said Cupid. "He has gone far. And he hasn't forgotten."

"He has every right to remember," said Tenbrook. "It was disgraceful how we treated him."

"I agree," said Cupid. "Ironic, huh? Now I work for him. Looks like you do too."

"For Christ's sake, I don't work for him. He showed up at my office one day. He introduced himself as James Stafford. Talked about how he'd heard so much about me, about my athletic exploits, about the big game. I didn't recognize him. He set me straight. He said he had a business proposition. Then he left me an envelope with ten crisp thousand-dollar bills and vanished before I could ask him what the hell was going on or give it back to him."

"And now you're running errands for him," said Cupid.

"I haven't the slightest idea what I'm doing. His goons showed up and told me to deliver this package and made some vague threats in case I failed. Jimmy took me to his playboy sex palace and told me his life story. He virtually begged me to accept his help. Then he dropped some warn-ings about what might happen if I didn't. He even made some reference to my wife and daughter."

"That's the way Jimmy-Roy operates," said Cupid. "Real nice at first. Then he gets mean."

"All I know is that I have enough problems. And this one scares me more than the other ones put together."

"With good reason, my man," said Cupid. "And you want me to untangle the mess you're in, I'm in, we're all in. You overestimate my powers. Let me do some speculating.

Maybe Jimmy's interested in you because he's drawn a bead on Everett Pillars. Maybe he has some sort of deal working with Everett and he thinks you could help him grease the wheels in some way. Hell, I don't know, maybe he thinks you're his ticket into Middleton high society."

"That's a lot of maybes. Anyway, I'm not part of Middleton high society."

"But you got the Tenbrook moniker. That opens all kinds of doors."

"Not anymore."

"Listen. I didn't tell him anything he didn't already know,"

"I'm not looking for someone to blame," said Tenbrook. "What I want is for someone to get me out."

"I'd like for someone to show me the way out too. But Jimmy's changed. He's dangerous. Once he's got his fingers into you, there's no getting loose. You take that first step. After that, there's no stepping back. You're in over your head, Ten. He can put a world of hurt on you."

"What am I supposed to do?"

"The way I understand it, Everett's planning some big development. He's in a pinch and needs some tide-over money. So he comes to Jimmy for financial CPR. Jimmy to the rescue. But Jimmy smells blood. There's never enough on his plate. He never takes a bite without wanting more. He's into everything from pole dancers to pork bellies. So he quote-unquote lends Pillars the money. But the hitch is he doesn't want to get paid back. He wants equity. He wants to transition out of the businesses he's in and get into sanitary businesses and this is one way to do it."

"I still don't understand how I fit in," said Tenbrook.

"I have the same problem. My theory is that there's something else going on here. Jimmy orchestrating something. He's bringing us all together again so he can see us squirm. How far is he wanting to go? I don't know. But

I promise you Jimmy knows. Maybe he just wants us to know what it felt like when he was small. Tell you one thing. Delivering this package to me was superfluous. He's got errand boys to do that for him. This was just to establish that you're on the team."

"Ridiculous."

"But not funny. Oh, you're on the team, all right. Tell you what. When Jimmy first showed up, I thought I was saved. You know what I was doing for a living at the time? I was a janitor. I'd tried to make it down the straight and narrow. I was smart. I had been a football star. I had the white talk down. On the phone you couldn't tell me from an Anglo-Saxon. You should have seen the looks I got when I'd show up for a job interview. For some strange reason, I never got asked back. I couldn't ever seem to land nothing. So I gave up and started pushing a broom. I accepted the fact. I was what I was. I don't talk like I'm talking to you anymore. I talk the way people expect me to talk. 'Yo, man, don't be jivvin' me no mo. Chilly my grilly, dawg up in the hood, muthuhfuckuh ma damn self.' That sort of shit."

"So, Jimmy came along and rescued me. He actually showed me some kind of respect. And he filled my pockets. Time passed, I found out that Jimmy wasn't no friend. I heard stories about guys who worked for him going off to the land of permanent nod. I found out that Jimmy doesn't like you to do well, doesn't like you to get comfortable. He starts finding fault. He doesn't like the way you dress or the way you chew your gum. He doesn't like to see you having fun. He starts cutting you down. You figure out what he wants and then he doesn't want it anymore. All at once there's no pleasing that man. He keeps you off balance. You can't just sit on the sidelines snorting Omar, you got to stay on your toes. One day things are coasting along, copacetic. The next day you start having stomach troubles. You start gettin' no rest. When he hits, it's over before you know you been hit. I've seen it happen. I promise he's close by just now, watchin' us. He's gonna want to know how you performed, how flexible you seemed, how agreeable. He's got both of us in a pinch. I love you man, but I can't help you."

"I'm going to get Jimmy his money back and wash my hands of him," said Tenbrook. Cupid sighed and that brought on a coughing fit.

"You got that money?"

"Not all of it."

"See? Jimmy's got you by the ying-yang. Just like me— and Everett."

"I'll scrape the rest together." Cupid shook his head.

"That's what I kept telling myself. Somehow the spending keeps outrunning the scraping. You want some advice? Don't listen to advice. Don't trust no one. Don't trust me."

"That's one of Everett Pillars' favorite sayings."

"Looks to me he forgot that one when he got in touch with Jimmy."

Tenbrook got up to leave. The odor of incense clung to his shirt. He wondered if he looked as aged as Cupid did. They stopped in front of the photo of the two of them holding up the championship ball.

"Remember when Pillars got into that game?" said Cupid. "He'd never been able to play until then on account of that rheumatic whatever he had when he was a kid."

"And he went crazy, making up for all that lost time."

"What did he make—eight tackles in that game?"

"That was a preview of his business style," said Tenbrook.

"His old man used to give me twenty dollars every time I made a TD."

"That must have made you feel great."

"Made me feel small," said Cupid. "Funny when you think about it. You and I were the men."

"You covered a football field like a sharp-shinned hawk," said Tenbrook.

"Pluckin' your passes out of the sky. Weren't we voted most likely to succeed? And here we are together again—in shit. What you think about that?"

"I'm going to find a way out."

"Just don't come looking for a way out from me. I got my own torments."

They stood at the door. Cupid looked through a curtain covering the glass pane on the door.

"We're both goners," said Cupid.

"If I'm a goner, I'm not going out gracefully," said Tenbrook.

"That sounds like you. 'Tenbrook, Tenbrook, he's our man. If he can't do it…' No, you're going out the way Jimmy decides you're going out. Say, don't forget, Henry boy. You didn't win that big game. You just threw the ball. I caught it." Tenbrook grinned. He pumped his arm and flung a phantom pass that sailed back twenty-five years. Cupid watched its progress, timed his jump and held a hand high to receive it. But he barely got off the ground and the ball was nothing but air.

Chapter 19

By midsummer, the earth was already baked and honeycombed with fissures. The cool season grasses were drying up and turning brown in the heat. Ponds that had overflowed the year before were shriveled up like scabs. Beans had prematurely yellowed. According to Troy, corn was about ready to "decide" whether to form kernels on the cob. It was going to be a bad summer. Except for the weeds and native grasses. They were flourishing. They loved the drought. Hob-nailed, goose-stepping weeds, seed-bearded, flagellating weeds, horse tail and pokeweed on the march.

Tenbrook crept forward on his four-wheeler looking for musk thistles to spray. He stopped at a hillside covered with flowering weeds—yellow moth mullein, bright orange milkweed, clusters of pale blue spiderwort. It looked like a coral reef. Thistles with iridescent blue blossoms dotted the pastures. They were ready to release a storm of seeds that would float off on downy parachutes in search of more fields to invade.

Spraying was at odds with Tenbrook's wish to live in harmony with nature. But thistles could take over if you didn't fight back. Every year he got a notice from the county warning him of fines if he didn't control them. They were formidable, malevolent. They kept coming at you. Tenbrook found new thistles blooming beside rosettes he'd killed the spring before. They grew out of cracks in stone and hid behind the boughs of cedar trees. Armed with prickly, metallic leaves to discourage browsing, they embodied the aggressive fecundity that made nature seem perverse and inimical at times.

But Tenbrook enjoyed his war on thistles. It was a benign way of venting murderous instincts. An hour passed like a minute when he was spraying. It gave him a respite from the harpies of deadlines and debts. And it thrust him into intimate contact with his little patch of land. He'd accumulated a mental scrapbook of familiar spots—the limestone outcropping where a spring seeped clear water even in winter, the bald depression he liked to believe was a buffalo wallow, the packrat's hovel in a grove of cottonwoods. He knew the spots where gamma grass grew and clumps of catclaw briar, whose leaves curled up like tiny hands when you touched them and mullein like giant candlesticks. He knew a rock where copperheads sunned.

Financial necessity had forced him to move to the porous, spavined farmhouse in the country. But Tenbrook had billed the move as a quest for renewal, an escape from the straitjacket of Middleton society. The real estate agent had told him—after he'd signed the papers—that this was the third time she'd sold the property in a decade and that if he ever wanted to sell, he knew where she was. Troy Bilbrey had chuckled when Tenbrook told him.

"Did she tell you that the former owner of your place tried to make his fortune raising chinchillas?" he said. "People move to the country thinking they're going to find theirselves. But they bring their city baggage with them. Country don't change them, but it sho nuff do drive a lot of them away."

"I may fit that description," said Tenbrook. It was true. He'd nursed the delusion that a change of scenery would redeem him. Kate had gone along with the move, but Tenbrook knew that it had contributed to the wedge that was growing between them. She hated the isolation, the spiders and mice, the windows that rattled in wind, the cold drafts, the pervasive aroma of mold.

"You're different," said Bilbrey. "You've got prospects. We gonna make a farmer out of you yet." Tenbrook wondered what his neighbor saw in him, but he was happy to be a project. He wanted to learn. He wanted to distance himself from the ledgers of city life.

An aroma of mint filled the air as Tenbrook drove over masses of ironweed, vetch and goldenrod. Clouds of midges rose and fell in the sunbeams. Dragonflies hovered and darted above bee balm beds. Swallows flew overhead, swerving, gliding and diving for the grasshoppers and moths stirred up by the machine. He passed the bleached skeleton of a cow that had been hit by lightning, its last meal of undigested grass still lying in a ball within the vault of its ribs.

The sound of his four-wheeler flushed three coyotes from a patch of shattercane. They didn't bolt, but bounded leisurely away, then turned and looked at Tenbrook with curiosity rather than fear. They looked like dogs about to wag their tails.

"Come on over and I'll scratch your ears," said Tenbrook. Coyotes and other predators were proliferating along with the weeds in the drought—foxes, feral cats, hawks and owls. There was no shortage of stuff for them to eat. According to Troy, one acre could support a thousand mice and rats.

The coyotes had become brazen. They showed themselves in open fields during the day and left their scat in Kate's garden, close to the house, turds twisted with rodent hair or purple from blackberries they'd gorged on. At night, they filled the valley with loon-like wails. They were probably hard on the quail. But Tenbrook couldn't bring himself to shoot them like his neighbors did. He watched the coyotes turn from him indifferently and trot away. Their coats were mangy. There were too many of them. Disease would correct their success.

The clatter of neighbors' mowers drifted on the air. Earlier, he'd watched Bilbrey's winnower with its spinning daisy wheels laying the hay in rows. Now Troy was out baling, scooping up the cut grass and dropping it bound in huge round bales that looked grave and inscrutable, like the monoliths of Easter Island. Bilbrey waved, stopped his tractor and walked over to the fence.

"Gwan gadeen," said Tenbrook when he reached him.

"Gwan gadeen."

"How you been?"

"Still breathing," said Bilbrey. "Got something to tell you. I done sold this here place. Some rich dentist in Potaxey bought it." Tenbrook was stunned.

"Somehow I can't picture it," he said. "This valley will lose its soul without you. And you'll miss it, Troy."

"I'm a-gonna need the money," he said. "My liver's eaten up with cancer."

"No," said Tenbrook. "God, Troy. I'm sorry."

"Not half as sorry as I am. But it's gonna come, sooner or later. There's a time to poke the fire and a time to leave the fire alone. I've had a good run. They give me six months to a year. I plan to do a lot of livin' in that time. Gonna take Retta Lou to Vegas, for one thing." Bilbrey rested his leathery hands on the barbed wire that separated them. He plucked the wire like a guitar string. "The Devil's Hat Band, that's what some folks call this here wayr," he said. "You did this right. Tighter than the instep of a hen."

"You showed me how."

"You did the work."

"I made some mistakes. I didn't do the corner posts right."

"You can't learn nothin' without mistakes." They stood for a moment without speaking.

"I wonder what a fellow would have to pay for land around here," said Tenbrook.

"Now you're talkin' like a farmer," said Bilbrey. "Never ask straightforward. Act casual, like you don't care, like you're asking for some other feller. Never ask a man how many head of cattle he's got. That's like asking him how much money he has in the bank. I'll tell you this, though. A feller who wants to buy land around here better be ready to start at $5,000 an acre." Tenbrook gave a low whistle. At that price his forty acres was worth $200,000. He looked up and caught Bilbrey watching him with a grin. "Just thought you'd like to know. Anyway, you can't buy land for farming at prices like that. I figure this dentist is gonna subdivide it and sell off tracts."

"There goes the neighborhood," said Tenbrook. "How am I going to get along without you, Troy?"

"I'll still be available on a consulting basis. Hate to tell you what I bought this quarter section for forty years ago." They watched Max, who'd just gone on point before a clump of buckbrush.

"He's deadly on meadowlarks," said Tenbrook.

"There was a time we'd consider a litter of hunting dogs and if we didn't like the looks of them, into a gunny sack and into the pond they'd go."

"Some of the folks in Middleton wouldn't approve," said Tenbrook.

"It's expensive to keep a dozen no-account dogs alive for fifteen years," said Troy.

"Still, it's harsh," said Tenbrook.

"Could you do it?"

"Not to a dog."

✳✳✳

Later that day, Tenbrook sat in his chair at the edge of the hill in front of his house, the secular province of his farm. He watched a cloud boiling up like a giant cauliflower, white froth tumbling over the sides of the quaking mass as it billowed upward. At last, it leveled off, forming an anvil head that covered half the eastern horizon. A small plane flew over with a chainsaw buzz. It probed the edges of the cloud as if the pilot were tempted to plunge into its center. Then it banked, swooping low and landed on the grass strip over at Conestoga Bluff.

The sky beyond was gas-jet blue. Tenbrook thought about the $200,000. In the abstract, it sounded like a windfall, a bailout. But where would they live if he sold? And he'd put his own soul into that piece of land. He'd be spiritually bankrupt without it. On the other hand, if for some reason he ceased to exist, it wouldn't matter. It would help make Kate and Channy secure. Such thoughts visited him from time to time.

A mockingbird called from the bleached branches of a sycamore: "rattely drat, rattely drat, chum cudely, chum cudely, brrrt, brrrt." The curdling cloud reached its climax, held unchanged for moment, then began to collapse, dissolving into ghostly vapors, leaving only a few fugitive streaks across the sky. A cold squall blew over the hilltop, making the cottonwoods shiver, tearing off a few leaves as if it were already November. Then all was still again, except for the intermittent popping of Chinese firecrackers and the occasional whine of a bottle rocket. At dusk's descent, spectral moths appeared, haunting the cooling grasses. Cries of screech owls filled the air. A cuckoo clucked. Then the faint sing-song of oil-derricks, reactivated because of the spike in oil prices. "Air-ball, air-ball, sar-row, sar-row," they sang like wetland birds. Dust hung like fog above the gravel road. The trees along Coal Creek leaned over the edge of the bean field like bearded beasts about to devour the crop. In the distance, the lights of Middleton burned and twinkled like embers. Some nightbird Tenbrook couldn't place flew over the house, croaking.

It was the Fourth of July. Kate, Toby and Channy had left to buy fireworks. The coffee house courtship was over. Toby and Channy had become "an item." Toby had come to the door one evening to take Channy on their first date. Tenbrook tried to discourage the young man by revealing Channy's former marriage to a lizard.

"He's not talking about marrying me, Dad," said Channy. "We're just going to the movies." Since then, Toby had become a fixture in the Tenbrook house. Tenbrook had taught him how to make a martini.

"Pour one-half ounce dry vermouth into a mixing vessel filled with ice," he said, demonstrating. "Move the vessel in a circular motion so that as much vermouth as possible passes over the ice. Then pour the vermouth out. Add three ounces of gin and stir with a bar spoon in a clockwise motion, agitating the ice against the glass. See? If the ice and the gin are moving at the same speed, you are not succeeding."

"Always there are two," said Toby. "A master and an apprentice."

"Plato?" said Tenbrook.

"Star Wars," said Toby. Toby was a bit of a chef and sometimes cooked fajitas or stir-fry for the family. When Tenbrook heard the young couple's a cappella laughter from the second floor, he hoped that some of their youthful magic would rub off on him and Kate.

As darkness gathered, Tenbrook's mood returned to familiar territory. He had accomplished nothing. He hadn't mastered any skill. He had failed to wrest one original thought from the flux of existence. Life was a trial and he hadn't acquitted himself. Sometimes he still had the nightmare that he'd forgotten to study for a final exam.

A barrage of fireworks erupted from a neighbor's yard. The horizon began to pulse with Independence Day pyrotechnics. Serpents of light squirmed across the sky shedding showers of sparks. Multicolored blossoms erupted, leaving pale haloes and veins of phosphorescence, followed by muted thunder. An alien sound split the air, the terrific blam of a high-powered rifle, then a loud smack above Tenbrook's chair. Just then, Kate, Toby and Channy returned. They had spent their entire budget on a single, monster explosive.

"It's called the Galactic Fantasy Doom Bomb," said Toby. He read the label outloud: "Thirty-six-shot 500 gram aerial repeater! Pyrotechnic blast! Red, green and white comets shoot up into beautiful large chrysanthemum bursts. Glittering mines with multi-colored pearls, golden tail comets that burst at the top with crackling crossettes. This item whistles during most of the performance with a firecracker type crackle barrage at the end."

"It sounds like the ultimate Fourth of July orgasm," said Channy.

"Watch your language," said Kate.

"There was a girl at the fireworks place who was wearing a t-shirt that said 'Give me head until I'm dead,'" said Channy.

"We tried to bring Channy up according to good, strong Christian values," said Tenbrook.

"The girl was telling her friends the story of Cronus eating his children," said Channy.

"That's pretty high-brow for our neighborhood," said Tenbrook.

"The funny thing is it wouldn't be that surprising to read some version of the Cronus story in the *Reaper* one of these days," said Channy. Tenbrook opened beers and passed them around. Toby set the Galactic bomb down at a distance.

"I think you should offer a few thoughts on the meaning of Independence Day before you set that thing off," said Tenbrook. Toby assumed an orator's stance.

"I hereby dedicate this Galactic Fantasy Doom Bomb to American military might and our God-given right to destroy any nation or other power that dares to get in our way."

"Here, here," said Tenbrook. "Or is it, 'Hear, hear?' Whatever. Patrick Henry couldn't have said it any better." Toby stuck a match and held it to the fuse. The fuse burned smartly for a few seconds than sputtered.

"Damn," said Toby. He struck another match and lit what was left of the fuse. It burned down into the bomb, but the bomb didn't go off. "Damn! There's nothing left to light."

"It went 'Pfft!' instead of 'boom!'" said Tenbrook.

"Seventy-five dollars down the drain," said Kate.

"We could light a fire and toss it on," said Toby.

"No," said Tenbrook. "Let it just sit there, a dud, to remind us of the limits of American power."

They finished their beers and watched fireworks fill the sky,

"Aren't they beautiful?" said Channy. "Wouldn't the world be emptier without them?" She smiled at Tenbrook and put her head on his chest. "See, Dad? I still have a little of the kid left in me." They cleaned up and went inside and sought out their various beds. In the morning, Tenbrook found a hole in the wall like the boring of a carpenter bee. With a screwdriver, he dug out a 30.06 slug from the wood.

Chapter 20

The shot might have been a random one, fired by one of the trigger-happy denizens of the valley to celebrate this great nation's independence from the yoke of George III. But it was hard not to suspect that it was a message from Jimmy, turning up the heat. The idea of a bullet whizzing within a few feet of his head didn't fill Tenbrook with concern for his own well-being. But what if Kate or Channy had gotten in the way of some poorly aimed bullet? That idea angered him.

Tenbrook entered his woods the next day, officially looking for blackberries, but also seeking some space for thinking. He was going to have to come up with a strategy. Foraging stimulated thought. But he was too late for blackberries. The berry bushes had been picked clean by birds and coyotes. The few berries that remained were shriveled and hard as stones. But the sandhill plums were ripe. Branches of the plum trees sagged with purple, grape-sized fruit. Tenbrook had planted the trees the first year they moved to the Missouri Compromise and some were already taller than he was. They'd spread, forming thickets that were supposed to be good habitat for quail, an impenetrable refuge from predators.

Tenbrook had just started picking plums when something caught his eye. There was a dark patch on a small nearby ridge that didn't look natural. It was an opening, too big for a coyote den. Tenbrook set his sack down and went to have a look. A hole had been dug in the side of the ridge and it was partly obscured by a crude patchwork of dead branches. He parted the branches and looked inside. What he discovered was a small, neatly excavated chamber. Inside were a few propane tanks, unmarked plastic bottles, a propane burner, some tubes and vials. He caught a whiff of something acrid. Then he heard a murmur of voices nearby.

Tenbrook froze. His heart pounded the way it did when he'd bow-hunted and a deer came within range. He stood still and breathed deeply. He waited. He concentrated on calming the surge of adrenalin. Slowly he moved and looked for a path without obstructions that wouldn't betray him. He listened, facing the voices. Then he stepped back. Crouching, he made his way without a sound on the soft debris of the forest, past the blackberry bushes, using them as a screen. He walked away from the voices in a circle through a cloud of midges rising and falling in a shaft of sun light. He crossed a shallow ditch and reached a patch of sumacs. Once he was out of range of the voices, the woods assumed again a solemn quietude. It was as if the wind had become trapped within its confines and when he breathed it seemed as if the concentrated wind entered his lungs.

He heard the voices again. He crept closer, dropped to his knees and crawled to a sprawling rose bush. Through its thorny branches, he could make out Roland and Benny lounging in the shade of a cottonwood tree. Pale vapor rose from a two-burner stove. An assault rifle leaned against the tree.

"Some say that ever 'gainst that season comes…Whatever."

"The bird of dawning singeth all night long," said Benny in a groggy voice, taking a puff on a glass pipe.

"So I have heard and do in part believe it," said Roland with a yawn.

"I'm worried, Rolly," said Benny, taking another puff.

"What are you worried about, good penny?" said Roland.

"I'm worried about that body," said Benny.

"The body dies, the body's beauty lives."

"I'm worried that the coyotes might dig it up."

"No way. We dug down deep, full fathom five. In a couple of weeks there'll be daisies blooming there."

"You're not using your head, Roland," said Benny, straightening up and shaking his head. "We should have dissolved it in acid."

"Where were we going to get acid?"

"Point well taken," said Benny. He held up the mouthpiece. "I pronounce this the Chateau Lafite of crystal meth."

"'Tis the e pluribus unum meth."

"What do you suppose Jimmy nets for a batch like this?" said Benny.

"Have you ever thought about skimming a pinch?" said Roland.

"I'm going to pretend I didn't hear that."

"We could be rich."

"We are rich," said Benny. "We could be dead."

"It's not against the law to dream."

"We have job security. The stage is a stingy master."

"True," said Roland, reaching for the pipe. "Nor does Jimmy begrudge us this lagniappe."

"We must take care not to overdo it," said Benny. "Not only for fear of arousing Jimmy's wrath, but for reasons of health."

"We can quit any time we want to."

"The question is in wanting to," said Benny. "I saw a guy on the street sweeping with an invisible broom the other day. That could be you or me in a couple of more years."

"In China, when they execute you, they make the family pay for the bullets," said Roland.

"How does that pertain?"

"And they give the family the spent cartridges."

"You have to hand it to Jimmy," said Benny. "He has no conscience. He'd waste a nun to protect a dollar bill."

"First prize, one week in Philadelphia."

"Second prize, two weeks."

"We're not making sense."

"You're harshing my mellow."

"Yet this is righteous meth."

"We have heard the chimes at midnight."

"They don't write lines like those ones anymore."

"We can't go on, we will go on," said Benny. "Those lines too are good."

"Sometimes, I feel as if I've been reciting someone else's lines all my life," said Roland. "Sometimes I think that if there was a button that would blow up the world, I would push it."

"And obliterate this fair globe?" said Bennie. "Tut, tut. That's the meth talking. If you don't tend your stove, you might blow the two of us up." Roland got to his feet and stumbled to the stove. Tenbrook edged away. When he could no longer hear the voices, he stood for a moment without moving. Then he picked up a short, stout log lying on the ground. He pumped his arm a few times and then let the branch fly. He heard it crash. There was a moment of silence, followed by an outburst of expletives. Then the assault rifle erupted with a random volley that cracked through the woods. Tenbrook turned and walked away, laughing quietly, pleased that his throwing arm still had its stuff.

Chapter 21

Gwen was waiting for him outside when he drove up. She was wearing a plain pale-blue dress that went straight to her ankles. It looked like something an Amish woman might wear for a shopping trip to Walmart. This must be her religious costume, thought Tenbrook, and as he watched her trotting to the car he remarked how much sexier she looked dressed like a chaste matron than she did in the showy, tight-fitting, cleavage-revealing outfits she usually wore. She still had a thoroughbred body. Her long athletic legs and flagrant breasts were more provocative when hidden, but unmistakably there. Beneath the hem of her skirt he caught a glimpse of wicked-looking snakeskin boots.

"I expected you to be wearing a wimple," said Tenbrook when she got into the car. Gwen leaned across the seat and gave him a kiss, leaving a scent of lilac on his cheek.

"Fuck you, Tenbrook," she said. "I haven't taken my vows yet." She took a pocket mirror out of her purse, checked her lipstick and smoothed an eyebrow as if she was putting the finishing touches on a work of art.

"You know, I have a walk-in closet with rows of dresses, suits, skirts, gowns, costumes for funerals and cocktail parties, aprés-ski outfits and uniforms for civic committee meetings," said Gwen. "I've still got my wedding dress preserved in a zipped-up plastic bag. Shoe boxes by the dozen.

Three fur coats. Riding jackets. Once a year, Josephine from Nelly Quaint's comes over to examine the inventory and tell me what new styles I must have. Isn't that pathetic?"

"You look stunning no matter what you wear, Sister Gwen," Tenbrook said.

"Good, I don't want anyone to be able to resist me, especially you. Seriously, Ten. I'm really happy you agreed to do this."

"Believe me, my heart's not in it. Kate thought it would be good for me."

"She wants to get you out of the house."

"She wants me to stop brooding and get 'involved.' I don't want to get involved. 'Don't Get Involved' is my motto."

"Have you ever thought about living in a monastery?" said Gwen. "I do believe you'd be happy wrapped in sackcloth brooding in a cave on a mountain top."

"I've thought about that. But what would I do for the cocktail hour?"

"Tell me the truth, Ten," said Gwen. "Do you believe in anything?"

"I don't know," said Tenbrook. "Believing turns people into witch-hunters. And so much of the Christian stuff sounds like pagan stuff. You know, Jesus sounds like the Corn God. I do believe in Original Sin, though. I feel guilty, but of what?."

"My husband doesn't believe in anything but himself."

"It must be nice."

It was late February, the undecided month. Migratory birds were already showing up, testing the barrier of cold air that still blocked their return to the north. One day the temperature hit sixty-five. People were shopping in t-shirts and shorts. The next day an arctic wind swooped down, blowing horizontal snow.

The retreat for new members of the vestry was to be held at the Wagon Wheel, a farm outside of Middleton that had been converted to a facility for meetings, weddings and various therapeutic events. Tenbrook and Gwen headed west out of town, past the high school, where students were putting on a play about a young gay man who'd been beaten to death. Fred Fister, the red-headed homophobic preacher, was outside with his flock, protesting the production, holding signs proclaiming the abomination of homosexuality: "God Hates Fags."

"They ought to shoot that man," said Gwen.

"Someday someone will," said Tenbrook.

"God, I hate Kansas," said Gwen.

"It's a terrible place," said Tenbrook.

"Then why don't you get out?"

"Oh, I love it."

"Misery is bliss, huh?"

"Why don't you get out?"

"I think about it all the time," said Gwen. "I want to but I don't want to. I'm unhappy but I don't want to be happy. I have everything I ever dreamed of and I don't want any of it. Sometimes I just wish you'd take me away."

"We tried that."

"And it didn't work. Sometimes, I think I've found something with the church. I actually tell myself that I'm going to give my life to Christ. And then the bubble bursts and I laugh out loud. It seems like such a joke. Tell me the truth—What do you think of Father Ned?"

"I think he's a fraud. I bet he doesn't even believe in God. But I loved his "Size Matters" sermon on stewardship. I once heard him say that the creation of the universe was a sexual act."

"Go easy, Ten."

"Okay. If you believe in Ned, I believe in Ned."

"You have to believe in something."

"I'm not so sure about that."

✳✳✳

A northwest wind buffeted the car as they drove out of town and entered the bleak countryside. Cattle and horses stood in the bleached pastures with their rumps to the wind. A few ragged, mutton-chop clouds flew across the sky. Scraps of black trash bags clung to the barbed-wire fences, flapping like snared birds. Fragments of tires that looked like small carcasses lay by the road. A crow flew up with strings of entrails in its beak. They passed abandoned farmsteads, barns with gaps between their slats, a one-room schoolhouse stuffed with hay, a series of faded Burma Shave signs: "Doesn't…Kiss you…Like she useter? Perhaps she's seen…A smoother rooster." A caravan of antique tractors with iron wheels marched across one hilltop. There were for-sale signs everywhere along the road: eggs for sale, kittens for sale, miracle cures for sale. "One Kansas Farmer feeds 128 people—and you" boasted one sign. Pennants flapped in the empty lot of a failed used car dealer. The torn banner said, "Everything Must Go." On the front door of a boarded-up service station, someone had painted, "Three That Make Us Great: God, Guts and Guns."

"That's Kansas for you," said Gwen. "The three G's."

"A hundred years ago there would have been four families living on each section out here," said Tenbrook. "Farming supported all those people. Then things changed. Farming became big business." They passed a limestone structure with a collapsed wall. "That was a station on the Santa Fe Trail."

"Everett owns the place across the road," said Gwen. The pasture was covered with small oil derricks, half of which were pumping. "Look what he's done to that land."

"Think of all the money pouring in."

"He's in business with a gangster," said Gwen. "Did you know that?"

***

The Wagon Wheel was situated in a broad river valley. Hereford cattle dotted the hillsides on either side of the road that wound through massive, gnarled cottonwoods. Rust-colored quarter horses grazed in the open spaces. Father Ned's big red Harley was parked by the front door of a stone barn when they drove up. Ned, wearing blue jeans and a Grateful Dead sweatshirt, greeted them at the door. Inside, members of the vestry were eating pizza out of boxes and making church-style "fellowship" talk.

After lunch, Father Ned asked everyone to join him in a circle. Once they'd joined hands, he introduced Ternbrook as the new member.

"The theme for today is 'connection,'" said Ned. He invited the members of the vestry to speak. An insurance salesman talked about the importance of connection in his business. But connecting with Jesus Christ was what really counted. Someone else complained that people were too "connected" to their cell phones. The prophets went off-line to the desert to communicate with God.

Father Ned made a sensual, gurgling sound of pleasure with each comment. After they'd exhausted the subject of "connection," he invited them to offer prayers. A change came over them, as if they'd been transformed into evangelical preachers. Voices rose and fell in sing-song notes. They closed their eyes, gave thanks, sought forgiveness, and called on the Lord to intercede in conflicts and crises. They used words like "thy," "beseech," "oblation" and "vouchsafe." Each one had a distinct style—giddy, pleading, magnanimous, oracular. And though the specifics were banal (one concerned some issue facing a rural water district, another sought guidance in the selection of new slipcovers) the invocations were passionate. Tenbrook wondered: Was it the license to become another self that drew these ordinary people into the communion of believers?

When it was Gwen's turn, she called on the Savior to answer her doubts, to assuage her anguish and make her an agent of kindness. The prayers progressed around the circle. Tenbrook tensed. The hands he held on either side sweated. The woman who held his right hand offered thanks to the altar guild for the flowers the previous Sunday and then squeezed to indicate that it was his turn. Tenbrook had nothing to say. He was the weak link in the chain, a circuit breaker. He felt like a child called upon to perform in front of the class. There were a few coughs and restless movements. At last the woman on his left squeezed his hand to exempt him and began voicing a prayer herself.

Father Ned called the vestry to order. The secretary read the minutes of the last meeting. There was the ritual pecking at the budget. The senior warden announced that there would be a potluck dinner the next Sunday evening. Then Ned gave a little homily about the "purpose-driven life," employing the parable of the lighthouse and the battleship.

When he concluded, Ned introduced Ben Swadmore, a "facilitator" who'd been recruited to help them hammer out a mission statement. Swadmore invited everyone to join him in a great adventure, a journey of self-discovery.

"When people come together, energy is created that's greater than the sum of the individuals," he said.

To get the ball rolling, Swadmore asked the vestry members to self-introduce by describing their individual ministries. One wanted to save the polar bears, one read to the blind, one sought an end to war.

"I don't know that I have a ministry," said Tenbrook when it was his turn. "I've never thought of myself as a minister. I guess I'm just one of the sheep."

"Being one of the sheep is a kind of ministry," said Father Ned. Swadmore called for mission statement ideas. The members responded: Giving, Seeking, Serving, Witnessing, Forgiving, Loving.

Someone compared the church to a sandbox in which members of the congregation played, sometimes together, sometimes alone, making things, changing shapes, sometimes even destroying structures and starting all over again. Someone compared the church to a flock of geese headed to an unknown destination. First one goose led, then another. The church was like a molecule, a spaceship, a business whose product was salvation. Someone worried that composing a mission statement was limiting and in a sense egotistical.

"It puts us before Christ and the liturgy. It makes the church sound like Rotary."

"I'm glad you said that," said Father Ned. "I want radicals on the vestry. I want to hear talk about revolution. I want Karl Marx and Che Guevara in this space. People: Get out of your comfort zones."

After an hour of soul-searching and sifting, they came up with a tentative statement: "Building a Loving Community that Seeks and Serves Christ in Others." Father Ned began sermonizing on the subordinate importance of ritual and doctrine. He was about to announce what really mattered when he suddenly stopped speaking. There was a long silence. A few of the members looked up to see what was wrong. Father Ned looked gravely around the room.

"Someone is thinking, 'Bullshit,'" he said. "Excuse my language, but I can feel it. Someone in this room has lost his faith, someone feels alienated from the church. And yet this someone isn't comfortable with disbelief. That's the person I cherish. That someone may be more spiritual than any of us. That someone may be a saint. That someone may make us reexamine the truths that we embrace but which may have grown stale, to renew our faith. You know, faith is like soil that must be turned by a plow. It needs to be disturbed to thrive. Don't forget—Jesus himself was an outsider. Jesus was a terrorist. He died but he didn't die. He's not finished. He's a work in progress. He's working himself out through us." Father Ned closed his eyes. It was good that this change agent had come, he said. Good that he thought, "Bullshit." Jesus probably said "Bullshit" when he listened to one of Ned's sermons. Some of the disciples probably said "Bullshit" when they listened to one of Jesus's.

"I rejoice in bullshit," said Father Ned. "I give thanks for the mysteries of faith."

***

The sky was filled with geese when Gwen and Tenbrook left the meeting and headed home. The birds were milling around, uncertain which way the weather was going to turn.

"Look," said Tenbrook. "The vestry, heading south."

"That's you in the lead," said Gwen. "The man of sorrows,"

"Maybe Father Ned is clairvoyant after all," said Tenbrook. "Because 'bullshit' was the exact word that passed through my mind when he was giving his little spiel. I don't know where he got the idea that I was spiritual, though. Kate must have told him that. I suspect he was trying to flatter me, to seduce me. Even if he's not chasing Kate, he knows I don't like him. Kate will kill me, but I'm not going to make it on the vestry, Gwen. I'd poison the well. I felt like screaming when we were holding hands." Gwen laughed.

"I won't blame you if you drop out," she said. "Sometimes when all those people are popping off about the Holy Spirit, I feel like pulling my skirt up and spreading my legs just to see what kind of Christian spin they'd put on that."

"Was he putting in a good word for Everett with that stuff about plowing the soil?"

"You know I hate what Everett did to our land."

They drove on in silence. The treeless hills stretched away to the southern horizon, pristine and glowing in the winter sun. Suddenly, Gwen yelled, "Stop!" Tenbrook gave her a questioning look. He slowed down and pulled off the road. "Turn around," she said. Tenbrook made a U-turn and drove back a few hundred yards until they reached a roadside cattle pen. They crossed over some abandoned railroad tracks and stopped by a faded sign that proclaimed Wasonkee, pop 16. But all that was left of the town was a small, immaculate cemetery bounded by a wrought iron fence. They sat with the motor running while Gwen looked out the window. Beyond the cattle pen, a dirt road dipped to a valley and disappeared into a glade of cedars. Gwen sighed.

"Have you ever wanted to turn off on a road like that just to see where it goes?" she said.

"All the time."

"I feel like that right now. Let's do it."

The road was deeply rutted. They crept downhill, riding the ridges. They crossed over a stone bridge, then ascended the hill beyond the dry stream bed. The road climbed until they reached a level promontory. They stopped by a broken windmill. The hills beyond seemed to be moving their shoulders slowly. In the distance, they saw a small herd of antelope grazing. The animals looked up, startled. They sprang, scattered and ran a short distance, then stopped, looked at the intruders and began grazing again. Tenbrook turned the engine off.

"This is Kansas," said Tenbrook. "Emptiness to the Nth power. I like it."

"That's the way I feel inside and I don't like it," said Gwen. "I'm just a bunch of fragments. I don't know what I'm going to do next. I'm burning up inside. One minute I think I'm going to run away and start a mission in Guatemala. The next minute I want to get drunk and give somebody head. I'm about to explode. I wish I would. But nothing happens."

"I suspect you're not as unhappy as you think you are."

"I am that unhappy. Something's missing in me. I can't change. At first, I wanted to be an artist. Then I wanted to be a saint. I settled on being a trollop. The only thing I know how to do is fuck. I've done a lot of that. I've dragged my body all over Middleton County doing it. That's the only time I feel together and free at the same time. Unfortunately, the feeling doesn't last. And you know, none of those fucks was as good as the one you and I had in the back seat of your parents' Ford convertible twenty years ago. Remember our first time? It wasn't so much like sex. I felt transported, weightless, you know. It was spiritual in a way. It's never been like that since."

Tenbrook turned to look. Gwen had pulled her skirt up. Slowly, she slid her panties down over her knees and looked at herself, not provocatively but with a kind of detached curiosity.

"I don't want to go to my eternal reward without fucking you one more time," she said. Then she leaned toward him until their shoulders touched. Her eyes were half-closed, her mouth parted. The next thing he knew, they were tangling, tongues thrashing, hands groping. Then his face was between her legs and she was moaning, "Jesus," "Fuck," "God," as if they were connected in some kind of mystical trinity. And then he was inside her, her legs wrapped around him, and she gave a little cry. For a moment, Tenbrook had the illusion that they were not coupled in the present, but had been transported back, transformed, beginners again, rejuvenated, breathless, and he remembered her trademark fingernail caresses which hadn't changed in the years. Then they arched together in a frantic, unthinking, throbbing rush and with a final shudder, they were done. For a moment they enjoyed the delusion that they were the first couple in paradise to perform the forbidden act.

"Take that, Everett Pillars," said Gwen. "Anything that feels that good can't be a sin."

"I haven't been able to do this for months," said Tenbrook.

"Then Kate shouldn't mind us recharging your batteries."

"Kate will know the minute she looks me in the eyes."

"Maybe she won't look," said Gwen. "Wear a mask. Just hang in there. You'll forget it happened in a couple of days." She sat against the door, her hands behind her head, smiling. Her dress was still lifted. "I'd like to just linger here a bit," she said, reaching over and touching him, running her fingernails over his thigh. "Remember? You couldn't get my bra off. I had to help you. First time, best time. Well, where do we go from here?" she said. She laughed when he looked alarmed. "Don't worry, Ten. We're not going anywhere. You're not going to get AIDS or herpes. And I've had my tubes tied. You don't have to worry about me calling you in the middle of the night. It was one shot for old times' sake. My lips are sealed. I used you and you used me. So we're even."

He watched her massaging her foot, stroking it as if it were an exquisite instrument and he was struck by its whiteness, as if it had been held under water for a long time. He was thinking about the courtship labyrinth—about rejection, seduction, deception, ecstasy—all in the homely service of procreation, about the hours of anticipation spent for a climactic moment. If she can hold his gaze she has him, and so she makes her earrings shake, smiles with her open mouth, plays with her hair…The mindless two-stroke rhythm of a reciprocating engine, pulsing, compensating, revving, variable-pitched thrusts and withdrawals, urgent and spasmodic, a threshing machine gone wild. It was a sublime, delusional rough strife ride, the man thinking he's taming a feral beast, the woman that she's snared a foolish man, yet both feeling for an instant like stars flung out from the black maw of anti-matter at the speed of light, then extinguishing in a cry. The delusion that they have been the first to taste the forbidden fruit, that they have gotten away with something, that they have smuggled gold out of Egypt.

The fringed female orchid, somewhat ovoid, corolla lobes reflexed, rare…the male randyweed, lance-oblong to elliptic, hoods short-stipitate…Translucent mass of golden pollen…Last spring, a pair of geese had nested on Tenbrook's pond. They came at him fearlessly when he got too close, honking and menacing him to protect the nest. After a few weeks, they appeared one day paddling serenely with five puffball goslings bringing up the rear. He and Kate had been elated. Two days later, the goslings were gone, taken by snapping turtles, hawks or maybe a bobcat. It seemed like a tragedy to Tenbrook and Kate, but it didn't seem to bother the pair of geese. They went about feeding on the tender shoots of grass as if they hadn't even noticed the loss of their young. They'd fulfilled the mandate of nature. It was their obligation to produce offspring. It was up to nature whether their offspring survived. Tenbrook doubted that God cared that much about the fall of a sparrow. So many of them fell, squandered—for what?

He and Gwen struggled in the confines of the car to put the clothes back on that had been so easy to remove. They sat for a moment looking at the prairie that stretched in every direction below the knoll where they had parked. The ranchers would be burning the grass in April and if you made that drive at night you would see flames creeping across the rim of the earth, a rite as old as the prairie itself, renewing the roots of the tall grasses and in the morning hawks would be patrolling in search of dead woodrats and snakes.

"They burn too often," said Tenbrook.

"What do you mean?" said Gwen.

"It destroys the habitat of the prairie chicken. They overgraze it. They try to wring every last nickel out of that grass."

"Everett would tell you that's the name of the game."

"Just think, Gwen," said Tenbrook. "All over the world parishioners are gathering in church basements for fellowship, followed by potluck dinners. Everyone will bring a covered dish. There will be tuna casseroles and sheet cake. Prayers mingling with banter. Ice tea turning into wine." Gwen gave a girlish laugh. Then she began quietly to sob.

"This is my blood which is shed for you for the remission of sins," she said. Tenbrook reached over and took her hand.

"Somewhere around here in the early days, there was a sect called the Soul Sleepers," he said. "They believed that the spirit was a substance that slept in the body until the racket of the Resurrection woke it up and freed it."

"You and I are the Soul Sleepers, Ten," said Gwen. For a moment, he felt restored, at peace. Then he heard the first whispers of guilt. A weight pressed on him. He couldn't move. He was finished. He'd transgressed. He'd been cast out. He was falling and he heard a metal door closing with the sound of doom. But it was only the sound of the wind in the windmill's broken blades.

Chapter 22

Kate's cousin Chocky was the first to die that year. He fell in mid-March at his favorite post in the backyard, presiding over the smoker where slabs of honey-glazed ribs were slowly cooking, beer in one hand, cigarette in the other. His wife saw him from the kitchen window, raising his hand like a child in a classroom asking for permission to speak. His legs gave way in slow motion. Mandy ran from the house and by the time she reached him, Chocky was dead.

The funeral was held in a confectionery-looking church finished in white plaster that glistened like icing on a cake.

"We believe that Chocky is already in heaven," said the preacher, "restored to a body very much like the one he inhabited here on earth, doing the same things he loved to do on earth."

"Like smoking and drinking and pigging out on ribs?" said Kate on the way to the grave site.

"Scripture promises abundant life," said Tenbrook. "It's all-you-can-eat in heaven. And the barbecue is fat-free."

"I can hardly wait to die," said Kate.

Happy talk about the afterlife depressed Tenbrook. Promises of reunions with loved ones and eternal rapture sounded like wishful thinking. The idea that his body, which was already betraying him, would be miraculously restored to its youthful vigor seemed laughable. They passed a bloated raccoon lying on the roadside, feet in the air.

"That's the afterlife," said Tenbrook.

"The preachers tell us what we want to hear," said Kate. "By the way, what kind of parents would name their child Chocky?"

Chocky was always on a diet. Tenbrook remembered going with him to Porky's. Chocky would order a little cottage cheese and cole slaw, poke at it with ostentatious lack of interest. Surreptitiously, he'd devour it, then sit there and watch the others, like a pariah dog waiting for the lions to stop gnawing on the carcass of a wildebeest.

"You're not finished, are you?" he'd say when someone stopped eating. "Those ribs ought to be bleached white when you're through with them." He sounded genuinely angry, as if some sacred code had been violated. Then he'd jump up, stride to the order window and come back with a plate of ribs. He'd pull them apart and attack them. After he cleaned off the meat, he'd suck the bones and hold one up to demonstrate the proper way to address a rib. Then he'd go back to the window for some fries and burnt ends.

"That was Chocky," said Tenbrook. "He used to say that beer has food value, but food doesn't have beer value. I'll miss the poor guy."

The sky was crystal blue, painfully bright when they lowered Chocky into the ground. The family sat beneath a green canopy. A small bulldozer with a box blade was parked at a discreet distance, waiting to push a mound of soil over the grave.

"For those of us whom Chocky has left behind, this is a sorrowful occasion," said the preacher. "But it is a joyful one for Chocky. He has embarked on a great voyage and passed over to the other side. For he has gone to be with the Lord and will spend eternity in a place where there is no pain or sorrow." Tissues were passed around and there were a few tears. One of Chocky's daughters laid a teddy bear on top of the coffin. A flock of blackbirds passed in a tight pattern overhead. Tenbrook watched them flare, fly off and merge again like filings drawn together by a magnet. A momentary pattern, then a random scattering. A gust of wind rattled the steel supports of the burial service canopy.

It was a season of funerals. Visits to churches and funeral homes became a routine feature of Tenbrook's life. Friends greeted him with their grieving masks on. They shook their heads, looked down at their feet and muttered platitudes: "She's gone to a better place." "We lost a good one." "To know her was to love her." "At least he didn't suffer." "The good Lord called him home."

After Chocky, it was Bonnie Westphal. She'd been in a virtual coma for three years. Three black women, a mother and her two daughters, had been taking care of her, turning her wasted body daily to prevent bed sores, feeding her, tending to her hygienic needs. Once considered a great beauty, Bonnie for some time had been referred to as a "vegetable." The consensus was that her death was a blessing.

The Tenbrooks went to Bonnie's visitation. A solemn undertaker guided them to the line that filed past the coffin.

"She looks so peaceful," someone said.

"Just like she used to."

"What a pretty dress."

"They did wonders with her hair."

"Such an elegant coffin."

"It's just what she would have wanted."

Tenbrook looked at the shrunken, wax-like figure, its face a withered flower. Bonnie wore a florid pink gown shot through with golden threads. Her head rested on a satin pillow. The mortician had fixed a serene smile on her thin lips. She looked like a mummified debutante or bride. For a second, Tenbrook had the illusion that she was breathing. The coffin looked like a candied Easter egg. A medallion identified it as a SlumberQueen II.

At the funeral the next day, Bonnie's son Donnie gave the eulogy. He produced a letter from his deceased father, delivered by a heavenly messenger. He read from the letter.

"You're probably wondering why I called this meeting. On the whole I'd rather be in Philadelphia. But heaven's not so bad. I'm looking forward to seeing the rest of you here, that is, those of you who make the cut." Donnie looked up over his reading glasses, cueing the audience to laugh. He read his father's reminiscences of his courtship of Bonnie and their first kiss. Rain kept them inside for a week on their honeymoon, but they somehow managed to find ways to keep one another entertained, wink, wink. He asked the congregation to concentrate and send a big hug up to his father in heaven. He walked up and down the aisle, holding his hand out, touching the outstretched hands.

"Oh!" he exclaimed suddenly, falling back as if smitten by an electric jolt. "Dad just sent me a big hug back from heaven. Thank you, Dad."

After three or four funerals, Tenbrook began looking forward to the next one. He thought he'd developed a respectably doleful demeanor and enjoyed the brief oases of time to brood on his own predicaments. Occasionally, a perverse impulse came over him, a temptation to display extravagant grief. He imagined himself at a funeral, beginning with quiet sobbing, building to an operatic wail of lamentation, beating his breast, collapsing into a kind of epileptic fit.

"Don't even think about it," said Kate. "I'll divorce you if you do."

The drought that summer seemed to complement the funeral epidemic. A pall of apocalypse fell over the town.

Middleton's prophets of doom attributed the drought to climate change. Letters to the *Middleton Reaper* were full of Judgment Day forebodings. "Hot enough for you?" wrote one reader. "Or must you have a few more biblical plagues to convince you that something is amiss?" Predictions circulated: The streams would dry up. Famine was at the doorstep. Another Dust Bowl was on the way. Middleton would become a desert.

Even when he wasn't sitting in a funeral parlor or a church, Tenbrook thought he smelled lilies, roses, chrysanthemums and the pungent odor of freshly turned earth. Every chair felt like a pew. Always in the background he heard elderly sopranos warbling the dismal hymns: "All to Jesus I Surrender," "Be Thou My Vision," "There is a Balm in Gilead," "In the Garden." Over and over he heard the refrain, "He walks with me and He talks with me." In dreams, he saw caskets floating down an aisle like barges on a stream, then images of the Griefmaker covered with monstrous buildings. The due date of the balloon mortgage on his house was inching towards him like a burrowing mole. The bad economy had struck Tenbrook's business. His meager income had plunged. And Kate really would divorce him if they lost the house. On several of the funeral programs, he saw James Stafford's name among the donors of flowers.

"If death has no substance, it can't exist," said one of the funeral preachers. Tenbrook was unconvinced.

✱✱✱

"Angie died," Kate said one afternoon when Tenbrook came home from work. Angie had been their neighbor when the Tenbrooks lived in Middleton.

"No," said Tenbrook. "Just like that?"

"Jack called. He told me she'd had a heart attack."

"She was too young for that," said Tenbrook.

"It's funny," said Kate. "We lived just fifty feet apart back then. I saw her every day. We talked while we worked. We exchanged gardening tips. I talked to her more than I talk to my friends. But I never really got to know her."

"She minded her business," said Tenbrook. "She didn't tell you how to vote. She didn't tell you what color to paint your house. She didn't ask you for money to find a cure for cancer or to save the baby seals. You didn't end up hating one another. She was a good neighbor."

Angie and Jack had asked the Tenbrooks over for "a cup of cheer" one Christmas.

"Once you've done this, it becomes a tradition," Angie said. But the conversation had been strained. They couldn't find common ground. They never invited the Tenbrooks again and the Tenbrooks never paid them back.

Angie and Jack had a circle of friends who gathered on summer nights on their patio across the alley from the Tenbrooks. The friends made easy conversation. It had a regular rhythm—a round of sotto voce murmurs followed by an outburst of Angie's jungle-bird whoops of laughter.

"I admit it used to annoy me," said Tenbrook. "But I'll miss that laugh."

Some of the plants in Angie's garden were memorials to her son, Chad. Chad's death had been ruled a suicide, but Angie didn't buy it. She'd talked to him the night before the police found him, an empty glass with traces of milk and cyanide by his bed. Chad had seemed fine, upbeat. And where was he going to get cyanide? Chad had told her that the bar where he worked was owned by an underworld figure who dealt in prostitutes and drugs. Angie suspected that Chad had overheard something he wasn't supposed to hear, that the crime boss's thugs had paid him a visit and offered him a choice between getting beaten to a pulp and drinking the poisoned milk. The police hadn't shown any interest in her theory. So she'd planted tulips and marigolds by a little sign that said "Chad's Garden" as a way of keeping him alive. And she stuck a little dime-store pinwheel in the ground to remind her of her son's free spirit.

"I took some cornbread and pea soup over to Jack," Kate said. "He looked so sad. He was so appreciative."

"He won't have anyone to walk that ridiculous shaggy dog with him," said Tenbrook.

"The garden will go to hell."

"I remember you and Angie standing in the alley, holding your spades, your faces covered with sweat and dirt," said Tenbrook. "Women of the soil. It's hard. One day, you're sitting with your friends in the backyard, cackling at their jokes. The next day a siren comes. And the party's over."

Angie had been married to a brutal drunk the first time around. She'd left him and sued for divorce. When she went to her minister for his blessing, he told her that divorce was anathema and that she should go back to the abusive husband. That had been the end of Angie's affiliation with the church. Her funeral was a casual, non-denominational, family-style affair. Angie's daughter sipped from a can of Coke. None of the men wore ties. Three of Angie's friends paid tribute to her. They recalled the long lists of jokes she used to e-mail them and her outspoken, opinionated personality. One praised her for her "fierceness." Another, who'd also lost a son, said that the only time she'd ever lied to Angie was when she told her she believed that Chad was "somewhere, still."

"I don't believe in life after death," she said. "But I told her I did. Now I hope I'm wrong and she is right."

Then her friends named the plants in Angie's garden. Camellia, Philodendron, Gardenia, Magnolia, Clematis, Honeysuckle, Amaryllis, Marigold, Primrose. They sounded like magic words, charms to bring the dead back to life.

After the funeral, Tenbrook and Kate drove down the alley between their old Middleton house and Angie's for a look at Angie's garden. It had already fallen into neglect. Kate bent down and picked up a handful of dandelions. Thorny creepers crept over the ground.

"This little patch of earth," she said. "Angie had tended it with so much love. That's tansy. That's pennycress. Those aren't city weeds. Where did they come from?" A breath of wind passed through the dead flowers, stirring Chad's pinwheel to life, making the leaf-like curls of plastic turn. They made a dry, scratching sound like some fluttering bird or winged insect trapped in a jar.

Tenbrook got down on his knees and started weeding. Some of the plants had prickly leaves. They fought back. They scratched his skin. His sleeves got covered with burrs. Tenbrook didn't care. He tore at them. Kneeling hurt his knees. Dirt crusted his fingernails. He didn't care. He pulled the plants up by the roots and tossed them in a pile.

"The horn of plenty is filled with weeds," he said.

Chapter 23

Pillars was no longer the "Pillars of Society." After he'd plowed the Griefmaker he'd become an outcast in Middleton. People referred to him as Attila the Hun. His friendships evaporated. Strangers muttered curses when they passed him on the street. His troubles multiplied. His phone calls went unanswered. He couldn't line up tenants for a spec office building. Someone suggested that he lower his rents. "And leave my profit on the table?" he said.

He was on the phone barking out orders to a subcontractor one morning. Gwen was sitting on the sofa in his office, giving herself the routine insulin shot. Suddenly, she let out a deep sigh and went rigid. She slumped against the arm of the couch, her eyes rolled back. Pillars threw the phone down, jumped up, tripped over a chair. He called her name. He got no answer. "Gwen!" he shouted. He sat down beside her, shook her, supported her with his arm, massaged her neck, rubbed her forehead. No response. He ran to the door.

"Mary!" he cried in a voice Mary had never heard before. "Come quick. Bring water." Mary came running with a pitcher and a glass. Pillars tried to get Gwen to take a drink. He splashed water on her face. She didn't respond. With Mary's help he got her on her feet.

"I'm not going to wait for an ambulance," Pillars said. He and Mary carried her to the car. By the time they got to the hospital, Gwen was in a coma. She'd had some kind of seizure. Either the medicine had been bad or Gwen had struck a vein that carried it too directly to her heart or brain. Orderlies rushed her to the emergency room.

Word traveled fast and soon the waiting room was filled with friends and curious sightseers. Platitudes of commiseration mingled with whispered asides about the Pillars' excesses and transgressions. Speculations about Gwen's chances and the possibility of brain damage flew around. A few visitors were managing genuine sniffles. "We will never see the Gwen we loved and knew again," someone said.

Pillars, wearing a rumpled jacket and mismatched pants, looked in shock himself. He sat down, stood up, wandered around the room, disappeared, reappeared, shook hands, made strange gestures of bafflement. He stared blankly at people who tried to offer him condolences.

"She kept me out of trouble, she was my port in a storm, she kept me straight," he said over and over, already speaking of Gwen in the past tense. Father Ned was there, cracking jokes, grandstanding, offering disjointed prayers and pious pronouncements about "God's plan," working the crowd, prancing as Tenbrook had so often seen him prance for Kate. Tod stood aside wearing a sardonic mask, refusing to play the expected role. When people asked him how his mother was doing, he said, robotically, "She's stable," with ironic stress on "stable," as if to emphasize the meaninglessness of the assessment and the insincerity of the visitors' concern. A delivery boy showed up with pizza.

"That's suicide in a slice," cracked Father Ned.

"Builds character," said Tod defiantly, taking a slice and shoving it into his mouth.

Gwen held on for ten more days. Two women who barely knew her appointed themselves guardians, showing up every day to watch for changes in her vital signs. One provided reports on the Internet. On day three she reported that Gwen was able to follow the movement of a finger with her eyes. On day seven she was unresponsive. Pillars hoped for a miracle. He felt tormented by parasites feeding on his grief and well-wishers who urged him to pull the plug. When he approached the room one day he heard one of the guardian women speaking to Gwen in a low voice, "I don't know whether to pray for you or to wish you were dead." He stormed into the room, yelled at her and ordered her to leave. As she hurried out she gave him a stricken look. He saw that she'd been weeping, perhaps suffering some grief of her own.

The church parking lot overflowed the day of the funeral. Men in black suits directed traffic off the paved lot onto the adjoining snow-covered field. The altar was crowded with flowers. The organ played a wistful dirge. An engraved program, which some of the mourners used to fan themselves in the overheated church, paid homage to Gwen, her high-spirited personality, her restless quest for experience, her beauty and generosity. The air thickened with the aroma of lilies and narcissus. A low hum of excitement passed through the pews. It was like a cocktail party without the booze. Unspoken was the suspicion that Gwen's death was somehow retribution for Pillars' plowing of the Griefmaker. Pillars was thinking, "So this is what I built this church for? Gwen has to die to fill this church?"

A hush fell when Father Ned trotted up to the pulpit looking like a chaste choirboy in his starched white robe with the gold embroidered chasuble. He gazed out at the congregation with a beatific, paternal smile.

"Words are inadequate at a time like this," he said. Then he began to pour out the verbiage. "I can't speak to this loss directly. I have to tell a story. One day in retribution for my sins, I woke up in seminary…" A twitter of laughter passed over the congregation. This has to be about him, thought Tenbrook. His ego won't let him give the funeral to Gwen. Ned told the story of a doctor who'd worked in the African bush, practicing medicine on the second floor of a shack. A sign in various dialects said, "The doctor is upstairs."

"He cured thousands of African of diseases," said Ned. "When, on account of neglecting his own health, he died, they sent the sign back with the coffin. People interpreted the sign as an affirmation that the doctor was 'upstairs,' that is, in heaven."

So this was Father Ned's way of pandering. Gwen was in the heaven which Ned didn't believe in and all was right with the universe. But Tenbrook had sold Ned short. Ned's face suddenly reddened and he spoke in an angry, choking voice.

"How could God let this happen?" he exclaimed. "Either God is not in charge or else he is malevolent." He shook his head and looked over the congregation as if in appeal for what he should say next. Coughs and rustlings passed through the pews.

What was Ned thinking? Was he about to proclaim a heresy that many suspected him of harboring? Was he going to say that adultery was a sin, but that you needed to sin to be forgiven, that without sin, Christ would be superfluous?

Ned looked down and muttered something about how creation hadn't always been an arena of cruelty. He was quiet for a moment. Then he rambled on. He swayed slightly as if in a state of rapture. He looked heavenward. This was how he had them in the palm of his hand for an hour every Sunday, even the non-believers. It was all magic, hocus pocus, the outlandish costume, the bishop's crook, the cut glass cruets, the golden collection plate. One moment his voice soared as if he were about to wind things up. Then back down to earth he'd come. He wandered in the wilderness, searched for a theme, then off he'd go on another riff about Lazarus or water turning into wine, trying to hit one out of the ballpark.

"When they take a guppy out of a pet shop aquarium, the other guppies mourn," he said. "They tell each other, 'They got Fred. Why did it have to be him? Fred was the best.' They don't realize that Fred has been *chosen*. We need to look beyond our own aquarium. Gwen was the best. She has been chosen too." At last he gave up and wound it down.

"The most important sermon that will be preached here today is the one Gwen is preaching to each of you," he said. Then he quoted the words of some sage: "Everything will be all right in the end. And if it's not all right, it's not the end." Tenbrook looked outside at the field blanketed with snow. That field had once been his patrimony. He had coveted it. Now he felt himself letting go. A kind of poison seemed to be draining out of his body. He felt a shaft of compassion for Ned. Wasn't there a bond between him and Ned and Gwen, even a bond of sin? She'd been struck down near the solstice. Already the days were growing longer. The seeds buried in the frozen ground were stirring with the memory of their purpose. The worst of winter was past. Perhaps there was hope after all, even for a man who believed in nothing. He felt the sudden urge to take communion from Ned's hands. Maybe the currents of hostility in the community would be harmonized for a blessed moment, the wounds healed. Maybe the furrows Pillars had plowed would be ironed away some day and the prairie would be restored. Maybe quail would make a comeback.

Who could say? Maybe the sky would be covered by flights of passenger pigeons once again. When he took the wafer from Ned's hands he imagined that the bread was the body of Ceres's daughter, who had gone down to the underworld, punished for eating a pomegranate seed. She would come back home next spring.

They sang a hymn that had its origins in some provincial sect. It began solemnly, a dirge in a soul-catching minor key. Halfway in, a change of key intruded, a riff of gaiety borrowed from a peasant jig. The hymn became a song. It sounded more like a pagan summons to dancing than the usual weary drones that dominated the hymnal. It brought to mind rustic dancing, the lifting of a skirt, a little irreverent kick of the heel, a gay swerve from religion and solemnity, a summons to rejoice and give thanks, a reminder of the human spirit, the refusal to give up, the will to keep on living and dancing no matter what cruel game nature or God played with hapless human beings. The congregation sang with gusto. Spoken words wouldn't have had the power. Only singing would do. "Alleluia," they sang. "Alleluia," whatever "Alleluia" meant. Tenbrook's voice also rose. Next to him stood Kate looking distant and inscrutable. Her eyes were among the few in the room that were dry that day.

Chapter 24

The Bilbreys were celebrating their fiftieth anniversary. Kate had declined to join Tenbrook. She was fond of the Bilbreys but cake and ice cream socials made her want to scream. Well-wishers were milling about in the Bilbreys' front yard when Tenbrook arrived, men in faded, crisply ironed overalls, women in flowery frocks, a few wearing white mesh bonnets. They looked like characters in a country fair painted by some Dutch master. Troy received his guests wearing his starched Purina Chow shirt and jeans held up by suspenders. In one hand was his plastic spitting cup. His lower jaw hung open like a pelican's, filling up with tobacco juice.

Troy and Retta Lou had eloped when he was twenty-one and his bride was nineteen. A justice of the peace in Raton, New Mexico, married them. Their honeymoon was the ride back home in Troy's '54 Ford. They'd moved in with Troy's parents and Troy helped his father on the dairy farm until he'd saved enough to make the down payment on his eighty acres. Since then their lives had been devoted to work, seven days a week, no vacations. Not once in fifty years had they left the county.

"We didn't have a wedding cake, and we didn't have a reception," Retta Lou wrote on the anniversary invitation. "We always said that if we made it to our fiftieth, we'd have our reception and lots of cake." An imposing array of cakes was spread over a long picnic bench—butter cake, pound cake, cupcakes, ring cakes and sponge cakes, an orange glow chiffon cake, a checkerboard fantasy cake, all contributions of neighbors, along with Retta Lou's own three-tiered Golden Glory wedding cake, wrapped with spun sugar and crystallized violets.

Tenbrook imagined a birthday party at the Middleton Country Club. There would be a bar with gleaming bottles, bartenders in white jackets pouring silver and golden potions into tall glasses, squeezing lime wedges into translucent gin and tonics, decorating whiskey sours with lemon twists and maraschino cherries. In the Bilbreys' society, cake was the elixir, the manna, the temptation and delight, the sanctioned escape from routine chores. The doctor had given Troy six months to live, yet there he was, backslapping and hugging, laughing it up, feeding his face with cake.

The Bilbreys' yard was a menagerie of fiberglass deer, plastic flamingos and brightly painted whirlygigs. A scarecrow draped in a clawfoot bathtub held a fishing pole striped like a barber's pole. An ancient Evinrude outboard motor hung from the back of the tub. In large red letters on the side of the tub Troy had written, "Red Neck Bass Boat," with the "R" painted in reverse. The Bilbreys' clapboard house was painted a stark white that shone when the sun struck it. Like all the farmsteads in the county, it was a footnote to the grand, gambrel-roofed barn. The farmers put their livestock's accommodations ahead of their own. Troy's implements were on display—his combine, his planter, his mower. That and his acres represented his material wealth. All destined to be auctioned off someday soon.

Tenbrook thought of his city friends with their manicured lawns, gazebos, croquet courses and water gardens. They'd smirk at the cornball tackiness and utilitarian homeliness of it all and dismiss the Bilbreys as bumpkins whose idea of entertainment was likely a Tupperware party or a tractor pull. The dirt beneath their fingernails and the manure on their boots would have repelled his city friends. But to Tenbrook, his Middleton friends were leading fake lives, preoccupied with the burdens of affluence, the difficulty of finding reliable cleaning ladies, the merits of condos in the Caymans, their golf handicaps, the injustices of the Alternate Minimum Tax. Tenbrook rejoiced in having escaped them and their civic pieties, the mean-spirited gossip, the platitudes and pronouncements—"So nice to see you," "Oh, don't get up"—and the boasting indulged in by those who'd left him financially behind.

His new rural friends talked about tangibles—shoats and heifers, bulls and boars, Massey Ferguson and John Deere, Tordon, Crossbow and 24-D. He admired their ingenuity in fixing things, their innate understanding of how mechanical things work. They couldn't afford to hire someone to do something for them. Farming margins were too thin. You had to be able to do everything yourself. You had to be an accountant, a mechanic, a plumber, an electrician, a carpenter. You had to be able to talk interest rates and loan terms with the banker. You had to know how to slaughter a hog. When they talked about the weather, it wasn't small talk. There was a pragmatic urgency about it. They cursed the elements and prayed to them. Weather made them or broke them. Rain that kept them from planting in spring might save their crops in July. How many times in a dry summer had each of them watched a cloud dragging a gray gown of precious rain stop and veer away a quarter mile short of their fields?

In April, after a total crop loss, they'd be out planting again. Tenbrook knew one farmer who'd lost his land to foreclosure. The next year, he'd leased some acreage and borrowed money for another roll of the dice. It was no joke that "bought the farm" was a euphemism for death. Clint, Zeke, Leroy, Verlyn, Virgil, Dwayne. Their names evoked a world of soil and engine parts, fertilizer and animal guts. There among the birthday crowd was Jasper Nichols, whose face looked like melted plastic, disfigured by the explosion of a propane tank he'd been hauling. And Loren Hobbins, who dangled a useless hand that had been mangled in a reaper. Dwayne Christian's shirttail got caught on his tractor's power takeoff, flaying him down to his scrotum. There they were, laughing like children, eating the forbidden cake. As if all you had to do in life was to keep your sweet tooth happy and keep rowing your boat merrily down the stream. There was Jed Penny. He'd bragged to Tenbrook about his eight-year-old granddaughter who'd shoved her arm up to the elbow into the birth canal of her 4-H sow to help deliver a litter of pigs. He was as proud of his little girl as if she'd been presented to society at a debutante ball. Associating with real people like them made Tenbrook feel a little more real.

He helped himself to a rib from one of the tinfoil bins. It was dripping with grease and sweet barbecue sauce. At the country club, waitresses in starched uniforms would be passing silver trays with water chestnuts wrapped in bacon. Wasp-waisted women with face-lift smiles would be helping themselves to dainty finger sandwiches filled with cucumber slices and salmon pate. Tenbrook remembered two of those pedigreed ladies who got into a fight, shouting obscenities and hurling hors d'oeuvres in the Raphael Room, on account of both having showed up for a party wearing the same outfit from Saks.

"Hecky darn," said Troy when Tenbrook caught up with him. "How's the gentleman farmer?" He recounted a few of Tenbrook's legendary mishaps to the men nearby, a ritual they'd all heard many times before. The kidding stopped just short of ridicule. Tenbrook didn't mind the jokes—they were outside the arena of his ego. Troy's audience wasn't the one that sat in judgment on him.

"I don't see you eating any cake," said Retta Lou, wagging her finger and giving him a scolding look. "Get up off your vernacular and eat." She pointed him in the direction of the cake table.

"We'z double-chin deep in cake," said Troy. Tenbrook picked up a paper plate, took a small slice of cake and ate it demonstratively. Retta Lou, watching, gave him an approving wave.

"That's what I would call a fait accompli," said Troy.

"Or a raison d'etre," said Tenbrook. The guests around the cake table were talking about the mountain lion almost everyone in the neighborhood claimed to have seen.

"Raise your arms up if you run into one," someone said. "Make yourself look tall."

"A hundred-pound mountain lion can take down a three-hundred-pound man."

"A mountain lion's got to eat every three days and I'm not talking about eating a bowl of kibbles."

"Sure it wasn't a dog? Them golden retrievers can be mistook for a mountain lion."

"I know the difference between a dog and a cougar."

"I'll tell you this. If you want a dog that'll stand up to a cougar, it's a Jack Russell, small as a Jack Russell is."

"My dog, Sadie, she just sits on the porch. Course, she can still kill a chicken if she gets the chance."

Talk turned to the drought.

"I lost seventy-nine out of ninety chickens."

"Them Cornish crosses don't stand up to the heat."

"They grow so fast their legs cayn't hold them up."

"I got about three tomatoes worth picking."

"It's so dry, trees are fighting over dogs to water them."

"If we don't get some rain, everything's gonna flat burn up."

"They got twelve inches in Centreville, just fifty miles east of here."

"I put green goggles on my cattle," said Troy.

"Joke comin' on,' someone said.

"Got them to eat everything including last year's sunflower stalks," said Troy. "Only problem is, they been eatin' my fence posts too."

A little boy passed Tenbrook with two cardboard panels attached to his arms.

"Are you going to try to fly?" said Tenbrook.

"Yes," answered the youngster, a little sheepishly, but resolute.

"Don't you think you ought to tie a string to him, just in case?" said Tenbrook to the boy's grandfather, who was following close behind, camera in hand.

"Probably so," grinned the granddad. When he reached the summit of the hill beside Troy's house, the youngster ran towards Tenbrook, his arms thrust back by the wind. It must have hurt, but his expression was beatific. Halfway down the hill, he took a little hop and for an instant he was airborne.

"Bravo!" cried Tenbrook.

Up by the house, Troy's workclothes were flapping in the wind. Every Saturday morning, Retta Lou hung them out to dry, one pair of blue overalls and a blue shirt for every day of the week. Season after season, year after year, every weekend they performed that hallelujah dance. A bounty harvest and rock-bottom prices one year, a blighted crop and skyhigh prices the next. A cornucopia followed by a black hole. Too much or not enough. And every morning, before sunrise, Troy in his uniform, ready for the harness again, waiting on the decisions of corn.

Fifty years, thought Tenbrook. Would he and Kate last that long? Retta Lou and Troy had stuck it out. Maybe they had no choice, no leisure to grow apart. Nursing calves, fighting the weather, greasing the machinery. A time to sow and a time to reap. No time to worry about fulfilling themselves or racking up status points. They had little to show for their labors other than skin cancers, limps and bruises. Every kind of malady had visited them and their friends except maladies of the self. Tenbrook doubted if there was a neurotic among them.

After all the cake had been consumed and the last cup of decaf had been drained, they would hug and bless one another and go their separate ways, without bothering to ask if it all added up. And would they really end up with a smaller pile of riches than his country club friends who knew how to turn pieces of paper into gold?

It would be a full moon that night, the fertility moon, the honey moon, the plenipotentiary moon of June. On such a night the Bilbreys had been married fifty years ago. Now they were calling in the harvest, while the future was bearing down on Tenbrook like a rip tide as he row, row, rowed against the stream.

Chapter 25

Jimmy showed up in his limousine. He didn't get out. He honked the horn and waited. Tenbrook came outside. The dark window slid noiselessly down. Jimmy was at the wheel.

"I have one last favor to ask," he said without looking at Tenbrook. He handed Tenbrook another package wrapped in duct tape. "Sequester this in your friend's vehicle. Do this, and your future is secure. Remember, I'm your benefactor. Don't disappoint." For the first time, Jimmy looked at him. His fleshy lips formed a warped smile. His eyes shone as if made of glass. "I want Everett Pillars' fingerprints on that package," he said. "You figure out how."

Tenbrook watched the limousine glide away and with it any ambiguity or choice. The way forward had been cleared. He wasn't going to betray Pillars, however much he held against him and wanted him to fail. He would "sequester" the package in his shed and there it would remain. And he wasn't going to go to the police or do anything that would entangle Kate and Channy in his own unraveling.

He'd taken out a $100,000 mortgage insurance policy some months before. He'd made a late-night survey of Jimmy's compound. He'd had a practice session with his pocket-sized 38. He looked at doom as if it was a gift. He'd been given the opportunity that he sought. He visualized and rehearsed the steps. It was like writing a story.

A disk arrived in the mail. On the jacket it read: "The Drug Deal—starring Cupid Carver and Henry Tenbrook." He put it in the player and saw himself entering the Kidrow residence. Inside, the picture was grainy, but he could make out himself and Cupid greeting one another with a fist bump and he heard himself saying, "It seems I'm supposed to deliver this."

A few days later, the Mercury came flying down the driveway, bouncing and sliding on ruined shocks. Kate was in town at her soup kitchen. Channy had just left for school. This time they didn't bother to knock. They burst in, slapping baseball bats against their palms. Benny walked up to Tenbrook, looked him over and shook his head.

"You wouldn't listen, would you, dickhead?" he said. "You didn't deliver." Tenbrook looked at him but didn't answer.

"Answer him, Delivery Boy," said Roland.

"I didn't realize he was asking a question," said Tenbrook.

"You like secrets, Dick Head?" said Roland

"Not particularly," said Tenbrook.

"You're gonna love this one," said Roland. "The secret is, you're a Dick Head."

"You're not scared, are you?" said Benny.

"Of course I'm scared," said Tenbrook.

"Here's the chance to conquer your fears," said Benny.

"You wasting your time," said Roland. "He's stupid."

"Do you answer to the name of 'Stupid?'" said Benny. "Or are you too stupid to know that you're stupid?" Benny reached in his jacket and pulled out a small bottle filled with white liquid.

"We're in a kind of hurry," he said. "You can drink your milk like a good little boy and go into a nice peaceful sleep. Or you'll have to play ball with us."

"It'll be like batting practice," said Roland. "Hitting fungoes."

"You'll be the ball," said Benny. "It won't be pretty. Sometimes it takes us half an hour to hit the ball out of the park."

"'Course, we start at the knees and save the head for last," said Roland.

"Your lovely wife and daughter won't be able to recognize you," said Benny. Roland made a slow swing with his bat.

"Batter up," he said.

"You might try to run," said Benny "Go on. Steal home."

A curious mood came over Tenbrook. He felt relaxed. Fear somehow melted away. He started to laugh.

"What the fuck are you laughing at?" said Benny.

"That's gonna cost you," said Roland. Tenbrook felt loose, ready to see what was coming next.

"I'm sorry," he said. "I was laughing because I was actually feeling grateful to you. Your timing is perfect. I consider myself lucky. Thank you. If there is an afterlife, I will always remember you with fondness and gratitude." Roland and Benny looked suspicious, confused.

"What the fuck are you talking about?" said Benny. "You crazy?" Tenbrook was surprised at himself. But he felt as if he'd found a groove.

"You men are busy," he said. "Let's get on with it. I'm ready if you are. I think I'll pass on the good-night milk. If I did, my insurance policy might not pay off. So, let's take the batting practice route. Have at it, gentlemen."

"This guy is fucking with us," said Roland.

"Let's see much how he likes it after we hit a couple of singles," Benny said. He assumed a batter's stance and took a practice swing. Outside, there was a sudden uproar of engines, the sound of slamming doors.

"What the hell?" said Roland. He went to the window. Half a dozen trucks had converged in the yard. Men with shotguns moved toward the house. Someone pounded on the door.

"Anybody home?" said a husky voice. The door handle rattled. Troy opened the door and stood there with a short-barreled shotgun at his side.

"Hope we're not interrupting," he said. He approached Benny with a friendly smile, his hand out.

"Troy Bilbrey here. Don't believe we've met. We was gonna go squirrel hunting with Mr. Tenbrook. Care to join us?" Benny showed his crooked teeth.

"We're just leaving," he said.

"Don't rush off," said Troy. "You can't very well rush off. We kinda got you boxed in. What's with them bats. Lookin' for a baseball game?"

"Ya," said Roland. "Know where we can find one?"

"I think we can field a team," said Troy, pointing the shotgun at Roland's chest. "Jimmy let you two monkeys out of your cage so you can play at being tough? You boys don't look so good. Maybe you need a check-up. Sure you gotta go?" Benny edged around Troy and started backing toward the door, his Adam's apple flexing. He wore a look of impotent outrage.

"Come on, Roland," he said. "Let's get out of this shithole."

"We was hoping you'd recite some of your big talk for us," said Troy.

"We'll save that for next time," said Benny.

"Best not be a next time," said Troy, prodding Benny with the butt of his gun. Benny turned and went out. Roland followed. Troy and the others followed them and moved their trucks.

"Them fellers try hard, don't they?" said Troy, after Benny and Roland had driven off. "I told you not to get mixed up with Jimmy. How did you get into this mess, son?"

"It's a long story," said Tenbrook.

"These stories always are," said Troy. He picked up the bottle and sniffed it. "That don't smell too good," he said. "They'll be back, you know. There'll be a next time. I'm not sure we can keep them away."

"That's not your job," said Tenbrook. "I've caused you enough trouble. I was glad to see you, though." He looked at Troy's backups. "And you guys. You've been good neighbors."

"You're not thinking about moving away?" said one of them.

"I don't want anyone to get hurt on account of me," said Tenbrook.

Troy and the others filed out. Tenbrook heard their trucks start. Then all was silence again. He felt as if he hadn't been breathing. He'd seen a side of Troy he hadn't known. Troy was tougher than he thought. Tenbrook looked at the bottle Jimmy's men had left, opened it and sniffed. A strong, sickly odor that almost made him retch. He wondered if this was the same elixir Angie's son Chad had been forced to drink. He was about to pour the contents out. On a second thought, he put the bottle in the freezer behind some frozen vegetables.

The next day, the *Reaper* reported two deaths in Bottomtown. A husband and wife, dead of undetermined causes. No signs of batting practice, thought Tenbrook. Cupid and Evie must have taken the magic milk. He walked through the breakfast room. Something outside caught his eye. He went to the window. The shed was on fire. He stepped outside and watched it burn. The fire hissed and popped. Tenbrook didn't care. It suited him to see the shed go up in smoke. It helped simplify things. Jimmy's package was going up in flames along with all of Tenrook's unfinished projects. Maybe this is the way things play out, he thought.

He turned and looked at the house. It seemed further away, as if it was receding, as if it belonged to someone else, as if it wasn't his mortgage that was coming due, as if Kate was someone else's wife who was losing her affection for someone other than him. He felt detached. He imagined Kate and Channy, turning faucets on and off, opening and closing closet doors, brushing their teeth, combing their hair, choosing a costume for the day, going through the motions, acting out their roles in the drama of their lives. For Channy, college, a career, marriage, kids lay ahead. For him and Kate—what? A slow decline ending in the nursing home, or a train wreck, cancer, divorce? The Tenbrooks, he thought sadly. Just another entry on an abstract of title.

The house looked toy-like, fragile. It wouldn't stand a chance against a tornado. A burglar with a pry bar could easily force entry and walk off with the Tenbrook's second-rate collectibles. Mice were scratching around the foundation even now, looking for openings. The dust that drove Kate crazy was sifting through the air, leaving a soft film on every surface, covering plates and glasses, finding its way into the kitchen cabinets and the clothing drawers.

Across the road beyond the field loomed the bright green wall of voracious wild growth. In the shadows of the woods, the dull rot of immortal decay. Legally, the woods belonged to him. But the real owners were the boring bugs, the gnawing rodents, the insatiable fungi. Technically, the Tenbrooks' house belonged to them too. How long before it would return to the earth, fed on by termites and worms or collapse before the bulldozers of some developer to make way for another country club development?

Still, his plan was taking shape. It was evolving without oversight, almost without thought, moving forward on its own wheels. It would save Pillars and at the same time rebuke him for his rape of the Griefmaker. The accounts would balance. Tenbrook felt energized, light-headed, like he used to feel on the playing field, dropping back into the pocket. He had nothing to fear, nothing to lose. Let the blitz come. He could sidestep it. The bleachers were filled with fans and they were rooting for him, but he was oblivious to the noise of the crowd. That's what he'd suited up for. It wasn't peace of mind after all. It was that old rush, the chance to put some points on the board.

Later that day, he looked out the back window and saw Channy and Toby playing Frisbee. They'd broken up a few days before, an agonizing, tearful rite. But there they were laughing, playing, carefree. The storm had passed over. With each toss, one of them would disappear from view for the catch, then reappear with the disk in hand for the next toss. Back and forth the Frisbee sailed, now Channy, now Toby. Never the two together in a single picture frame. One more pair expelled from the Garden. How did they keep on going? How can love just stop?

That night he had a dream. He and Channy (age five or six) were on a train somewhere in Eastern Europe. He'd waited too long to take his seat and suddenly the train was leaving. He ran and jumped aboard at the last instant and went to his seat, number 38. When he got there Channy was gone. He ran for help, but he couldn't communicate with anyone. Someone translated, the conductor shrugged. He'd have to get off at the next station and wait for the next train back. Tenbrook begged them to call and see if Channy was there. Another shrug and a show of empty hands. He got off at the next station and waited for hours. When he got back, Channy wasn't there either. He ran through the station, confronting passengers and ticket clerks trying to describe his daughter, but no one understood or cared. All he got were blank looks or looks of annoyance.

He spent the rest of his life going from village to village looking for his daughter, carrying a picture that grew worn and anyway represented a girl frozen in time. Who could imagine how she would change with each passing year? Wherever he went he attracted opportunists who grasped his plight and promised information in exchange for money. Near the end of his life, in a village of gypsies, desperate and memory faded, he found a woman who might be Channy, though she spoke only her cacophonous native tongue. Something in her eyes convinced him she was his daughter and somehow the woman seemed to understand what he needed of her. She took Tenbrook in her arms and comforted him as he wept.

The next day, when he returned from town with a box of ammunition, Tenbrook saw Ned's truck parked behind the barn—hidden there, he thought. He went inside and called to Kate. No answer. He tried the door to their bedroom.

"You can't come in," she cried. At last he knew for sure. The final piece of the puzzle. They'd been getting it on after all. Betrayal didn't make him angry. He welcomed it. The last link was broken. He was released. A sad freedom. It made him realize how isolated he'd become.

Tenbrook loaded his pistol and headed to Conestoga Bluff. A light rain fell. He drove slowly. The windshield wipers whispered, "Dvorak, Dvorak." Back and forth they swept, a moment of clarity followed by a blur of mist. Clear, obscure. The moon shone dimly behind a veil of clouds, but the usual crowd of stars showed between breaks. Two players played among the galaxies. He was one of the pieces on the board. He had no say in the game. But what if the rule-makers violate their rules? Can't the pawns just walk off the board?

When the police arrived at Jimmy's mansion, they found four bodies. They'd gotten a call about a shooting and had converged on the bluff house. It was a scene of surreal chaos—pit bulls lunging against their chain link kennels, half-naked bimbos scattering like frightened chickens, a few muscular men in suits trying to escape in dark SUVs and some Middleton dignitaries in various stages of undress, trying to look inconspicuous. They discovered a horde of weapons in a metal-clad outbuilding and beneath the mansion a vast concrete bunker with lab equipment, exhaust fans, bundles of marijuana and packets of white powder. Festive lanterns were strung about the compound. Ol' Blue Eyes was crooning "That Old Black Magic" from speakers within the still unfinished house. Aroma of cannabis hung in the air.

Jimmy was attired in a shiny tuxedo, like the toastmaster at a celebrity roast. Beside him lay Roland and Benny. They'd caught Tenbrook's bullets just as he'd caught one of theirs. Tenbrook wore his high school letter sweater with the number "17." At first, that seemed like a sad evocation of his glory days, as if he thought it might endow him with superhuman powers. But that wasn't Tenbrook. Everett's guess was he intended it as a self-mocking jest. Even when he was throwing touchdown passes—his record, 28 of them, still stood—his expression was always enigmatic, passive, detached. He never flashed a victory smile. He seemed contemptuous of how easy his natural ability made success for him back then. He went out of his way to make things hard. But it was easy to wonder if his ears were ringing at that perfect moment with echoes of cheerleaders crying, "Tenbrook, Tenbrook, he's our man, if he can't do it, nobody can."

Kate had a spell of sadness after Tenbrook's death. She kept having conversations with him, not big ones, just ordinary chit-chat, making plans, wondering what he would say about this or that. She felt cheated. He hadn't added things up. Sometimes in the supermarket, she'd hear a tune that reminded her of some scene they'd shared. She'd look out the window and think she'd caught sight of him walking away. She'd think he was a good friend, unsuited for business, always looking for some handle of meaning that wasn't there. He ran from opportunities. But maybe he felt fulfilled by restoring the Griefmaker to Pillars debt free. Maybe that was the liberation and acquittal he sought. The irony was he died in debt to Jimmy. She couldn't imagine him feeling comfortable with leaving a debt unpaid, even a debt to a crook. She couldn't imagine that he died at peace, but who does? Maybe he had a last laugh.

She didn't believe in life after death. But she thought that there was a kind of immortality in her recollections of the dead. "Gone but not forgotten," as the inscription on the tombstone says. But the dead exit stage right without a bow or a round of applause, just as the new cast shows up, reciting its own vain, doomed lines. The first cry a newborn baby makes says, "Goodbye."

Still, Kate liked to think that when Tenbrook's eyelids closed he had a moment—not of understanding, because life is meaningless and there's nothing to understand—but of peace. She imagined him waking up in his woods refreshed…Out of a whirlwind of golden dust, a mountain lion emerges, more sphinx than cougar, with scaled wings of bronze. It steps from the shattercane, approaches with measured steps and licks the wound. Then, fixing its talons in Tenbrook's ribs, it beats its wings and lifts off to the sky. From a nearby pasture, a meadowlark sings. And then another. And the green grass grows all around.

Chapter 26

They drove along a fencerow of the Griefmaker to the edge of the woods. The land that was once wild prairie was now regimented in rows of milo and beans. Tod sat beside his father, locked in silence, a rifle held between his knees. Pillars parked the four-wheeler, got out, stepped over the fence, and called Tod to come along. They entered the woods. Pillars followed a deer path through a swath of nettles, parting cables of vines that drooped from the limbs of cottonwoods and elms, sidestepping pale purple blackberry brambles. Tod walked sullenly behind him. He wore a camouflage jacket, paint-spattered jeans and black military boots. He carried the rifle on a sling. His hair stood up as if electrically charged. Pillars could hear his asthmatic breathing.

It had been a long time since Pillars had visited the woods. He and Tenbrook had hunted deer there in their youth. Now, for the first time, he was struck by the absolute division between the cultivated field and the unruly woods, two alien kingdoms separated only by a broken-down barbed wire fence. Chaos reigned in the kingdom of trees. You couldn't speak of purpose there. Fallen branches were scattered across the ground. Trees toppled by storms, split by lightning, lay with their roots in the air. Ragged weeds crawled across the black soil, trivial rivulets broadened into gorges, and there—a solitary hawthorn tree in extravagant bloom. Where had it come from? Nothing in that place expressed logic or order. For once, he noticed things, details that were interesting, not for their convertibility to cash, but just for their stubborn existence: the bark of a hackberry tree pebbled like Braille, a woodpecker drumming a message on a hollow tree, the branches of a dead cottonwood creaking like a rusty hinge.

"Be careful," Pillars called out, without turning around. "Those are stinging nettles." Most of Tenbrook's woodland knowledge had been lost on him, but he remembered the nettles. When he pointed them out to Tod, he had the odd sensation that his voice sounded like Tenbrook's.

It was dark as twilight in the woods. The canopy was a gothic hovel of tangled branches that let only scraps of sunlight through. Shadows of leaves fluttered like birds across the ground. A squirrel scolded them from its nest of leaves high in the crotch of a hickory. They stopped at Jenkins' trailer. Through a window covered with cataracts of rain dust Pillars could make out the vintage Playboy centerfolds taped to the walls. The sheets had curled at the edges and been eaten away by insects and time.

"When I was about your age, Tenbrook and I took a couple of girls out here," Pillars said. "We had big plans to score. My girl went into the woods to the ladies' room. She must have relieved herself in a patch of nettles, because when she came back, she was wailing, 'Oh, my ass…Oh, my ass.' We didn't know what was the matter. We took her to the emergency room. Tenbrook called that the Night of the Nettles. So much for our plans to score." Pillars laughed.

"Is that supposed to break the ice?" said Tod.

"That's supposed to demonstrate that I was once your age."

"No need to patronize me," said Tod. Pillars didn't have the heart for a blowup. He let it go.

Tod asked if their outing was part of the "Save Tod Initiative."

"That's right," said Pillars. "Take your boy hunting instead of hunting your boy." He thought he saw a faint smile, but Tod mastered it and it was gone in a second.

"Just for the record, if you're trying to straighten me out, I don't want to be straightened out," said Tod.

"I'm not trying to straighten you out," said Pillars.

Jimmy's death had freed Pillars from the loan, which was unrecorded, an instrument for laundering cash. But the economic downturn had torpedoed his development plans and his enthusiasm for the Griefmaker project had evaporated anyway after Gwen's death. He'd been completely unprepared for the loss of his wife. He hadn't understood how much he depended on her, how much she'd sustained him. Now there was no one to talk to, no one who'd listen. He was gripped with loneliness, a condition he'd never experienced before. His self-image—the can-do bulldog— had gone up in smoke. He felt weak, outcast. He looked in the mirror and saw a man disheveled, distracted, lost like a sleepwalker. His landfill and quarry went into receivership. The bank foreclosed on his vacation home. His mansion looked abandoned. The yard went to seed. Skeletons of unfinished buildings covered the Griefmaker like ruins left by a war. The sign that promised the World of Oz theme park had been knocked down by a high wind. Jenkins stayed on but the rest of his staff were let go.

All he had now was Tod and Tod despised him. For a long time, he couldn't bear even to look at Tod, with his frail arms, his pasty, acne-covered face and his perpetually insolent look. Pillars needed to build bridges with the boy, but he couldn't bring himself to like him. He suspected that Tod was "queer." (He refused to use the word "gay.") But he kept seeing Gwen in Tod's features. Tod was the only connection he had left with Gwen. Gwen had tried to console him with the thought that Tod was only "rebelling." Pillars' retort was that he was paying for Tod's rebellions. He regretted that argument now.

Tod's loss had been greater than his. He and his mother had had an easy, intuitive rapport. He trusted her. She understood him. His mother's death seemed to have made Tod more angry than bereaved. He looked unhealthy. His fingernails were bitten down and there were thin cut marks on both of his wrists. It was hard to imagine him walking into Middleton High and opening fire on his classmates and teachers. But how could you be sure?

They passed a wooden rowboat, a beautiful hand-made craft with elegant lines. Tenbrook had talked about restoring it, another of his unfinished projects. Now the bow had split, weeds were growing between the broken ribs. The transom had caved in and moss grew on the rotting bottom. "You waited too long," Pillars said out loud, as if Tenbrook were walking there beside him.

They crossed a ditch which Jenkins and his ancestors had used as a dump. It was like a museum of obsolete farm implements—the warped remains of a combine and a cultivator, a steel disk harrow, the chassis of an antique tractor, a rusted threshing machine, an overturned manure spreader. Floods had deposited tree trunks across the bottom of the ditch and left plastic trash bags caught on exposed roots along its walls. A sign for Mail Pouch tobacco was covered with coyote scat. Half buried in mud and detritus Pillars spotted a cream separator, a washing machine with a wringer attachment and a refrigerator with the circular compressor on top. Empty tubs of fertilizer and jugs of herbicide were scattered about, along with torn lawn chairs, a rotten mattress and some scorched glass bottles that Pillars suspected belonged to an abandoned meth lab. He touched an ancient thresher covered with scallops of rust, and a flake of metal fell away like a feather.

"This place looks like your mother's art collection," he said, regretting it immediately.

Pillars remembered that Tenbrook had gutshot a deer near the spot years before. The wounded animal, charged with adrenaline, ran down one side of the ditch and up the other and hid in the woods to die. Tenbrook never found it. And he'd never hunted deer again. Pillars had thought it was a sign of weakness. He regretted that judgment too.

Tenbrook had laughed at him for getting Tod the rifle after he'd wrecked the Mercedes.

"It sounds like a reward," Tenbrook said. Pillars hadn't even heard him.

"The trick is to take the mystery out of guns," he'd said. "Make him think of the gun as a tool, like a shovel." Tenbrook had just smiled. He was laughing at me, Pillars thought. Laughing at the way I knew everything back then.

They came to a treeless wetland.

"This is Jenkins' Wishing Hole," said Pillars. "Jenkins used to sit down here in his duck blind drinking schnapps and he'd come back with stories about all the mallards he'd shot. I've never seen a duck land here but Jenkins claimed thousands of those phantom birds." Tenbrook spent hours in the blind with Jenkins, listening to his tall tales, neither of them caring about getting their limits, content to wait for the big green heads to come boiling in, driven south by a cold front, falling from the sky like leaves.

"The funny thing is, Jenkins once was a big-time duck hunter," said Pillars. "He taught Tenbrook and I how to shoot. He was the best duck caller in the county. I guess at some point he figured he'd killed enough ducks. He'd just as well shoot imaginary ducks as real ones."

Pillars also regretted that he'd so often walked away from the Hole and left Tenbrook and Jenkins to their pointless musings. He didn't like to waste time. Now it seemed as if he'd missed the best part of time. Jenkins was full of woodland lore. He could lead you to a trove of mushrooms or a nest full of turkey eggs. Pillars smiled when he remembered that Jenkins had claimed to have seen a mountain lion on that spot.

They reached a clearing in the woods, a rectangular gash—Jenkins' shooting gallery. At the end of the narrow corridor was an ivy-covered berm to stop bullets. Jenkins still kept the area well mowed and sprayed so that nothing grew there that might distract the shooter's aim. Sometimes Pillars could hear Jenkins firing shots in rapid succession, assassinating shadows, mowing down his enemies. For even Jenkins was sometimes visited by demons. The sighting table had been recently painted. It stood out like a misplaced piece of furniture which the forest birds had generously covered with droppings. Pillars found a pad of targets in the drawer of the table. He tore off a sheet, walked down the trail to the target stand and pinned the paper to the backstop with clothes pins.

"Let's have a look," he said, holding out his hand. Tod handed him the rifle. It was a Remington thirty-ought-six. The cross-hatching on the stock and the bluing of the barrel were pristine. It had never been shot. Pillars looked through the scope.

"Nice gun," he said. Tod picked up a stick, fidgeted with it and jabbed at a pile of leaves. Pillars pulled a box of shells from his jacket.

"Let's see how it shoots," he said. He handed Tod a pair of ear protectors. "You're never too young to go deaf." Tod took some shells from the box, fed one into the chamber and two more into the magazine. When he tried to close the receiver, the gun jammed.

"Don't force it," said Pillars, reaching for the gun. "It's better if you put all the shells into the magazine and then load it." He tried to keep the abrupt authoritative tone out of his voice. He pried the jammed shell out with his pocket knife, placed the three shells in the magazine and handed the rifle back to Tod.

"I hope I don't sound like a scout master," he said. "But always be aware of where the barrel is pointed. And don't forget that this bullet can travel a mile or more. Give it a try. Lock and load." Tod shoved the receiver forward. The shell slid smoothly into the chamber. He held the rifle up and aimed at the target.

"Safety off?" said Pillars. He reached over and pressed the safety off. He pointed to his ears.

Tod put the ear protectors on, raised the rifle stock to his cheek and squinted through the scope.

He held for a long time without firing. The rifle barrel waved erratically. He was shaking. His breathing was shallow and tense. He pulled the trigger. The barrel flew up. He winced from the recoil. He removed the ear protectors and scowled.

"It packs a punch," said Pillars. "It'll knock a deer off its feet." Pillars looked through his binoculars.

"A little high and to the left. You closed your eyes just when you pulled the trigger. Keep them open. Try breathing deep at regular intervals. And squeeze the trigger. Don't pull it."

Tod aimed and pulled the trigger again. Nothing happened.

"You've got to eject the spent shell and put a new one in the chamber," said Pillars. Tod frowned, but followed his father's instructions. He fired off two more rounds.

"Better," said Pillars. "Don't think about hitting the bullseye. Don't think at all. Try not to care. The harder you try, the worse you do. Detachment's the key. Breathing is all-important. Exhale, take a breath and hold it. And leave the chamber open for a minute. The cooler the barrel, the more accurate it's going to be." He was enjoying the role of teacher.

Tod fired off a dozen more rounds. They were all over the place. His breathing was more controlled and he kept his shooting eye open, but he couldn't keep the rifle steady. It still wavered and when he fired, he still jerked the trigger.

"Check the magazine and make sure it's empty," said Pillars. "I'm going to put a fresh target up." He tore another sheet from the pad and walked down the path to the target stand. He felt Tod's eyes on his back and guessed that he was experiencing the perverse impulse that having a gun in your hands provoked. He could feel the spot on his back below the shoulder blades where the lead would enter. He didn't care. If Tod shot him, the scores would be settled, he would have paid his dues. When he reached the target stand, he didn't glance back at Tod. He wanted to show him that he didn't mistrust him, that he wasn't afraid, that he didn't care. He tore off the old target, pinned the fresh one up and walked back. He handed the target to Tod.

"That sucks," said Tod, tossing the target aside and setting his rifle down. "I don't need this shit. I quit."

"Don't be discouraged," said Pillars. "You're just getting started. It's not supposed to be easy."

He picked up the rifle and looked through the scope at the target. The bullseye looked back at him, freakishly sharp. Aiming a gun always seemed to enhance his vision. He could almost make out the numbers on the concentric circles. Don't think, he thought. Detachment's the key. But how could he offer advice to Tod that he couldn't follow himself?

A tiny insect crawled up Pillars' arm. He raised his hand to slap it, but something made him stop. It's not that different from us, he thought. It has a brain, a heart, probably even a liver. It eats, shits, fucks. Look at it crawling up my arm. It has a will, goals, ambition. He chuckled. What's come over me? he wondered. He fired off three rounds, set the weapon down and looked through the glasses. All three shots were in a tight pattern, but they were off the bullseye, still high and to the left. He adjusted the scope and handed the rifle back to Tod.

"This is more fun that those video games you play, don't you think?"

"It's okay."

"I mean, when you shoot the gun, you feel it. It's physical. The recoil is real. When you hit a clay pigeon, it breaks. There's a connection between you and it."

"It's not that different," said Tod. "When you hit a target in a video game, it's not a fantasy hit. There's an impact. You can feel it too." Tod made a percussive sound that sent a mist of saliva from his mouth. He looked intense, as if he'd entered another space and was talking to himself. "The computer shudders. You feel it in your fingers." He made a comically demonic face and assumed an evil genius voice. "You can wipe out an army. You can unleash a cone of death that turns a city into rubble. You have so much power at your fingertips, Dude. New Zombies, Halo 3, Team Deathmarch. Heavy Rain, Counter Strike Force. I've played them all. I had an NPC-based character who was rampaging across the entire map, slaughtering everything. I killed him. I killed a sniper in a gilly suit. I've killed hundreds of Grunts and Brutes." He was laughing, amused at his own performance.

"That's a lot of killing," said Pillars.

"Kill or be killed—right, Dad? I've got a K-D Kill-to-Death ratio of 1.25. I got my Killtacular medal and my Killtrocity medal. I got so many experience points they forced me to prestige. I've done damage with a Needler and a Gravity Hammer. Eclipse Scythe, Cerebral Bore, the Glaive of Dark Sector...I'll take them over this rifle any day."

"The Glaive of Dark Sector," said Pillars. "Where do I get one of those?"

"You should be so lucky," said Tod, allowing the joke. "The Glaive's a three-pronged boomerang. It can dismember your enemy from a quarter-mile away."

"But isn't it sort of make-believe? I thought maybe you wanted to get into guns because they're tangible, real."

"There's nothing unreal about video games."

"But there must be some kind of mental trick you play to get yourself into that world. You know, evil empires, that sort of thing."

"You making fun of me, but that's okay. I don't really care."

"Not at all. I'm interested."

"Video games are just like life," said Tod. "You run into players who don't focus on the objective, just like in so-called life. They can do the stupidest things. I was playing Battlefield 2 once when a group of 32 fighters spawned at a control point next to a helicopter pad. One sniper shot another player. A third player got into the machine gunner's seat and started shooting his own teammates. The pilot didn't know how to fly. He turned the helicopter over. It blew up. It was crazy. What are you supposed to do with players like that? Incompetence. See what I mean? Just like life." Pillars thought: You sound just like me.

"Then you have the Griefers," said Tod. "They know how to play, but their objective is to disrupt the game. They like to pick up objective items and hide them. In Mod Zombie Master, the Map has a high amount of explosive barrels. Griefers pick them up and throw them at other players. Pow! Instant chaos. Rules broken. Game ruined. That's where all problems begin. Imagine playing a game where you don't know what the rules are, or where there aren't any rules, or where the players deliberately break the rules."

"I play in that game every day," said Pillars. That sounded like something Tenbrook would have said.

"See?" said Tod. "Video games make perfect sense. It's a spectrum. You have to make choices. Your actions give you your fame or your infamy. If you don't believe in your power, you lose it. If you follow the rules and have the skills, you survive. You may even prevail. If you make a mistake, you die."

"But there's a difference between virtual death and the real thing."

"Not so much. All it takes is a little imagination. The stakes are the same."

"I wonder if those kids who open fire on their classmates imagine that they can rewind the tape and bring everyone back to life."

"I think they understand they're in it for keeps. Usually they finish by shooting themselves."

"Good answer," said Pillars. He felt oddly exhilarated, as if he'd made a small breach in his son's defenses, as if he were getting through. Maybe for the first time, he was listening to Tod.

"Try another shot," he said. Tod loaded the rifle and fired a few more rounds. "You're tense," said Pillars. "Don't think about scoring. Let go." Tod fired. This time he held steady. After a few more shots, his shoulders relaxed. His grip on the rifle eased.

"That's better," said Pillars, looking through the glasses. "Actually, that's pretty good."

"You're surprised?" Tod didn't try to hide his grin.

"Not at all," said Pillars. "It's just that I'm not that great a shot. You won't get much aptitude from my genes. Tenbrook was a good shot. He could hit a dime tossed in the air with his BB gun. We used to have some pretty fierce competitions. He almost always won. Tenbrook would have been the one to give you a shooting lesson. He was a hell of a shot."

He hadn't been a good father. He'd put Tod down relentlessly, thinking he was engaging in some kind of motivational shock therapy. He'd make Tod play catch and then throw the football so hard it would hit him in the chest and knock the wind out of him and then he'd tell him to stop crying, to keep his eye on the ball, to be a man. He'd felt so sure of himself, that his way was the only way, that his principles were the ones you had to follow to achieve success. He used to boast about his tenacity and unshakable self-confidence. Now he'd lost his armor, his secret powers, his medicine bundle. And the strange thing was how much lighter he felt. He wanted to make some sort of confession, to ask Tod's forgiveness, to atone, to say that he'd failed as a father, that he hadn't taken enough interest in his son, that he was too wrapped up in dollars and cents. But the words wouldn't come. Maybe they would some day. He didn't want to kill the good moment he was having by trying to get more points on the scoreboard, by trying to balance the ledger in one afternoon. It wouldn't work. A voice he couldn't place was speaking to him: Locate the target in your crosshairs. Don't set your sights too low. What are the parameters of your plight? That sounded like something Tod might say. What was the name of that girl in the nettles—Nancy? Claire? Everything is significant—or nothing is. Everything changes, nothing is lost. Maybe the treasure chest was within reach.

"That was good," he said, after Tod shot a few more rounds. "Well done, Dude. What do you say? Ready to go?" Tod looked bewildered. He was shaking his head. He turned as if to go, then turned back. And the next thing Pillars knew, Tod was hugging him, sobbing. It had come to pass. Pillars felt as if a ghost was watching them. As they walked back, they heard a pheasant's two note mating call. The bird flushed from a weed patch beside the path. It must have been a survivor from the pheasant prison break the night he plowed the Griefmaker, a lone rooster, calling to imaginary hens. The pheasant was missing its tail feathers, probably from encounters with coyotes. When they got back to the four-wheeler, Tod noticed a strange shape in the sky to the south, a sinister black cord dancing and waving in wild gyrations.

"What's that, Dad?" he said. Pillars looked. As they watched, the specter dropped low and broadened to the shape of an inverted bowl. It seemed to be boring down into the earth, throwing up fragments of timber, parts of cars, whole trees.

"Twister," said Pillars. "Big one, headed this way."

Chapter 27

Just before he died, Tenbrook had a conversation with Channy. She told him she believed in the future. According to her, life will keep getting better and better because of advances in science and technology.

"But people don't get better," said Tenbrook. "People are the same today as they were when they lived in caves. Technology has made them even more monstrous and idiotic. They spend most of their time watching inane entertainments or having inane cell phone conversations or shooting strangers in movie theatres and malls."

"They?" said Channy, giving him an affectionate pat. "It's true, Dad. You belong to a different species." She told him that she thought life was a story. "It may be a story told by an idiot, but I can't help turning the pages. I want to see how it turns out."

"I believe in the past," said Tenbrook. "But you're right to take a positive attitude about the future."

"I'm confused," she said, apparently struck by his inconsistency.

"Join the club," Tenbrook said. "In life, you can find yourself on the wrong side of a story, for instance a story that requires you to kill someone to save someone else. Murder can acquire a kind of sanctity if you believe you've been called to commit it by a higher power."

"I didn't know you believed in a higher power," said Channy.

"I don't," said Tenbrook.

Channy wondered what had passed through her father's mind when he died. Did he think he was dying for a noble cause? Tenbrook killed Jimmy to save Pillars but he also effectively committed suicide. Was it an act of courage or a means of escape? There was a moment of revelation just before the lights went out? Or was his last thought when the bullet struck his chest something profound like "Oh, shit?" Tenbrook said that life was meaningless, but stories have to mean something. We make up stories and tell them to make life make sense, to answer questions that begin with "Why?" Dying in a gun battle would have appealed to Tenbrook: "I died to protect Kate and Channy, I died to redeem the Griefmaker." But his death wasn't a story. Channy wondered if her father had just had enough, if he just wanted to get off the stage.

Of course, no one shed a tear for Jimmy. Killing him was like killing a raccoon in the chicken coop. On the night he and Tenbrook died, SWAT teams swarmed the city, hauling in some forty colleagues of Jimmy's, including several Middleton cops. The *Middleton Reaper* ran a series under two-inch headlines, "From the Emerald Triangle to the Sunflower State: The Inside Story of Middleton's Cross-Country Drug Pipeline." Federal investigators had been watching Jimmy and his cronies for several years. The payoff came when police answered a domestic disturbance call. A man on parole with a pistol in his possession, which meant more time in prison, spilled the beans on Jimmy's operation, for which he was a functionary. He described a network that was ingeniously managed, but so vast that weak links and eventual breakdowns were inevitable.

Faced with the prospect of long prison sentences, Jimmy's other underlings opened up. Among them were some well-known businessmen, a former Middleton University basketball star and a rough collection of ex-cons with aliases such as "The Cockroach" and "The Jackhammer." One of the charmers was charged with beating a woman in a wheelchair over an unpaid drug debt.

The story was a sensation in sleepy Middleton. Jimmy's business involved marijuana and cocaine shipped from the "Emerald Triangle" area of Northern California to Middleton and methamphetamine manufactured in the bunker beneath his mansion. The police found reams of notes and ledgers written in a crimped hand documenting purchases and sales, charting prices, supply and demand, and detailed evaluations of various strains of weed: Bubba Kush, Sour Diesel, Northern Light, Jack and Ripper. Jimmy's operation included a number of semi-legitimate businesses for the purpose of hiding illegal activities and laundering money. Why would he and his associates risk getting caught and sent to prison when they could have prospered by running legitimate businesses? There was much musing in Middleton on that theme. The funny thing was that none of the culprits seemed that surprised at getting caught or even that much bothered by the prospect of a long sojourn in the slammer. This puzzled rational, conventional folks. They couldn't wrap their imaginations around the "Why?" of it. Maybe the bad guys were members of that subspecies that looks at life fatalistically, carelessly, that doesn't buy into the line between legal and illegal, given that "legitimate" businesses are always skating as close to the line as possible and that government is constantly getting caught breaking the law. Playing by the rules was for the tame, the frightened, the meek. No doubt they thought of themselves as Robin Hoods.

Benny and Roland turned out to be graduates of the Middleton University Theatre Department who'd failed to make a career out of acting. A photo in the *Reaper* showed them sword fighting in a production of "Romeo and Juliet" during their college days. The head of the theatre department remembered them as promising but somewhat unstable thespians.

Jimmy's circus was really a pretty pathetic, clichéd affair. There was nothing original about it. It had all the conventional trappings, culminating in the humiliating perp walks, the handcuffs, the orange jumpsuits, the defiant obscenities. The feds had extensive recordings of Jimmy tossing around code words such as "racks," "wheels," "pop the top," and "a box of parts." There was something almost childish about it, like a drama dreamed up by pre-adolescent boys playing pirates, cops and robbers, cowboys and Indians. The guy on parole who started spilling the beans got five years as his reward. But before he started serving his sentence, he got caught robbing a drugstore for sedative medicines and got re-sentenced to fifteen years. What a piece of work is man.

In a sense, Jimmy was the perverse reincarnation of Henry Tenbrook, the patriarch, adjusted for contemporary times: ambitious, energetic, insatiable. The only difference was that Jimmy was a crook. But some Middleton historians thought Henry Tenbrook the First was also a crook. And some who still seethed over the plowing of the Grief-maker didn't see that much difference between Jimmy and Everett Pillars.

A witness to the gunfight at Jimmy's headquarters reported that when Tenbrook aimed his pistol, Jimmy looked at him sadly, as if he was disappointed.

"I'm your biggest fan," he'd said. The irony was that Tenbrook didn't have to die to bring Jimmy down and save Everett. If Ten had stayed home that night, the mills of justice would have done that work for him. But justice wasn't Tenbrook's goal.

***

After Tenbrook died, Everett Pillars visited Kate. He may have been testing the waters, looking for a little encouragement. But he didn't find it. She looked more beautiful than ever, with her fine patrician face and exquisite frame. But she was arctic, frigid, unknowable. He had questions he wanted to ask her. He wanted to know if she'd loved Tenbrook. She gave him no opening. But she did want to talk. She told him that Tenbrook had come home that day. He'd called for her and knocked on their bedroom door. She was wrapping his birthday present and had locked the door. She told him he couldn't come in. That was the last time she heard his voice. Ned had trailered his motorcycle out to her house that day, she said, and had gone for a ride in the country. Pillars wasn't sure why she volunteered that information or even if she'd guessed what had gone through Tenbrook's mind when he saw the front end of Ned's truck sticking out behind the barn. If he'd looked and seen the trailer without the motorcycle, he might have understood that it was an innocent visit. But who knows if that would have made him change his mind. Tenbrook was as enigmatic as Kate.

A more seemingly mismatched couple than Pillars and Kate couldn't be imagined, but a few months later they got married. The Great Middleton Tornado had leveled the mansion. Pillars and Kate were living in a double-wide. Neighbors saw them from time to time walking the Griefmaker, hand in hand, Kate wearing loose-fitting overalls, a stained gray sweatshirt tattered at the wrists, a baseball cap and scruffy boots, the goddess of plain beauty pulling weeds, a pretty sight. Pillars had changed. He was gaunt.

His hair was shoulder-length and completely white. But he didn't look old. The crops were gone, the land was covered with a fine stand of native grass.

To his few friends, he confided that he'd been on "a long pilgrimage to sanity." He'd spent months in a drunken stupor after Gwen died. Lawsuits from creditors had piled up. A former secretary had threatened him with a patrimony suit unless he paid her a thousand a month. One day, he saw a story in the *Middleton Reaper* about a majestic elm that was going to be cut down to make way for a downtown office building. There was a picture of a woman who was camping out in the lower branches of the tree to protest. Pillars recognized her. She was the woman who'd put a hex on him the night he plowed the Griefmaker.

He drove downtown and found her sitting on a mattress she'd wedged between the limbs of the tree. Another woman was putting provisions in a basket that hung from a rope. They were engaged in a shouting match about who had the better pedigree as a witch. The woman in the tree claimed to be thirteenth generation. They stopped arguing and looked at Pillars. The witch in the tree asked him what he wanted. Then she recognized him. He told her that his wife had died, that he'd lost his business, that his house had been leveled by the tornado. That seemed to please her. He was desperate. He didn't believe in witchcraft stuff, but he asked her—begged her—to call off the dogs. She gave him a wicked witch's grin and asked for a thousand dollars. He was willing to try anything. He put the money in her basket, even though he was getting low on cash by that time. The other woman told her she should have asked for more. And then they started in shouting at one another again.

Sometimes when Kate and Pillars were out walking, he'd start talking as if he were addressing someone who wasn't there. He'd speak about his prairie restoration project, pointing out forbs that had sprouted as if each one was a precious gem.

"Look at that," he'd say. Dropping to his knees he cradled a tiny flower. "That's the prairie fringed orchid. The tree huggers said it was 'endangered' to keep me from plowing. And do you know what? I've brought it back. How's that for irony?" The first year he drilled the native grass seeds, he was out there with a shotgun trying to scare off the black birds that were eating the seeds. That spring, some kind of lacy plant popped up. It covered the place. He asked the government agent what it was. 'Ragweed,' he said.

"That's how much I knew back then." By the first of July a blanket of ragweed covered the Griefmaker. Pillars thought he'd created a plague. But right away the quail started coming back. There were at least a dozen coveys now. And the ragweed was almost gone. Native grass had beaten it out.

"I remember Tenbrook telling me that."

For a second, Kate thought it was Tenbrook talking. Pillars had nearly caught his tone of voice. He'd told her that he was somehow completing Tenbrook's work. She wondered if he understood that Tenbrook had tried to save him or if he thought that by restoring the Griefmaker he'd somehow saved Tenbrook.

"This grass is wonderful," he said. "You can plant some seeds today and bring back the world the way it was." He never came out and said it, but he had the sense that the Griefmaker had claimed him and turned him into a different man.

"You know, I've lived all my on this patch of ground and I've just begun to think of it as home."

A giant combine was creeping over a distant hillside. What was it doing out in the middle of winter? Pillars and Kate stopped to watch its progress, a harbinger of harvests to come. They walked past the creek where Tenbrook once had his deer stand. Pillars looked up and saw a bow hanging from a branch. Tenbrook's abandoned bow.

"I just want to cover everyone with happiness," Pillars said.

"That's a tall order," said Kate. A ragged figure like a scarecrow leaped up from a slough ahead of them. He must have been one of Middleton's homeless who'd made a camp out there and somehow was surviving the cold. He ran off to the south like a vaudeville clown. Pillars shouted that it was okay for him to stay, but the scarecrow didn't seem to hear him. He ran with a limp that gave his run the look of a crazy shuffle, tattered sleeves and coattails flapping, a ragtime dance. Just before he disappeared over a hill he made a nimble leap and gave a little festive kick.

"He's out here," Pillars suddenly exclaimed with a catch in his throat. "I guarantee you."

"I know he is," said Kate.

"I miss him," said Pillars.

"So do I," she said."

"He was the last of his kind."

"I guess you could say that about every one of us," she said.

Author's Note

Thanks for suggestions and encouragement to Martha Masinton, Maureen Carroll, Jim McKinley, George H. Gurley III, Gillian Gurley, Susan Gurley, Paula Schmidt, to Alexander Fischer for information about video games, to Louis Copt for cover art.

Acknowledgements

The letter from Tenbrook the Patriarch was adapted from a letter written by George H. Hodges, 19th governor of Kansas. Everett Pillars' speech at Jacamar was adapted from comments by Stephen Schwartzman, CEO of Blackstone. Witch's chant adapted from "Psycho Killer" by the Talking Heads.

About The Author

George Gurley wrote a column for the *Kansas City Star* and was Book Review Editor for a number of years. He also wrote columns for the Lawrence, Kansas *Journal World*. His poems and stories have been published in literary magazines such as "Poetry" and "New Letters." Two books of poetry: *Fugues in the Plumbing* (BkMk Press) and *Home Movies* (Raindust Press)… One book of columns (with Peter Simpson) *Press Box* and *City Room* (BkMk Press). Two plays: *Cures* and *Indian Givers*, both produced by Park College and directed by Pulitzer Prize winner Charles Gordone…Book Reviews in the *Wall Street Journal*. He lives on a farm in Douglas County, Kansas where he and his wife Susan have been working on a native prairie restoration project for 20 years. Winner of Kansas Bankers Association and Kansas Department of Wildlife and Parks Wildlife Habitat Conservation Award.

OTHER BOOKS YOU MIGHT ENJOY FROM ANAMCARA PRESS LLC

ISBN: 9781941237-33-5
$18.99

ISBN: 9781941237-30-4
$18.99

ISBN: 9781941237-32-8
$18.95

ISBN: 9781941237-82-3
$21.99

ISBN: 9781941237-18-2
$21.99

ISBN: 9781941237-08-3
$24.95

Available wherever books are sold and at:
anamcara-press.com

Thank you for being a reader! Anamcara Press publishes select works and brings writers & artists together in collaborations in order to serve community and the planet. *Your comments are always welcome!*

Anamcara Press
anamcara-press.com

www.ingramcontent.com/pod-product-compliance
Lightning Source LLC
Chambersburg PA
CBHW020751190726
48285CB00006B/1977